PENGUIN BOOKS

THE EARTHLY PARADISE

C. S. Forester was born in Cairo in 1899, where his father was stationed as a government official. He studied medicine at Guy's Hospital, and after leaving Guy's without a degree he turned to writing as a career. His first success was *Payment Deferred*, a novel written at the age of twenty-four and later dramatized and filmed with Charles Laughton in the leading role. In 1932 Forester was offered a Hollywood contract, and from then until 1939 he spent thirteen weeks of every year in America. On the outbreak of war he entered the Ministry of Information and later he sailed with the Royal Navy to collect the material for *The Ship*. He then made a voyage to the Bering Sea to gather material for a similar book on the United States Navy, and it was during this trip that he was stricken with arteriosclerosis, a disease which left him crippled. However, he continued to write and in Captain Hornblower created the most renowned sailor in contemporary fiction. At the end of his life he was living in California. He died in 1966.

C. S. FORESTER

The Earthly Paradise

PENGUIN BOOKS

IN ASSOCIATION WITH
MICHAEL JOSEPH

Penguin Books Ltd, Harmondsworth, Middlesex, England
Penguin Books, 625 Madison Avenue, New York, New York 10022, U.S.A.
Penguin Books Australia Ltd, Ringwood, Victoria, Australia
Penguin Books Canada Ltd, 2801 John Street, Markham, Ontario, Canada L3R 1B4
Penguin Books (N.Z.) Ltd, 182–190 Wairau Road, Auckland 10, New Zealand

—

First published by Michael Joseph 1940
Published in Penguin Books 1962
Reprinted 1981

—

—

Set, printed and bound in Great Britain by
Cox & Wyman Ltd, Reading
Set in Monotype Garamond

CHAPTER ONE

THE learned Narciso Rich was washing his shirt. He had dropped a wooden bucket over the side on the end of a rope, and, having filled it – with difficulty because of its tendency to float and the lack of motion of the ship – he had swung it up to the fore-deck. Although it was late afternoon, it was still stifling hot, and Rich endeavoured to stay as much as possible in the shadow cast by the mast and sail, but that was not easy, because the ship was swinging about slowly and aimlessly in the flat calm. The sun stung his bare skin, brown though the latter was, when it reached it. Yet Rich could not postpone what he was doing until nightfall, because the work in hand necessitated a good light – he was freeing his shirt of the insect pests which swarmed in it.

There were grim thoughts running through his mind as he bent over his revolting task. Firstly, he knew by experience that his shirt was far easier to clean than the leather breeches which he wore, and on which he would have to start work next. Next, he would not stay clean very long, not in this ship, where every man was alive with lice, and where the very planking swarmed with loathsome creatures which hastened out at nightfall to suck human blood. At this very moment, when he stopped to think about it, he thought he could distinguish their hideous stench among the other stinks which reached his nostrils. It was a strange piece of work for him to be doing. Not since his student days had he had to abase himself in this fashion, and for the last five years he had had servants to wait on him in his own house, after he had attained eminence in his profession. Without immodesty he could look on himself as in the first rank of jurisconsults in the triple kingdom of Arragon, and as certainly the second, and possibly the first, authority on the universal maritime code of Catalonia. Merchant princes from Pisa and Florence and Marseille – the very Doge of Venice, for that matter – had sent deputations, almost embassies, to request his judgement upon points in dispute, and had listened attentively to his explanations of the law, and had paid in gold for them. Now he was washing his own shirt under an equinoctial sun.

And – he admitted it to himself with all a lawyer's realism – it was his own fault. He need not have joined this expedition. The King had summoned him to consultation; a pretty tangle they had got their affairs into, His Highness and the Admiral, as a result of not consulting expert legal opinion when drawing up their first agreement, which was exactly what always happened when two laymen tried to save lawyer's fees. Rich remembered His Highness's inquiring glance; the subject under discussion was as to which able-bodied young lawyer would be best suited to send out to the Indies to watch over the royal interests and to try to straighten out the legal muddles there. A hot wave of recklessness had swept Rich away.

'I could go myself, Highness,' he said, with an appearance of jesting.

At that moment he had felt weary of the dull round of a lawyer's life, of the dignified robes, of the solemn pretence to infallibility, of the eternal weariness of explaining to muddled minds the petty points – often the same points over and over again – which to him were clarity itself. He had suddenly realized that he was forty, and ageing, and that the twenty years which had elapsed since his journey back to Barcelona from Padua had brought him nothing except the worldly success which seemed to him, momentarily, of small account. With pitiless self-analysis Rich, sousing his shirt in the bucket, reminded himself that at that time the prospect of wearing a sword at his side had made a definite appeal to him, as though he had been a hare-brained boy to be attracted by toys.

His Highness's lantern jaw had dropped a little in surprise.

6

'There is nothing we would like better,' he had said.

There had still been a chance of escape. Instant retraction would have left him at peace in his quiet house in Barcelona, and yet he had thrown away the opportunity.

'There is no reason why I should not go, Highness,' he had said, like a fool, and after that there was no chance of withdrawal save at the risk of royal displeasure, and the displeasure of King Ferdinand was more perilous even than a voyage to the Indies.

So here he was, eaten alive by vermin, and roasting under a tropical sun in a ship which seemed as though she would never again feel a breath of wind, so long had she drifted in these equatorial calms. He was indeed the only person on board, of all the hundred and thirty who crowded her, who was displaying any sign of activity. The Admiral and his servants were invisible in the great after-cabin, and the rest of the horde were lying idly in the shade of the bulwarks and of the break of the fore-deck. They were more accustomed to filth and vermin than he was; his fastidious nostrils could distinguish the reek of their dirty bodies and unwashed clothing as one strand of the tangled skein of stinks – salted cod, not too well preserved, and rotting cheese, and fermenting beans. The least unpleasing and most prevalent odour was the vinegary smell of spilt wine drying in the heat – the wine barrels in the waist had been badly coopered, and wine was continually sweating out between the staves, the supply dwindling daily, although to them it was of more value now than the gold they were seeking. The tremendous rain storms, accompanied, alas, by hardly a breath of wind, of the last few days, had brought them drinking water, but it was drinking water flavoured with sea salt and tar as a result of having to be caught in sails before being run into the casks. It was vastly unattractive water, especially to Spaniards with their discriminating taste in drinking water; Rich suspected the water of being the cause of the bowel complaint which was beginning to plague them all.

His shirt was finished now, and he put it on, revelling in the coolness of the wet material against his skin while he stripped off his breeches – it was repulsive and unpleasing to be naked. It was strange that among all the dangers and discomforts he had expected – the fevers, the poisoned arrows, the fire-breathing dragons, the tempests and rocks, he had never anticipated the vermin which now held so important a place in his thoughts. St Francis of Assisi, of blessed memory, had spoken of lice as the pearls of poverty. Rich, bending over his disgusting task, shuddered at the unorthodoxy of disapproving of anything St Francis had said, until he reassured himself with the thought that divine Providence had not blessed him with the Saint's humility. There was a whiff of heresy about that, too, now he came to think about it. But he pulled himself together sturdily; his immortal soul could not really be endangered by his cleansing the seam of his breeches. *De minimis non curat lex.* He could argue a good case with St Peter on that point.

These breeches were fiendishly difficult to clean; cold sea-water was not the most helpful medium in which to attempt it. Boiling water, if he could be sure of not hardening the leather, would be far more efficacious. Or a hot knife-blade, run along the seams. But there was no chance of heating a knife-blade or of boiling water; the cooking fire on the stone hearth in the waist was out, and had not been lighted for – how many days? Five? Six? – the days had been so much alike that he could not remember. The heat had been too great for the cooks to do their work, so the cooks had said, and the Admiral had believed them. The Admiral did not care whether his food was hot or cold, sweet or rotten; probably he did not even notice. Presumably he was not in his great cabin, dreaming over his charts, revolving fresh theories. Rich pointed out to himself that the Admiral, even if he were too gentle with the men, was hard enough on himself, and even though he was grasping in his efforts to adhere to the letter of that absurd agreement with the Crown, he was at least prepared to devote every thought in his head and every breath in his body to the furtherance of the objects of that agreement.

This southerly course which they were following – now – or would be following, if there was only a wind – would take them into a region of burning sun and brilliant moon; it had done so, for that matter, already. That would greatly increase their chances of obtaining precious metals. The golden glory of the sun and the silver brightness of the moon must obviously engender and stimulate the growth of gold and silver. The soil should be thick with them in this climate, when they reached land. The Portuguese had discovered more and more gold the farther south they pushed their exploration of Africa, which was a clear confirmation of the theory. Shiploads of gold and silver would make Spain rich and powerful. There would be content and plenty in the land. There would be bread on the table of every peasant, and the court of Their Highnesses would be the most brilliant in Christendom.

The Admiral saw this plainly enough. It would be a much shorter cut than the tedious methods of trade. The other Indian islands he had discovered had obviously been pretty close to the dominions of the Grand Khan. That wealthy region of Cibao that the natives of Española talked about must most probably be the island of Japan, often referred to as Cipangu, which was known to lie adjacent to the coast of China. For that matter the Admiral had reached the confines of the Grand Khan's dominions in his previous voyage. The great land of Cuba at which he had touched – the name obviously recalled that of Kubla Khan, whom Marco Polo had encountered in his travels to the East. Rich was aware that more than one wild theorist had put forward the suggestion that Cuba was just another island, vaster than any yet known, larger even than Sicily, but the Admiral did not agree. The Admiral was much the more likely to be right. He had proved himself right over the tremendous question of the

9

practicability of reaching the Indies by sailing westward, so that he was hardly likely to be wrong over the simple question as to whether Cuba was part of the mainland or not. Kubla Khan's court was wealthy, and his empire wide; trade with him might produce benefits, but nothing nearly as great as winning great shiploads of gold without the tiresome necessity of trading.

So Rich had thoroughly approved of this southerly course, which would carry them to the gold-bearing, barbaric countries and keep them clear of Cuba and Japan and the other Chinese territories. He was only a tiny bit doubtful now, and that merely on account of practical details. To the north of them lay a region where the wind blew eternally from the eastward; he had sailed through it, he had observed the phenomenon with his own senses. Always from the eastern quarter, sometimes from the north of east, very occasionally from the south of east, that wind blew. If there was a region where there was always a wind blowing, was it not likely that there was another where the wind never blew? They had had days and days of calm. If they were to push farther south still they might reach an area where the calm would be eternal, where they would drift helpless until they died.

Rich looked about him. Westward the sky was beginning to display the marvellous reds and golds of another sunset. Over-side was the deep clear blue of the sea, in which lay a long wreath of golden weed – a pleasing colour contrast. A little flock of flying fish rose from the sea as he looked, and skimmed along, and vanished again; the dark furrows they left behind them on the glassy surface vanished as quickly. In the bows, black against the colouring sky, stood the look-out, his hand resting on the forestay. Aft stood the helmsman, the tiller idle at his side. Far astern, almost on the horizon, he could see the brown sail and the red sail of their consorts, wallowing, like them, helpless in the calm. Lovely, and yet sinister, was how the scene appeared to Rich. Standing barelegged on the fore-deck of the *Holy Name,* his breeches in his hand, and with the sunset lowering round him, he felt a twinge of lonely fear.

At that very moment a little wind began to blow. He felt it first on his bare legs, damp with the water that had dripped from his shirt – a tiny coolness, the merest ghost of a breath. At first the coolness was all he noticed, never thinking of the cause. Then the big sail above him flapped a trifle, and then louder. Alonso Sanchez de Carvajal, the sailing master, was on his feet now on the poop, looking round at the sea and the sky, and up at the long red-cross pennant which was stirring itself at the mast-head. He bellowed orders and at the sound of his voice the sailors bestirred themselves, rousing themselves up from where they lounged on the decks, moving to halliards and braces with more cheerfulness than they had been accustomed to show during the last few days. The yards were braced round and the sails bellied a little to the wind. Already the motion of the *Holy Name* had changed, from the indolent indifferent lurching to a more purposeful swoop. Rich heard a sound he had forgotten – the musical bubbling of water under the bows. In itself that was enough to rouse him from his depression. He could feel his spirits rise as he hopped on one leg trying to pull on his breeches and not impede the sailors in their duties.

There was the Admiral on the poop now, in his blue satin doublet with the gold chain glittering round his neck, his white hair hanging to his shoulders. He, too, was looking round the horizon. Now he was speaking to Carvajal, and Carvajal was bellowing more orders to the crew. The yards were being braced farther round. They were altering course; Rich looked forward as the ship steadied herself. Right ahead the sun hovered close above the horizon in a glory of red and gold. The *Holy Name* was heading due west – the Admiral must have changed his mind at last about holding to the south-westward. To the westward probably lay the nearest land; Rich felt a little thrill of anticipation.

Alonso Perez came shambling past him – the Admiral's

servant, major-domo, and general factotum, stoop-shouldered and with arms disproportionately long. He stepped to the rail and cleared his throat noisily, standing waiting.

'Go!' came the Admiral's high clear voice from the poop, and Perez spat into the indigo sea.

The Admiral was by the rail on the poop, the fingers of his right hand clasping his left wrist. He was counting the number of times his pulse beat while the white fleck of mucus drifted back to him, which would enable him to estimate the speed of the ship through the water. Rich had helped in the initial tedious calculations by which the table of speeds had been constructed – for example, if the ship travels XCI feet while the pulse beats XLIII times, and the number of times the pulse beats in a minute is LXX, how many leagues does the ship travel in an hour? But there was no need to make those calculations now, because the table was constructed once for all, and mere knowledge of the number of pulse beats enabled anyone to read off the speed of the ship; and Carvajal's pulse, and the pulse of Diego Osorio the boatswain, had been compared with the Admiral's so that any ore of the three could take an observation.

It was highly ingenious – one of the many highly ingenious devices which Rich had admired since he had come to sea and interested himself in navigation. The astrolabe, which enabled one to guess which point one had reached of the earth's rotundity from north to south, was another ingenious device. By its aid a ship's captain could always return to a place he had previously visited, if only he sailed long enough along the line which ran through it parallel to the equinoctial line. If only – Rich was beginning again, as he had often done before, to try and work out a similar method of ascertaining longitude, but he was interrupted by his noticing that the ship's company was assembling aft.

He hastened after them, and took his place among the group of gentlemen and priests at the starboard side. The Admiral stood by the tiller, Carvajal at his side, the seamen in line athwartships, and the landsmen to port. Only the look-out and the helmsman took no part in the prayer. Heads were bowed. Horny hands made the sign of the cross. They prayed to the Queen of Heaven, the unlettered among them stumbling through the Latin words following the others. Rich glanced up under his eyelids at the Admiral, who was standing with clasped hands gazing up at the darkening sky. There was a happy exaltation in his face, a fixed and fanatical enthusiasm – everyone was aware of the Admiral's special devotion to the Blessed Virgin. His blue eyes were still bright in the growing darkness, his white beard ghost-like.

The prayer ended, and the massed ship's company began to break up again into groups. Overhead the stars were coming into sight – strange stars, with the Great Bear almost lost on the northern horizon, and new constellations showing in the south, glowing vividly against the velvet of the sky. Like another star appeared the taper borne by a ship's boy to light the shaded lamp that hung above the compass before the steersman.

CHAPTER TWO

THE blessed new coolness of the night gave sweet sleep to Narciso Rich, despite the foulness of his sleeping quarters with twenty gentlemen of coat-armour on the berth-deck below the great cabin aft, despite the snores of his companions, despite the lumpiness of his chaff mattress and the activity of its inhabitants. He told himself, as he stepped into the fresh air in the waist, just before dawn, that they must be nearing the fountain of youth, for he felt none of the weight of his forty years on his shoulders, and his bones had ceased to protest about that chaff mattress. Carvajal had told him of the curious type of bed used by the natives of the Indian islands – a network of interlaced creepers, secured to posts at either end, and called a 'hammock' in their pagan tongue – and Rich had once suggested that they would be ideal for use on board ship, where space was limited and motion violent, but Carvajal had pursed his lips and shaken his head at such a preposterous notion. Chaff mattresses had always been used at sea, and always would; and Christian sailors could do better than to adopt ideas from naked unbelievers.

Rich dipped his bucket and rinsed his face and hands, ran his comb through his hair and beard, and looked about him. The sky was lavender-hued now with the approaching dawn, in such lovely contrast with the blue of the sea as to rouse an ache in his breast, and that blessed breeze was still blowing from the east, driving the *Holy Name* steadily westward over the rhythmic rise and fall of the sea. He walked over and glanced at the slate hanging beside the helmsman. There was bunch after bunch of little strokes recorded there – they must have made at least twenty leagues during the night. Quite soon they must reach land, and they were a hundred leagues or more farther south than Española – one of the southern islands which Polo had heard about, Sumatra, perhaps, with its sandalwood and spices.

A ship's boy came pattering up, barefooted; the last grains were running out of the hour-glass and he turned it and lifted his voice in a loud cry to Diego Osorio. The ship's day was begun, and by coincidence just as the first rays of the sun were gleaming over the sea, touching the crests of the waves into gold. Carvajal came up on to the poop, crossed himself before the painted Virgin by the taffrail, and looked keenly at the slate. He nodded curtly to Rich, but he had no words to spare for him at this time in the morning, for it was during this cool hour that the work of the ship must be done. Soon he was bellowing orders at the sleepy men who came crawling out of the forecastle to join those already on deck. Twelve of them were sent to work at bailing out the ship – seven of them as a living chain passing up buckets from the bilge to the rail, and five returning the empty buckets again. It was a slow and weary process, which Rich had watched daily for five weeks, and every day the work was harder, because in these seas there lived creatures who bored holes in the bottoms of ships, as clean as an auger.

Rich had dallied with several ideas bearing on the subject, both to reduce the labour of bailing and to evade the necessity for it. There was the Archimedean screw, about which he had read in an Arabic mathematical treatise. A single man turning a handle might do more with such an apparatus – if it could be set up in a ship – than twelve men with buckets. Or there were pumps about which he had vaguely heard – the Netherlanders and Frisians were using them to drain their drowned fields. Here, too, they might be worked by the force of the wind and keep the ship dry without any labour at all. And if the marine creatures bored through wood, why not protect the wood from them? A thin coating of lead, say, or of copper. Perhaps the weight would be too great for the ship to bear, and certainly the cost would be enormous, but it might be worth while thinking about.

It would be no use discussing such innovations with Carvajal, as he was painfully aware. Nor – Rich decided reluctantly – with the Admiral. The latter regarded him with suspicion, as a royal agent sent to try and devise methods of entrenching upon his cherished privileges as Viceroy of the Ocean, and in that he was not far wrong. Where he was wrong was in seeing traps laid for him in the most innocent suggestions, such as for copper-bottoming ships. The Admiral was in such a state of mind as to believe every man's hand against him.

The ship was fully awake now. Here came the friars in their robes, and after them Rich's recent cabin mates, the hidalgos, lounging out on deck, their swords at their hips; the two Acevedo brothers, Cristobal Garcia and his followers, Bernardo de Tarpia, still a little unsure of himself from seasickness, and the others. Their lisping Castilian contrasted oddly with the rougher, aspirated Andalusian of the crews and with the sweet Catalan which was music to Rich's ears. João de Setubal spoke the barbarous Portuguese, which put him on better terms with the Admiral, who spoke Portuguese well, but who, when he spoke Castilian, was liable to lapse with startling unintelligibility into his native Italian. When that happened it was not unusual for him to go on talking for several minutes without realizing what had happened, and for him only to be recalled to Spanish by the look of blank incomprehension on the face of the person addressed.

Here he came on deck now, wearing scarlet velvet – the fact that he could wear velvet in that heat was a clear enough proof of the way in which personal discomfort meant nothing to him – his gold chain and his jewelled sword and dagger. His four pages followed him – it was as if they were carrying a five-yard ermine train – and Perez with his white staff of office and Antonio Spallanzani his Italian squire. The hidalgos, Rich among them, fell into line and bowed deeply as he

16

approached, with all the deference due to the Regent of the Indies. He bowed stiffly in return – it was rheumatism which made him so unbending – and then turned, with head bowed and uncovered, to murmur a prayer to the Virgin by the taffrail. Carvajal awaited his attention at his elbow, and the Admiral, when he had finished his devotions, turned to him with a slow dignity. Carvajal made his report on the night's run, the Admiral's keen blue eyes running over the slate to confirm it. They had run twenty-one leagues. Two great shooting stars had been seen during the middle watch. At dawn the look-out had seen a flight of pelicans.

'Then land is near,' said the Admiral. 'Pelicans never fly far to sea.'

'Yes, Excellency,' said Carvajal, bowing again. 'But the western horizon was clear at daybreak.'

'No matter. We shall see land today. We are close upon it.'

The Admiral directed his glance forward, to where the look-out stood gazing ahead. There was a little petulance in the Admiral's manner, a little impatience, as though he suspected the look-out of not doing his duty. Rich felt a little puzzled, because the Admiral could have no certain knowledge that land was within five hundred miles of them in that direction; the Indies already discovered were far to the northward, and no one could tell exactly where were Java and Sumatra and the islands of the roc and the island of pearls where Sinbad had traded.

'It may even be in sight now,' said the Admiral. 'Here, Perez, go aloft and see for me.'

Perez handed his white staff in silence to one of the pages and shambled forward. He leaped with ungraceful agility up into the shrouds of the mainmast, and climbed like a cat or an ape up the unstable rope ladder. Every eye watched him as he reached the mast-head and steadied himself with one arm linked round a rope and shaded his eyes with his other hand. For a long time he stared to the westward over the indigo sea, looked away to relieve his aching eyes, and then stared again. Suddenly he waved his hand.

'Land!' he shouted. 'Land!'

The ship broke into a bustle of excitement. Everyone began to scramble for a better point of view. Two or three sailors sprang for the shrouds, and were instantly checked by a high-pitched cry from the Admiral. No one except the faithful Perez should set eyes on this new domain of his before its legitimate ruler should. He walked to the shrouds with the dignity that concealed his rheumatic gait, and slowly began the climb. His bulky clothes and his sword impeded him, but he never hesitated until the mast-head was reached. They saw Perez make place for him and point forward, and then, clearly dismissed, slide down the halliard to the deck. The Admiral stayed at the mast-head, the sun gleaming on his jewellery and his scarlet and gold. It was long before he began the descent again, longer still before he reached the deck.

'Gentlemen,' he said gravely to the group of hidalgos – gravely, but with a sparkle of happiness in his eyes. 'Yet one more miracle has been vouchsafed to us by the mercy of God.'

He crossed himself, and they waited for him to say more, patiently.

'This voyage, as you know, gentlemen, the third expedition to the Indies which I have commanded, was undertaken in the name of the Most Holy Trinity. The third voyage, gentlemen, and in the name of the Trinity. And now the first land we sight is a triple peak, three mountain-tops conjoined at their base, the emblem of the Trinity, Three in One and One in Three. I have named the land in sight Trinidad, in perpetual memory of this stupendous event. Let us give thanks to God the Father, and to the Blessed Saviour, and to the Holy Spirit.'

The harsh voice of the Dominican friar began at once to recite the prayer; heads were bared and bowed as they followed the words. And when the prayer was finished the Admiral turned to the ship's boys behind him.

'Sing, boys,' he commanded. 'Sing the Salve Regina.'

They sang like angels, their clear high treble soaring up to the cloudless blue sky, the deep bass of the crew blending in harmony with it. It was only after the hymn was finished that the Admiral, with a gesture, dismissed the excited ship's company so that they could climb the rigging and view the land in sight, but at the same time his eyes met Rich's and detained him.

'You see, Don Narciso,' said the Admiral, gravely, 'how clearly the hand of God is visible in this enterprise.'

'Yes, Your Excellency,' said Rich. He felt the same. The sighting of the triple mountain-top as the first incident of a voyage undertaken in the name of the Trinity might – so Rich's legal mind insisted – have been only a coincidence. But that land should be sighted on the very day the Admiral had predicted it, at a moment when Rich was acutely aware how insignificant were the data on which to base any calculations – that was also proof of God's providence. The two facts together made the deduction indisputable.

'We are no more than ten degrees north of the equinoctial line,' went on the Admiral. 'It will be the gold-bearing land whose existence was postulated by my friend Ferrer, the jeweller, as well as by the ancients. Pliny and Aristotle both have passages bearing on the subject. It seems likely enough to me that this will prove to be the land of Ophir of which the Bible tells us.'

'Yes, sir,' said Rich.

The possibility of the new land being Ophir seemed to him not too great. It was only a possibility, not a probability. If it were so they must have progressed at least two-thirds of the way round the globe, and their noontime must differ by sixteen hours from that of Cadiz. If only by some fresh miracle they could know what was the time at that moment in Spain! Or if only their hour-glasses could be relied upon to give accurate time over a period of weeks, without a cumulative and unknown error of hours! So much that was doubtful would be settled by that.

'My hope is', said the Admiral, 'that we shall obtain such quantities of gold that there will be no need for dispute between me and the other servants of Their Highnesses.'

'We must hope so, sir,' said Rich. He tried to imagine how much gold would have to be imported before King Ferdinand considered it too much trouble to go into the accounts. He felt there was not that much gold in the whole world, even though Queen Isabella would be more easily satisfied.

'With Ophir found, and with shiploads of gold returning to Spain,' went on the Admiral, 'it will not be long before the Holy Places are free and the unbeliever ceases to defile Jerusalem.'

'I beg your pardon, sir?' said Rich, a little bewildered. This was something new to him.

'Did not Their Highnesses tell you?' asked the Admiral, surprised. 'The dearest wish of my heart, in achieving which I will die happy, is to set free the Holy Places. It is to that end that I intend to employ the gold of Ophir. I have visited the ports of the Levant, and I have studied the problem on the spot. With four thousand horse and fifty thousand foot three campaigns would reconquer the Holy Land for Christendom. I vowed my wealth to that end when I first reached the Indies, and I have no doubt of the assistance of Their Highnesses when the money becomes available.'

'Yes, sir,' said Rich, feebly. His mind struggled with the details of the plan – with the expense of maintaining an army of fifty thousand men for three years, with the question as to whether such a force would attain any success against the most powerful military state in Europe, and, lastly, whether Their Highnesses were likely to set the whole Mediterranean into a turmoil and wage a bloody war at the instigation of a vassal whose power they suspected even on the other side of the ocean. The whole scheme seemed utterly wild; and yet – six years ago the Admiral had discovered the Indies, in face of the hostile criticism of all the world. Today his prediction of the presence of land in a place where no one could be certain land existed had been dramatically confirmed. Nothing he said could be dismissed casually as an old man's maunderings.

'Nazareth!' said the Admiral in a kind of ecstasy. His mind was evidently still running on the same subject, but presumably in a very different way from Rich's. Yet his enthusiasm was infectious.

'It is a glorious project,' said Rich, in spite of himself.

'Yes,' replied the Admiral. 'And we are approaching the country which will provide the means to realize it. The land of the Trinity!'

There was dismissal in the gesture he made. His mind was wrapped now in lofty schemes like a mountain among the clouds. Rich bowed and withdrew. He was glad enough, too, to do so, for he was excited and impatient for his first sight of the Indies. He hoisted himself up on the bulwark, but the approaching land was still below the horizon from there, and he set himself to make the unaccustomed climb up the main shrouds – the whole rigging of the ship was still thick with clusters of men, like fruit in a tree. At the mast-head there were a dozen of the soldiers whom Bernardo de Tarpia commanded, and they grudgingly made room for him. Rich clung wildly to the yard, breathless and giddy. He was unaccustomed both to exercise and to heights, and up here the motion of the ship was greatly exaggerated. The horizon swooped round him for a few wild seconds until he regained his breath and his self-control. He wiped off the sweat which was streaming into his eyes and looked forward. There was the land; bright green slopes illuminated by the morning sun. The Indies! The most westerly and the most easterly limit of man's knowledge of the world he lived in. It was raining there to the northward – the sun behind him was lighting up a dazzling rainbow at that extremity of the island. From there southward there stretched luxuriant green hills; when the *Holy Name* rose on a wave he could see a line of white foam as the waves broke against the beach at their feet.

The sun was beating on his back like a flail; he wiped the sweat from his face again and continued his observations. It looked a rich enough country – that vivid green spoke well for its fertility – but it seemed virgin. No axe had ever plied among those forests. His straining eyes could see no sign of human habitation. Trying to compel himself to think clearly, he came to admit that at that distance he could not expect to see individual houses. But a town would be visible enough, for all that, and there was not the slightest hint of the existence of a town. A busy and prosperous coast would be thick with shipping, and there was no shipping in sight at all, not even – what was the word the Indian islanders used? – not even a canoe to make a speck on the flawless blue. Depression settled on him for a moment, which he told himself was unreasonable.

But God had vouchsafed a sign – the Admiral had announced to them the sight of the triple peak from which he had already named this new island. Rich swept his gaze along the skyline to identify the mountain. It was odd that he did not see it at once. He had looked from north to south; now he looked from south to north, more carefully. There was still no triple peak to be seen, and yet it ought to be obvious. The Admiral had been very positive about it indeed. It occurred to Rich that the explanation probably lay in the long interval which had elapsed since the Admiral had first seen the land. During that time the three peaks must have moved round into line relative to the new position of the ship.

With this in mind, he looked again. It was puzzling, for the ship had been heading straight for the land ever since it had first come in sight, and the relative movement could not have been great. Nowhere was there any outstanding peak which might be resolved into three summits from another point of view. With a little sinking at heart he began to realize another possibility – that the Admiral had not seen any triple peak at all, and had merely imagined it, the wish being father to the thought. That at least was humanly possible, and as far as he could see was the only hypothesis which fitted the facts; in that case, his study of logic assured him, he should work on that hypothesis until either it was disproved or a better one presented itself.

Nevertheless, it was disquieting, not merely to be at sea under an admiral who saw mountains which did not exist, but because – this was quite as disturbing – it tended to shake his faith in miracles. He had just disproved one for himself, and it was tempting to imagine that all miracles had a similar foundation in wishful thinking. That cut at the base of all religion, and led to doubt and heresy, and from that to polygamy and unsound theories on the distribution of property, to the fines of the Inquisition and the flames of Hell. He shuddered at the thought of the damnation of his soul, and clung to the yard in front of him, a little sick. The soldiers beside him were joking coarsely – their words came faintly to his ears as if from another room – about the naked women who were, they hoped, looking out at the ship from the island and awaiting their arrival. He tried to shake off his depression as he set himself to descend the shrouds.

As his feet touched the deck he found himself face to face with Rodrigo Acevedo, the elder of the two brothers.

'Well, doctor?' said Rodrigo. He was a tall, wiry man, of a bitter humour; his high arched nose and his flashing black eyes hinted at his Moorish blood, and he bore himself with an easy athleticism which made Rich conscious of his own ungainly plumpness, and this despite the fact that Rich had been at some pains to acquire that plumpness as increasing the dignity of a young doctor of law.

'Well?' said Rich, defensively.

'What do you think of the promised land?'

'It looks green and fertile enough,' answered Rich, still defensive.

'Did you see the great city of Cambaluc?'

'No. That must lie more to the north and west.'

'Yes. More to the north and west. How far? A hundred leagues? A thousand?'

Rich was silent.

'Five thousand, then!' sneered Acevedo.

'Not as far,' said Rich, hotly.

'And did you see the Grand Khan putting off to welcome us in his gilded galleon?'

'No,' said Rich. 'We have come this far south so as to avoid the Grand Khan's dominions.'

'We have avoided them in all conscience,' said Acevedo. 'Did you see any mountains of gold?'

'No,' replied Rich.

'None? You are quite sure? Did you see any mountain with a triple peak?'

'I went up the mast a long time after land was sighted,' said Rich, uneasily. 'The appearances had changed by then.'

'Yes,' sneered Acevedo again. 'Doubtless they had.'

'What do you think then?' asked Rich, his dignity reasserting itself. He was tired of being teased.

'I? I think nothing.'

Acevedo's mouth was distorted in a lopsided smile. Rich remembered what he had heard about Acevedo's past – of the Inquisition's descent upon the family of his betrothed; his prospective father-in-law had been burned at the stake in Toledo, and his prospective bride had been paraded in a fool's coat to make a solemn act of contrition before disappearing for life into a dungeon where the bread and water of affliction awaited her. The Holy Office must have questioned Acevedo closely enough. He was wise not to think; he was wise to come here to the Indies where the Holy Office would not have its attention called to him again so easily.

'That is sensible of you,' said Rich.

Their eyes met, with a gleam of understanding, before Acevedo was called away by a group clustered forward.

The backgammon boards were out, and the dice were already rattling there. Half the ship's company had already recovered from the excitement of sighting land and had plunged again into the diversions which had become habitual during the long voyage. The people were indifferent to their fates, careless as to where they were going, and that was only to be expected, seeing that three-quarters of them at least were on board either against their will or, like Acevedo, because Spain had grown too hot to hold them.

It was like the first voyage over again, when the ships had to be manned by criminals and ne'er-do-wells. For the second voyage there had been no lack of money nor of volunteers. Seventeen tall ships had sailed, with full complements, and a score of stowaways had been found on board after sailing, so great had been the eagerness to join, as a result of the marvellous stories the Admiral had brought back of the wealth and the marvels of the newly discovered lands. But during the years that followed bad news had drifted back across the ocean. The original garrison left in Española were all dead by the time the second expedition arrived, and death had followed death in terrifying succession. Death by disease, death by poisonous serpents, death even from the pointed canes which were all the weapons the Indians possessed. Then death by famine, death by the gallows after mutiny. The stories told by the broken men who were lucky enough to make their way back to Spain had discouraged the nation. The adventurous spirits now followed Gonsalvo de Cordoba to the conquest of Italy. King Ferdinand, struggling in the whirlpool of European affairs, had naturally been dubious about expending further strength on chimerical conquests. Twenty ships from the Basque ports had been necessary to convey the Princess Katherine and a suitable train to her wedding with the Prince of Wales. It was not surprising that compulsion was necessary to man the ships for this present third expedition.

Rich remembered the sullen evidence given by the wretched survivors whom he had examined. Every man had cherished a grievance, mainly against the Admiral. It was his digest of the evidence which had influenced His Highness to dispatch a lawyer to the Indies to investigate. Rich told himself that, like the eagle in the fable, it was he himself who had winged the arrow of his fate.

CHAPTER THREE

'By order of the Admiral!' announced the harsh voice of
Alonso Perez in the stifling 'tweendecks. 'All gentlemen on
board the *Holy Name* will wear half-armour and swords
today. By order of the Admiral!'

It was nearly dawn, and still comparatively dark. The
harsh voice awakened Rich from a tumultuous sleep;
the heat and the excitement had kept him awake most of the
night. He sat up on his chaff mattress in his shirt and listened
to the yawns and groans around him. Someone pulled the
deadlight away from the scuttle and let in a little more light
and a whiff of fresher air; the sky visible through the hole
was a rich dark blue. Twenty tousled men were stretching
and rubbing their eyes, their hair and beards in disorder.
Some were experimentally running their tongues over their
palates, savouring the foul taste in their mouths resulting
from a night in the poisonous atmosphere of the 'tweendecks.

He got to his knees – the deck above was too low to admit
of standing, with the 'tweendecks floored with chests – rolled
up his mattress and struggled to open the chest beneath it.
Cristobal Garcia lay next to him, against the bulkhead; he was
big and burly and bearded to the eyes and clearly in a bad
temper. An unexpected movement of the ship caught Rich
off his balance and rolled him against him. Garcia growled
like a wounded bear.

'I beg your pardon, sir,' said Rich, hastily.

He tugged the heavy bundle of his armour out of the chest
and allowed the lid to fall with a crash. Garcia yelped at the
noise in his ear.

'God, what a devilish din!' he said. He got on to his

27

elbow and eyed Rich sardonically. 'So our little fat Doctor of Law becomes a soldier today?'

'The Admiral's orders,' said Rich.

'The Admiral can work miracles by his orders, apparently,' growled Garcia.

Rich kept his mouth shut. It saved trouble, although he could have replied that he was entitled to wear the gentlemanly sword although he was merely a vintner's son; half the artisans of Catalonia could do so – much to the amusement of fine gentlemen – thanks to the peculiar laws of the kingdom. He comforted himself with the thought that although not yet forty he had already accumulated more wealth than was owned by all the segundones – younger sons – in this crowded space put together. He had acquired it honestly, too, and with no advantage over them save a good education. In the whole fleet he was perhaps the only man who had not been driven by necessity to join, the only man save the Admiral who had already made a name for himself in his own walk of life.

Yet it was cold comfort, all the same. He could not meet them in the lists, which was the only kind of argument they understood, he had never seen a battlefield, he could only just manage to sit a horse. More important still, they were completely convinced of their superiority over him in consequence of their ancestry. In their eyes he was hardly more of an equal than, say, an ape or a mule. Without one hundred and twenty-eight quarterings of nobility he could no more reckon himself their equal than he could reckon himself the equal of the archangels of God.

It was quite an athletic feat to wriggle into clothes and armour under the low deck while crouched on his mattress. He was sweating profusely by the time the leather coat and breeches were on, and the back and breastplates buckled about him. He grabbed his sword and his helmet and scrambled out, bent double.

There was the dull gleam of armour to be seen everywhere about the ship. He put on his helmet and felt its unaccustomed weight upon his forehead. He slung his sword by its broad leather belt over his shoulder and saw to it that its hilt was clear. The deck was crowded with crossbowmen in helmet and jerkin, and spearmen with helmet and leather shield. On the forecastle the bombardier and his two mates were cleaning the two swivel cannons ready for use. They had a barrel of gunpowder and a chest full of their enormous bullets, each nearly the size of a man's fist. The six hand-gunmen were aft, by the taffrail, each with his ponderous weapon and his rest. Of a certainty; it was all extremely impressive, and grew more so each minute as the hidalgos came crawling out of the 'tweendecks in helmet and armour. No embassy from the shore but could fail to be struck by all this display.

Rich could see, as he peered under the peak of his helmet, the gleam of more armour on the decks of the two caravels lying hove-to a short distance away. The fleet was close up to the land, and had been lying-to through the dark hours. Rich gazed across the intervening water; easy green slopes, lush vegetation, dazzling white surf where the ocean swell burst upon the beaches. The steady east wind blew, but it hardly tempered the sweltering heat; Rich in his armour and helmet felt as if he were being roasted alive.

Here came the Admiral, in his usual dignified procession, walking stiffly on account of his rheumatism. Orders were bellowed and stamping men hauled at ropes. Round came the ships, westward before the wind, heading close along shore. Now Rich could understand why the Admiral had so persistently, when the expedition was being got together, demanded only little ships – nothing more than a hundred tons. The two small caravels sailed far nearer the beach and had the land under far closer observation than could the *Holy Name*. A sailor in the bows of each vessel was heaving the lead and chanting the depths, but apart from the men engaged in the actual work of the ship, everyone's attention was fixed upon the land.

It was a silent shore. There were birds wheeling overhead, but save for the birds there was no sound, no sign of life. Only the expressionless green slopes and the monotonous surf; a dead landscape, changing and yet in no way different as they cruised along beside it. They had hoped for the teeming millions of Asia, opulent cities and luxurious princes – to impress whom they were wearing the armour that burdened them. Even at the worst they had hoped at least to see the laughing naked peoples whom they had discovered in the other islands, but here there was nothing. Nothing at all.

The Admiral was giving an order now, and the bombardier fussed over his swivel cannon. He ladled powder into the muzzle, and stuffed it down with a mop. He clicked his flint and steel over his tinder, blew at the spark, tried again, got his match alight, whirled it round to make it glow, and pressed it on the touch-hole. There was a loud bang and a puff of smoke. The birds screamed and a little cloud of them appeared above the trees on the island. The echo of the report ran flatly along the shore, and that was all. No welcoming human appeared; the armoured men stood stupid and silent on the decks.

'A lovely land, Don Narciso,' said the Admiral's voice in Rich's ear – he started with surprise. 'Green and fertile, like Andalusia in spring time.'

'Yes, Your Excellency,' said Rich, unhappily.

The Admiral was breathing great lungfuls of air. There was a fresh colour to his cheeks and a fresh light in his eyes. He wore his armour and his cloak over it as if they were gossamer.

'There is something rejuvenating about the air here,' said the Admiral. 'Do you not notice how fresh and sweet it is?'

'The sun is hot,' protested Rich, feebly.

'Naturally, seeing that at noon it is directly overhead at this time of year. But that calls forth the treasures of the soil, the fruits, the minerals. This will prove to be the richest quarter of the earth, Don Narciso.'

'We must hope so.'

'Hope? We know it to be so already. The ancients proved it, and the Scriptures tell us so. Last night, Don Narciso, instead of sleeping, I pondered over our new discoveries. I thought about this new balminess of the air, as compared with the windless and torrid regions of the ocean which we have crossed. I compared this blessed land with the stifling unhealthiness of those regions of Africa which the Portuguese have discovered and which lie as close to the equinoctial line as does this. There must be an explanation of the difference. Is it not likely to be that the earth is not a perfect sphere, as one might deduce from what one knows of the northern half, but drawn out and prolonged towards this point, like, say, the thinner end of a pear? Or perhaps on a smaller scale – one can naturally not be certain yet of exact proportions – like the nipple of a woman's breast?'

'The possibility had not occurred to me, Your Excellency,' said Rich, bewildered.

'But now you must appreciate it. Here we must be farther from the earth's centre, closer to heaven, remote from evil. I think we must be close beside the Garden of Eden, the Earthly Paradise, where the Tree of Knowledge grows, and where man is near to God.'

Rich stared up, under his helmet's peak, at the tall, gaunt Admiral and the ecstasy in his face. Yesterday they had reached Ophir, today it was the Garden of Eden. He could think of no passages either in the ancients or in the Scriptures to justify either theory. He was at a loss for words with which to make any pretence at a reply. But he was preserved from the necessity, for the Admiral's keen eyes had detected an indentation in the shore line. He turned to give orders in his clear, penetrating tenor, and the seamen leaped to obey him. The steersman dragged the tiller over; the sails were clewed up; the anchor was let go and the cable roared through the hawse-hole. Even Rich, with his mere theoretical knowledge of the sea, was impressed by the neatness of the manoeuvre – as

31

impressed as he was by the Admiral's sudden change from a dreamer of lunatic dreams to a sailor of profound practical ability. As the *Holy Name* swung to her anchor the Admiral turned to Rich.

'A stream comes down to the sea at that beach, Don Narciso. I shall send ashore for fresh water. Would you care to go with the landing party and take possession of the island in the name of Their Highnesses?'

'Indeed yes. I must thank your Excellency.'

There was no denying the thrill of excitement which ran through him at the suggestion. Rich forgot the weight of his armour and the heat of the sun; he fidgeted with his sword hilt while the sailors rigged the yardarm tackles with which to swing out the longboat from the waist. The cooper supervised the lowering of the empty barrels into the boat; six seamen scrambled down and took their places at the oars; Osorio the boatswain took the tiller. At a sharp command from the Admiral four of Bernardo de Tarpia's crossbowmen followed him. Then came Antonio Spallanzani, the Admiral's Italian squire, with the Admiral's standard, bearing the lions and castles of Leon and Castile, recently granted him, quartered with the barry wavy, argent and azure, charged with green islands, to represent his discoveries. Those lions and castles in the flag might be of use if ever a legal argument arose regarding the sovereignty over this new land. They would help to make out Their Highnesses' case – but although the Admiral might be suspected of much, no one had yet openly accused him of dreaming of an independent sovereignty.

They were waiting for him. Rich clambered down into the boat, ungracefully, conscious of many eyes upon him, and only realizing after he had settled himself at Spallanzani's side that if he had slipped into the sea his armour would have carried him straight to the bottom. The sailors tugged at the oars, and they went dancing over the sea towards the shore.

The Italian sat silent – he had a reputation for taciturnity – while they rowed past the anchored caravels, busy hoisting out their boats, and crept in closer to the shore. There was still only the golden beach and the white surf and the tangled greenery to be seen. The sailors rested on their oars for a space while Osorio stood up and studied the surf. He gave a hoarse cry; the sailors tugged sharply at the oars, and the boat leaped forward on the shoulder of a wave, hurrying on until its motion died away and the sand scraped under the keel and the white foam eddied back past them. The sailors leaped out, thigh deep, in the water, and hauled the boat up as far as it would go, until by a wave of his hand Osorio indicated to the two gentlemen that it was time for them to step ashore. Rich scrambled up into the bows and from there over the side; a dying wave swirled past his knees as he stepped into the water and his feet sank in the sand. He struggled up the beach, oppressed by the weight of his armour, until he was beyond the water's edge. The Italian was close behind him, and the crossbowmen followed, their crossbows on their shoulders. Spallanzani struck the shaft of the flag into the sand and took a paper from his breast.

'We,' he read, a barbarous Tuscan accent colouring his Castilian, 'Don Christopher Columbus, Admiral of the Ocean, Viceroy and Governor of the Islands of the Indies, Captain-General and Grandee of Spain –' it was a solemn formula of possession.

When he had finished Rich took off his helmet.

'This is done,' he proclaimed, bareheaded, to the four solemn crossbowmen, 'in the names of Their Highnesses Don Ferdinand and Donna Isabella, by the grace of God King and Queen of Castile, Leon, Arragon, Sicily, Granada, Toledo, Valencia, Galicia, Mallorca, and Seville, Count and Countess of Barcelona, Roussillon, and Cerdagne, Duke and Duchess of Athens and Neopatra, Marquis and Marchioness of Oristano and Goziano, Lord and Lady of Biscay and Molina.'

He had left out quite a number of the titles, but he had done enough to ensure the legality of the Royal possession, especially as the only witnesses were the crossbowmen, standing with ox-like stupidity in the sunshine. Osorio and his men had put out the boat's anchor, and were carrying empty water breakers up the beach. At a roar from the boatswain two of the crossbowmen joined in the work; the other two wound up their bows, laid bolts in the grooves, and walked forward to where the stream came bubbling down out of the greenery, to stand as sentries on guard against surprise. It was an elementary precaution to take, so elementary that Rich experienced a feeling of annoyance that he had not thought of it and ordered it himself.

He cleared the hilt of his sword and walked curiously up the beach, conscious now of a particular thrill at making these, his first steps in the New World. The little stream bubbled and gurgled, and he stooped and filled his hands and drank, over and over again, rejoicing in the water's cool freshness and in having enough to drink after six weeks of a ration of only three leathern cups of water a day. He walked on beside the stream, to be engulfed in the delicious shade of the vegetation, so dense and tangled that it was only by walking ankle deep in the pebbles that he was able to make any progress. He turned a corner and the forest behind him cut him off from the sea more effectively than the closing of a door. The sounds of the beach – the surf, and the voices of the watering party – ended abruptly.

Here he could only hear the sound of the brook and the clatter of birds' wings above him. Looking upward, he could see the birds flitting through the tangle of the branches, birds of gay colours, crying harshly to each other. Some brilliant red flowers grew just out of his reach to his left; there were some strange greenish yellow blooms growing on a decaying stump on the other side of the stream. The noise of his passage disturbed half a dozen more birds – like starlings, he thought at first, and then he saw that they were all of a sombre black, beak and claws and all, funereal birds, with something repellent about their metallic chirping.

There was a breathless heat here in the forest. The shade

had been grateful enough at first, but out in the open there was at least a wind, and here the air was stagnant and warm. The sweat streamed down from under his helmet, and his skin began to itch furiously inside his armour where he could not scratch. A mosquito sang into his ear and then bit his neck. He brushed it off, and soon he was busy brushing off flies from neck and face and hands and wrists. He burst through into a little clear space where the stream expanded into a small pool with marshy banks. There was a startled croaking of frogs, and a dozen splashes told how they had dived back into the pool on his approach. On the surface of the water lay two fallen trees, their exposed parts green with moss; so wide was the pool that the interlaced branches hardly met overhead, and, looking upward, he could see the blue sky again. Tall canes grew here, each twice the height of a man and thicker than his wrist. The gay birds with hooked beaks flew thick – parrots, they were. He remembered that in the Admiral's triumphal procession through Barcelona, when he was received by Their Highnesses on his return from his first voyage of discovery, there had been a great many parrots displayed. Probably there was nothing to be found at this landing place which was not to be seen in Guanahani or Española.

He turned back and made his way down the stream again. Were those bees, beating the air above the scarlet flowers? Rich looked at them more closely. They were tiny birds, brilliant in their colouring. He thought they were the most lovely things he had ever seen in his life. He plunged into the thorns in order to view them more closely, but they flew away, erratically, at his slow approach, and would not return. With a twinge of real regret he continued his way. A loud challenge greeted him at the edge of the wood, and he replied, a little self-consciously, 'Friend.' It was the first time in his life a sentinel had ever challenged him.

The crossbowman lowered his weapon and allowed him to pass, blinking in the sunshine. Someone was kneeling at the

35

water's edge, above the point where the men were filling their barrels. He had a flat pan in his hand, which, with a gentle rocking motion, he was holding at the surface of the water. There was gravel in the bottom of the pan, and under the influence of the current and of the man's raking fingers it was gradually being swept away. Rich recognized the man and guessed what he was doing – it was Diego Alamo the assayer, who had sailed in the caravel *Santa Anna* along with them. Alamo had dealt in gold and precious stones; he was learned in the languages of the East and with his knowledge of Hebrew and Chaldean might be useful when they made contact with Asiatic civilization. Under suspicion of being a crypto-Jew he had thought it well to accept the appointment of Royal assayer to escape the attention of the Holy Office.

Alamo with a skilful jerk flirted the remaining water from the pan and studied the layer of sediment closely, inclining the pan to this side and to that so as to catch the faintest gleam of colour. Then he shrugged his shoulders and washed the pan clean, looking up to meet Rich's eyes upon him.

'Ha, good day, Don Narciso,' he said, white teeth showing in a smile.

'Good day,' said Rich. 'Are there signs of gold?'

'Not so far. The country looks as if it might bear gold, but I'll certify that this stream has none.'

Rich forgot any disappointment he might feel at that statement in the pleasure of this re-encounter with a friend – Alamo and he were old acquaintances. He made the conventional inquiries as to whether Alamo had enjoyed his passage across the ocean – conventional and yet sincere. It was odd to ask those questions here, on the shores of the Indies.

'Well enough, thank you,' answered Alamo. There was a wry smile on his dark intelligent face; Rich guessed that Alamo was as much out of place among the seamen and gentlemen-adventurers of the *Santa Anna* as he himself was in the *Holy Name*.

Alamo rose to his feet, brushing his hands clean. The beach was a scene of animation now, with three boats lying in the shallows and a score of men carrying water casks. The two caravels lay beyond, black upon the blue, and farther out the *Holy Name* rode to her anchor.

'Have you been into the forest?' asked Alamo.

'Yes.'

'Did you see any minerals? Any rocks?'

'Only the pebbles and boulders of the stream bed. The forest is too thick to see more.'

Alamo was looking round the beach.

'Over there,' he said, pointing. 'The rock comes down to the sea there.'

They walked over the sand to the place he had indicated, and Alamo ran his hands over the rocky ledges.

'Gold is unlikely here,' he announced. 'These rocks are dead. They are smooth and lifeless – feel them for yourself, Don Narciso. It is the spirited, lively rocks which bear the noble metals.'

He climbed over the ridge and dropped on to the sand the other side. There were more rocks beyond, running out to the water.

'Now this is strange,' announced Alamo.

He went down on to his knees to examine his find more closely. Among the brown rocks there were patches and dabs and seams of black, and he pawed at them, clearly puzzled.

'This appears to be pitch,' he said. 'Bitumen. I have seen specimens brought from the Holy Land, but never before have I seen it *in situ*. Now how comes it here?'

He looked up at the forest and out at the sea.

'It is found on the shores of the Dead Sea,' he explained, 'at the foot of arid cliffs. It was with fiery pitch that God overwhelmed Sodom and Gomorrah, but the Moslems believe it to be formed by the great excess of salt in the water, under the influence of a burning sun. Now, is the ocean here more salt than usual?'

'It is not dead, at least,' said Rich. 'There is weed growing. And the gulls prove that there must be fish.'

'Quite right. I should have thought of that. Yet it is hard to think of any other explanation of this pitch. The Dead Sea lies in the midst of deserts. There is no life, no plants, no birds, although I am assured by credible authority that the story is incorrect that birds drop dead who fly over its mephitic surface. Two places more unlike than that and this it is hard to imagine.'

'Very hard,' agreed Rich, thinking of the lush vegetation and the teeming bird life around them.

'Has a Sodom been overwhelmed here, too?' asked Alamo.

'Not unless the name of God has penetrated here,' answered Rich, fairly sure of his theology on this point.

'Exactly. That is why I sought for a naturalistic explanation.'

Alamo walked on among the rocks of the beach, Rich straying a little apart from him along the water's edge. It was he who made the final discovery, and his sharp cry brought Alamo hurrying back to him. There was a little stretch of smooth sand here, at which Rich was staring; in the sand was a wide, shallow groove, and around it were the half-obliterated prints of bare feet. Rich had already made the deductions from the appearances.

'No ship's boat made that mark,' he said. 'There is no sign of a keel.'

Alamo nodded agreement, stooping to peer at the footprints.

'There is little enough left to see,' he said. 'But I should think that the feet that made those marks were longer and narrower than any Spaniard's.'

'Yes.'

'And how long ago were they made? An hour? Two hours?'

They looked at each other, a little helpless. Neither of them had the faintest idea.

'We can be sure of one thing at least,' said Rich. 'The people here are not as eager to meet us as were those of Cuba and Española.'

A bellowing behind them made them turn; the watering party was waving arms to them in recall. They picked their way back over the rocks.

CHAPTER FOUR

THE squadron was still sailing westward along the south coast of Trinidad, while the Admiral listened to Rich's report. His face fell a little when he heard that Alamo had found no sign of gold, but he grew cheerful again over the undoubted evidence that the island was inhabited and over the other details which Rich conveyed.

'Pitch?' he said. 'Bitumen?'

He ran his fingers through his beard as he pondered the phenomenon.

'What did Alamo say about it?'

'He said that it was found beside the Dead Sea,' said Rich. He was a little shocked to notice an inward quaver as he said it; he was actually dreading some new theory as to the fleet's whereabouts.

'That is so. It is found in Egypt, too, in the deserts that border the Nile.'

'There is no desert here, Your Excellency,' said Rich, stoutly.

'No.' The Admiral looked over at the luxurious green coast. 'Yet it makes me more sure of the Earthly Paradise being at hand – I shall write to Their Highnesses to that effect – but perhaps I shall have more evidence still by the time I can spare a ship to return to Spain.'

'I have no doubt you will, sir,' said Rich, strangely sick at heart.

The armoured men were lounging about the deck. Spallanzani had his lute, and was singing Italian love-songs to the accompaniment of soft chords from it, to an audience of hidalgos. They had eaten their meal of weevilly biscuits and rancid cheese with its flavour of cockroach. Rich remembered with regret the roast sucking pig on which he had dined his last day on shore, and was quite startled to note that all the same he did not wish himself home. This crushing heat, this wearisome armour, the foul food, the wild talk of Ophir and the Earthly Paradise – notwithstanding all these things he was happier where he was, here in the New World, than sitting in his furred robe in the Admiralty Hall in Barcelona listening to the crooked pleadings of crooked lawyers paid by crooked merchants. Seventeen years of it – the Consulate of the Sea, the Laws of Oleron, and the Code of Wisby, Justinian and the fueros of Barcelona; it was better to be able to raise his head and sniff the scented air of Trinidad.

A loud cry from a look-out brought everybody to their feet again. There was a canoe, a black speck under the glaring sun, full in sight as they rounded a headland. It was well out to sea, on passage between cape and cape; they could see the flash of the paddles as the men bent to their work. With the wind right aft the squadron overhauled it fast; it turned frantically to make for the shore, but the *Santa Anna* was there, cutting it off, and it headed back. Fifty yards from the *Holy Name* the paddles ceased work, and the canoe drifted idly on the blue.

Brown and naked, with streaming black hair, the Indians stared with frightened eyes at the huge hull drifting down upon them. One of them stood up, overcome with curiosity, in the desire to see better, revealing herself as a woman, quite naked save for her necklace. A loud roar of laughter burst from the ship – a naked woman was so rare a sight as naturally to excite laughter. She sat down abruptly, with hands over her face, and in her place a man rose to his feet, balancing precariously in the rocking canoe. He set an arrow to the string of the bow he held, raised the weapon and drew it to his breast, and loosed off the shaft.

Rich saw the arrow in the air; it struck his breastplate with a slight tap, and dropped on the deck with a faint clatter. It was an effort as feeble as a child's – the shaft was already spent in its fifty yards' flight by the time it reached him. His furred judicial robe would have been as effective protection as his steel breastplate. The arrow was merely a thin cane, crudely sharpened at one end, and with a single parrot's feather at the other. But the gesture had excited the Spaniards. A cross-bowman lifted his lumbering weapon to reply, and lowered it again at a hasty order from the Admiral.

'Put that crossbow down!' he called in his high tenor. 'We are at peace with them. Hey, Diego, there, beat your tambourine, and you boys dance to it. Show them that we mean no harm.'

It was a ludicrous scene, the ship's boys capering on the forecastle, and the sullen Indians gazing up at them uncom-prehending. The canoe was in the lee of the *Holy Name* now, and the wind was gradually drifting the big ship down upon it. The Admiral himself was up on the bulwark, jingling hawk's bells – hawk's bells had been found to be an unfailing attraction in the other Indian islands – and Alonso Perez was beside him, a red woollen cap in either hand held temptingly towards them.

'Jorge,' muttered the Admiral out of the corner of his mouth to a seaman close at hand. 'Strip off your coat and make ready to upset the canoe.'

The canoe was close alongside as Jorge swung himself over the bulwark and dropped amid a wild scream from the Indians. The canoe overturned, and the occupants were flung into the sea. They were glad to clutch the ropes thrown to them and to be pulled on deck, where they stood, dripping water, with the Spaniards clustered round them. Four of them were men and two women, the women quite naked, but three of the men were wearing cloths of coarse cotton about their shoulders – Rich examined the material. It was of poorer weave than any he had ever seen.

'Make fast the canoe!' called the Admiral over the bulwark. 'Put those paddles back in her!'

The Indians made a frightened group, their arms about each

other and their teeth chattering in fright, while the Spaniards pushed and elbowed to see more closely these strange humans, who felt no shame at nudity, who had never heard the name of God, who knew nothing of steel or gunpowder. Someone stretched out a hand and stroked a woman's shoulder; she shrank from the touch at first, but when it was renewed she gradually recovered from her shyness and smiled a little over her shoulder at the man who caressed her, like a child, but a new bellow of laughter made her seek safety again beside her fellows.

The Admiral pushed through the mob, resplendent in his scarlet velvet with his glittering helmet and armour; the Spaniards falling back to make room for him revealed him and his position of authority to the Indians. He was uttering strange words learned in Cuba and Española, and they responded to his soothing tone of voice even though they clearly could not understand what he said.

'Guanahani,' said the Admiral. 'Cibao. Cuba. Hayti.'

The names of these places meant nothing to them.

'Canoa,' said the Admiral, pointing over-side.

That they understood; they nodded and smiled.

'Canoa,' they said, in chorus, and one of them went on to say more, in a sing-song tone.

It was the Admiral's turn to shake his head.

'Their speech is not unlike that of Española,' he said to Rich. 'But it is not the same, save for a few words, like canoa.'

'Canoa,' repeated one of the Indians, parrot fashion.

The Admiral jingled one of his hawk's bells enticingly, and they eyed it with wonder. He offered it, and they shrank back a little. He took the hand of one of the men and put the bell into it, shutting his fingers over it, and then setting the bell a-rattle again by shaking the man's fist. An awed expression crept over the man's face as he realized that this bell was actually to be his. He could hardly credit his good fortune, cautiously opening his hand and finally jingling the bell delightedly. All the Indians were smiling broadly now.

Rich's eyes were on the necklace worn by the woman in the background. He stretched out his hand to examine it; she shrank away for a moment, and he tried to make soothing noises. But immediately she understood what he wanted, and stepped forward, proffering a loop of the necklace to him. He examined it closely. It was a string of pearls – two yards of pearls. The other Spaniards noticed what he was doing, and surged towards them, frightening her; a score of hands were stretched out for the necklace, when the Admiral turned fiercely upon them and they dropped back again.

'They are pearls,' said the Admiral after examination. He took one of the red woollen caps from Alonso Perez and offered it to her with a gesture of exchanging it for the necklace. She did not understand. He jingled a hawk's bell, and reached for the necklace again. Suddenly her expression changed to one of comprehension, and with two swift movements she uncoiled the necklace from her neck and thrust it, a great double handful, into his hands. Her puzzled look as he proffered the cap in exchange revealed that she had intended the necklace as a gift.

'It is the same as in Española,' said the Admiral. 'The heathen have no notion of barter. They think that because a stranger wants a thing that is sufficient reason for giving it.'

The surging Spaniards round laughed at such folly.

'She does not know what that cap is for, either, Your Excellency,' remarked someone in the background.

'True,' said the Admiral.

At his order Perez took off his helmet and the Admiral perched the cap on top of his mass of hair, stood back with a gesture of admiration, took the cap again and put it on the head of the trembling woman. The other Indians chattered at the sight, teeth flashing in smiles.

'And look at this, Your Excellency. Look!' said a Spaniard, loudly.

One of the Indian men had something hanging on a string

round his neck, a little fleck of something with a yellow glint. It was a tiny fragment of gold, smaller than half a castellano but gold all the same. Rich heard the quick intake of breath all round the ring. Gold! The Admiral strode up, his expression so hard and fierce that the Indian raised his arm to ward off a blow.

'Where did you get this?' demanded the Admiral.

The Indian still cowered away, and the Admiral, with an obvious effort at self-control, changed his tone.

'Send for Alamo from the *Santa Anna*,' he said, aside, and then, turning back to the Indian, he smiled winningly. He raised his eyebrows in an obvious question, pointed to the bit of gold, and then away to the island. The Indian thought for a moment and pointed westward. There was a general murmur from the crowd – there was gold in the west.

'Much?' asked the Admiral, making a gesture with widespread arms. 'Much?'

The Indian after a moment of puzzlement extended his arms in agreement, to the sound of a renewed murmur from the crowd. There was much gold to be found; but Rich, watching the by-play, was not quite so sure. The Indian was clearly doubtful of the significance of the question asked him. He might be meaning that the gold was far away, or even, conceivably, that it was hard to come by. Years of sifting evidence had given Rich an insight into the extraordinary ways in which misunderstandings can arise.

The Admiral was jingling another hawk's bell and offering to barter it for the gold, and the Indian made the exchange gladly as soon as he grasped what the Admiral wanted.

'This piece of gold would buy five hundred hawk's bells,' commented the Admiral; he reached for another scarlet cap and set it on the Indian's head, to the accompaniment of a renewed chorus of admiration from the others.

'They like caps equally as much as hawk's bells,' said the Admiral to Rich. 'In that they are more like the cannibal

45

Indians of Dominica than those of Española. That is what one would expect.'

The longboat, rowed as fast as a dozen stout arms could drive her, had returned now from the *Santa Anna*, and Alamo reported himself to the Admiral. He looked at the string of pearls which the Admiral gave him for inspection.

'They are pearls undoubtedly,' he said, feeling their texture with his lips. He shaded them from the sun with his body to see their lustre. 'Yet they are different from the pearls of the Orient. Their tinge and lustre are not the same.'

'Are they valuable?' demanded the Admiral.

'Oh, yes. Half their value has disappeared because of the clumsy way in which they have been bored, but I would give you a good price for them in the Calle del Paradis. As rarities, even if for no other reason, they would stand high. And there are some good specimens here, too. These two match well and are of superb lustre. A queen could have no better ear-drops.'

'And what of this gold?'

Alamo took the fragment of metal, poised it on a finger-tip, tested it against his teeth, turned it to obtain a flash of the sun from it.

'That is gold,' he said. 'Without my acids and scales I cannot assay it, but I am certain it is pure and virgin. It contains no base metal, in other words, and it is in a state of nature, as it was found.'

'And where would that be?'

Alamo shrugged.

'In the bed of a stream, most likely. Or in sand or loam close to a stream. Gold found in the heart of a rock is never in pieces as large as this.'

'Thank you. Now speak to these men in the tongues of the East.'

Alamo addressed the Indians in a language of which Rich understood no word. Nor did the Indians, to judge by the blankness of their expressions. Alamo tried again, this time in the Arabic with which Rich was faintly familiar, but without result. He spoke to them in Greek, of which Rich had a working knowledge, and then again in a language faintly reminiscent of Arabic to Rich. The Indians' faces remained impassive.

'That is Hebrew, Greek, the Arabic of the East, and the Arabic of the West Your Excellency,' said Alamo.

'Thank you. We can let them go now,' said the Admiral.

He took more caps, and set one on the head of each Indian. He pressed a hawk's bell into each of their hands, and then he waved them over the side to where their canoe, gunwale deep, floated at the end of a line.

'Go in peace,' he said, as they still stood awestruck at the magnificence of the presents pressed upon them. He drew one by the wrist to the ship's side to make his meaning plain. They slid down the line into the water-logged canoe; one of the women took hold of a big shell tied to the gunwale and with it began to scoop the water swiftly out – it was obvious that they were perfectly accustomed to having their cranky craft capsized. The line was cast off, and the men took the paddles. Slowly the canoe stood away from the ship, heading in for the land. The scarlet caps danced over the water, bright in the light of the setting sun. The Indians never looked back; Rich, watching their course, saw the canoe turn abruptly aside in fright, like a shying horse, from the caravels as the big sails were trimmed to the wind again.

'With kind treatment and presents,' said the Admiral, coming to stand beside Rich, 'we can hope that they will tell their fellows and send them to us. We need pearls and we need gold.'

Not merely for any mad scheme for reconquering the Holy Land either, thought Rich. He knew how precarious was the Admiral's hold on the Royal favour, despite the presence of his two sons – one of them a bastard, too – as pages at court. 'We have made a start,' he said, cheerfully.

'So we have,' said the Admiral; in his two fists was the long string of pearls, luminous in the failing light.

CHAPTER FIVE

In the lavender dawn next morning, when the ships had hardly gathered way after lying-to all night, the look-out cried that he saw more land. It was a low peak on their port bow; to starboard the southern coast of the island of Trinidad terminated in a similar peak, with a narrow strait between, towards which the easterly breeze was briskly pushing them. The Admiral came with his limping step to see for himself. He gave two hurried orders, hailing the caravels himself, in his high voice, as they converged upon the *Holy Name* towards the strait. Rich did not understand at the time all that happened next. He saw the anchors let go and the sails got in, and the longboat manned to go up the strait and take soundings, but before the boat could cast off the sailors in the ships were running and shouting with excitement. The anchors were not holding on the rocky bottom, there was a fierce current running here of which they could have no knowledge until they tried to stop, and the wind was still pushing briskly against hulls and rigging. Stern first, and with anchors dragging helplessly, the ships were moving fast towards the unknown passage – a fact which Rich found it hard to realize at the time, and of the danger of it all he was quite unconscious.

He saw the *Santa Anna* lurch as her anchor caught, saw her cable part, and saw her swing round and race them on their course towards the strait. The rocks to the right, all a-boil with surf, seemed to be coming nearer, dangerously near. The Admiral was shouting orders; Osorio was running forward with an axe, and the Admiral himself was hounding the panicky sailors up the shrouds. The cable was cut, the mainsail dropped. High and clear the Admiral's voice called to

48

the steersman. Over went the tiller. For a few more harrowing seconds the ship, nearly aback, hesitated; they could hear the surf on the rocks. Then slowly she turned and gathered way. She lurched in a sudden boil of current, and a moment after she was running free, as if nothing had happened at all, on a sea mirror-smooth, with the rocks far astern and the land already far distant on either hand.

The Admiral was smiling as he returned from setting the men to work at preparing the spare anchor and cable.

'Sailors are ignorant and superstitious,' he said, limping up to Rich. 'On seas where no Christian has ever sailed before I suppose it is excusable. When they found that anchors did not hold and that we were in the grip of a current they imagined all sorts of things. They thought we were near Sindbad's loadstone mountain, being dragged by the attraction of our iron. Or they thought we had reached the edge of the world and were about to slide off. They thought of everything, in fact, except the need for getting the ship under control again.'

'*You* thought of that, Your Excellency,' said Rich. The incident confirmed what he knew well enough already, that the Admiral was a first-rate seaman with a clear head for any emergency.

'That is thanks to the Blessed Virgin,' said the Admiral, simply and devoutly. 'She has never deserted me. Not even in worse perils than that. But that was a strange current between those islands.'

He shaded his eyes from the sun and looked back at the perilous passage.

'So it appears,' said Rich.

'The caravels are safe. They were nearer the centre of the strait. It was well that we hove-to last night,' commented the Admiral, half to himself. 'I shall call the new land the Isle of Grace. And the strait must have a name, too, for my chart. The Serpent's Mouth!'

'Your Excellency is ingenious at devising names. But of course you have had much practice.'

The Admiral flushed a little at the compliment. He smiled confidentially, and made a deprecating gesture with his hand; the smile almost became a grin.

'Even of the devising of names one can grow tired,' he said. 'And the places must have names. To me they are each distinct enough, but in my letters to Their Highnesses I must have something by which to call them.'

At that human moment Rich felt himself to be more in sympathy with, and fonder of, the Admiral than he had ever been before. He must have been in this mood at the time when he made his famous demonstration with the egg. The Admiral showed in a far better light as a practical seaman and as a man of the world than as a highfalutin theorist. But one at least of his theories – that there was a route to the Indies across the ocean – had most certainly been proved correct.

'I could wish,' said the Admiral, 'that we should see more Indians. We need to trade. And we shall need labour for the mines.'

He called a request to Carvajal, and the *Holy Name* headed once more towards the coast of Trinidad, a seaman at the lead to ascertain the safe limit of their approach. The land was tantalizingly just too far away for close observation.

'Might I – ' began Rich, and then he hesitated, surprised at himself, before he took the plunge. 'Might I take the longboat closer in to shore?'

'I would be glad if you did,' said the Admiral. 'You must take every possible opportunity to be able to report favourably to Their Highnesses on the wealth of these islands.'

Rich had no time to repent. It was a surprisingly short interval before he found himself in the sternsheets of the longboat, indubitably invested with his first command at sea, and experiencing a tremor of fearful excitement in consequence. The old sailor Jorge sat at the tiller beside him, two more sailors were at the sheet, and forward there sat five gentlemen of coat-armour, glad of the opportunity of escaping for a while from the confinement of the ship and ready in consequence to acquiesce in the command with which the Admiral had tacitly invested him. Rodrigo Acevedo was one of them, however – there was a hint of a smile in his handsome swarthy face as he met Rich's eye which told Rich that Acevedo was aware of the inner doubts which were troubling him.

The wind was off the land, blowing briskly enough, and the boat lay over gaily on her side as they headed parallel to the shore, the sailors handling sheet and tiller deftly as they translated Rich's vague directions into action. The coast curved here in a wide bay, shelving so gradually that even the longboat had to keep two hundred yards from the beach, and everywhere the monotonous green vegetation came down to the very water's edge – green, eternally green. There were irregularly shaped hills in the background, but never a sign of a clearing, no hint of smoke to betray the habitation of man. The wind blew more briskly yet, and the sky was overcast, yet it was stifling hot. As Rich stirred uncomfortably in his seat he felt the sweat trickling in the folds of his clothes. A rainstorm changed the colour of the hills from green to grey; it came drifting towards them over the grey sea. Soon it was upon them – they heard the hiss of the drops upon the water as it approached. The first drops rang sharply on the helmet which Rich wore – he had discarded his armour – but immediately the distinctive sound was blurred in his ears by the roar of the rain beating everywhere about them. Entirely exposed as they were, they could neither think nor see. The rain fell in cataracts, blotting out both ships and shore from view, soaking them and dazing them as it drove into their faces.

Rich was still conscious of Jorge moving beside him. He was still attending to his duties, presumably by touch and instinct, and his example diverted Rich from his first instinct to order the longboat to run back for shelter to the ship. Rich set his teeth; he would not be the first to give in. As captain, even though it was only of a longboat, it was his duty to make no complaint about the conditions, and the thought of Rodrigo Acevedo's earlier amused tolerance acted as a new stimulant. It was worth suffering discomfort if the hidalgos – *hijos de alguna*, sons of somebody – had to share it. They might be better swordsmen than he, better horsemen; they might think of him as a pot-bellied little lawyer, but sitting in the rain was a thing anyone could do without either practice or grandfathers. He wiped the rain out of his eyes to peer at the five gentlemen huddled in mute discomfort in the bows, and grinned to himself and settled down to endure.

For an hour they crept along through the downpour, and then, when the rain had almost killed the wind, it stopped as suddenly as it began. Within a few seconds the sun was shining in all its majesty, and the wind, hot and sticky, had almost died away. Rich stood up to wring the water from his clothes; the thwarts steamed in the glaring sunlight. There was no change in the appearance of the shore – the hills may have grown a little loftier, but they were still clothed in their eternal green. He scanned the coast carefully, and looked to seaward, where the *Holy Name*, in all the glory of her coloured sails and ensigns, preceded the two caravels on her slow northerly course. Only then did he pay any attention to the group in the bows, and, even so, he waited for them to speak first.

'God, what rain!' said Bernardo de Tarpia. His hair hung lank over his cheeks, his trim beard was a mere ludicrous wisp. The water trickled out of the skirts of his coat as he stood up.

'What of the food?' asked Cristobal Garcia. 'I suppose the bread is no better than a pudding.'

'No, gentlemen,' explained Jorge. 'It is a tarred sack in which it is kept.'

'It is hard to decide', said Garcia, 'whether a flavour of tar is preferable to rainwater.'

'Tar or no tar,' interrupted Rich, fumbling in his pocket, 'I mean to dine today on fresh fish, newly broiled.'

'Fresh fish!' exclaimed Garcia.

'That is what I said,' said Rich, demurely. 'It will be odd if we cannot catch enough for our dinners here.'

The little bundle he produced from his pocket contained lines and hooks; he felt a gratified glow as he heard the delighted exclamations of his crew. He thought of the other contents of his chest in the 'tweendecks in the *Holy Name* – his anxiety during the three weeks between his deciding to join the expedition and its sailing had at least stimulated him into wondering what might be of most use in the new world, and he had stocked his chest accordingly. These penniless younger sons, their heads full of battles and gold mines, had done nothing of the sort.

He doled out lines and hooks; a biscuit from the bag was crumbled into paste for bait.

'Please God,' said Garcia, piously, 'that the fish here like the flavour of weevils.'

With shortened sail, before the faint air, the longboat crept slowly over the glassy sea. The gentlemen fished as enthusiastically as the seamen; it was amusing to note how they cheered up at the thought of fish for dinner, and how earnestly they plunged into the business. Two months of weevilly biscuits, of stinking dried cod, and of boiled barley porridge and stale olives made the prospect of fresh fish ineffably attractive. But Rich could guess how they would round on him, their tempers sharpened by disappointment, if no fish were caught. He bent his head secretly and prayed earnestly to St Peter – he had prayed to St Peter for good fortune in fishing often before, on pleasant outings in the roadstead of Barcelona, but this time there was an edge to his prayer. He wanted desperately to catch fish.

St Peter was kind. They caught fish in plenty while the wind died away to nothing. They landed and built a fire and toasted their fish on sticks before it – not very efficiently.

Rich wondered secretly to himself what comment these young men would have made if in their fathers' houses they had been served with fish half charred and half raw, but here, stretching their legs on land for the first time for months, and in the blessed shade at the edge of the sand, they ate with gusto, and with only moderate curses for the mosquitoes which bit them. Rich could see a new light in their eyes when, full fed and comfortable, they regarded him now. There was a faint respect for him as a giver of good things; he sat with his back against a tree and his helmet on the ground beside him and felt happier than he had done for months.

The ships still lay becalmed on the blue, blue sea under the glaring sun.

'We can explore for a little while,' he announced. 'Who'll come with me?'

They all wanted to, seamen and gentlemen both, looking eagerly to him for orders.

'Two men must guard the boat,' decided Rich. 'Will anyone volunteer? Then you must stay, Jorge. And you, Don Diego. Come on, you others.'

As they plunged into the forest Rich decided to himself, remembering the disappointment in the eyes of those left behind, that the hardest task of a man in command was the arbitrary allotting of distasteful duty. He was glad he had not hesitated, but had given his orders instantly without allowing time for argument. He was conscious that he was learning fast.

The forest was dense and nearly impenetrable; in places they had to hack a path through it with their heavy swords, for the gurgling watercourse they followed was too small to allow easy passage along it. They sweltered in the stagnant air, plunging knee deep into slime and rotting vegetation. Gaudy birds clattered among the branches over their heads. Bernardo de Tarpia uttered a sudden sharp cry, slashing with his sword – a red and black snake coiled and writhed at his feet. It was a lucky blow which had taken off its head before it could strike; they had all of them heard stories of those red and black snakes of the Indies and the death they could inflict. A huge goggling lizard ran frantically among the branches away from them. Then they saw monkeys, scurrying among the tree-tops for all the world like mice on the floor of a barn. They laughed at their antics and the monkeys chattered down at them in reply.

'There is everything here save the Grand Khan and the mines of Ophir,' said Rodrigo de Acevedo in an undertone to Rich, but Rich would not allow himself to be drawn; he could not enter into a discussion of that sort while in a position of responsibility.

And at this place where they had stopped for a moment there seemed, for the first time, to be a possibility of humans near them. There might almost be a path through the undergrowth here, nearly imperceptible, probably only a wild beast run. Rich looked up at the sky; there was a wisp of cloud there which was quite stationary – in the absence of wind they could continue the exploration without fear of being parted from the *Holy Name*.

'Follow me quietly,' he said to the others, and he turned his steps up the path, his sword in his hand.

But they could not hope to move quietly in the forest. Dead wood crackled under their feet, low twigs rang on their helmets, their scabbards rattled and their accoutrements creaked. There was precious little hope, Rich realized, of ever surprising a party of Indians in this fashion, especially after he stumbled and fell full length. As he picked himself up someone came running down the path and stopped and looked at them – it was a little Indian boy, naked and pot-bellied. He put his fingers in his mouth and stared, the sunlight through the branches making strange markings on his brown skin. His features began to work, and it was clearly only a matter of seconds before he started to cry.

'Seize hold of him!' hissed Garcia into Rich's ear.

'Quiet!' muttered Rich in reply over his shoulder.

He held out his hand, peacefully.

'Hullo, little one,' he said.

The little boy took his finger from his mouth and stared all the harder, postponing his tears.

'Come to me,' said Rich. 'Come along, little one. Come and talk to me.'

Clearly while he spoke gently the child would not be frightened. He racked his brains for things to say, chattering ludicrously, and the little boy slowly began to sidle towards him, with many hesitations.

'There!' said Rich, squatting down on his heels to bring their two faces on a level.

The little boy piped out something incomprehensible; his eyes were fixed on Rich's helmet, and he stretched out a small hand and touched it.

'Pretty!' said Rich. 'Pretty!'

The little boy replied in his own strange language, still engrossed in the helmet. When at last his interest died away Rich cautiously straightened himself.

'There!' he said again, and pointed slowly up the path. 'Mother? Father?'

He began gently to walk forward, and the little boy put his hand in his and trotted with him.

They came out into a little clearing. There was a tiny wisp of smoke rising in the centre, marking the position of a small fire. On one side there were five strange houses of dead leaves, but no human stirred; as they stood grouped at the edge of the clearing they could hear no sound save that of the birds and the insects. The little boy tugged at Rich's hand to draw him forward, and then raised his voice, calling. An Indian woman broke from the forest beyond the clearing and came running heavily towards them. She, too, was naked, and far gone in pregnancy; she caught up the little boy in her arms and stared at them, asking urgent questions of the child meanwhile.

Rich spread his left hand again in the instinctive gesture of peace, even though his right still held his drawn sword.

'We come in peace,' he said. He tried to make soothing noises; the little boy pointed at the glittering helmets and chattered shrilly to his mother.

Now there was a bustle and stir in the forest; a score of Indians came forth into the clearing, old and young, men and women and children. Rich, looking to see if any of them were armed, saw that one man carried a little cane bow – as feeble as a ten-year-old child's – and two small cane arrows, and two others carried headless cane spears, against which ordinary clothes – leaving leather coats out of account – would be adequate protection. He took off his helmet.

'We are here,' he announced, forcing his voice down into quiet conversational tones, 'in the name of Their Highnesses the King and Queen of Castile and Leon.'

The Indians smiled, with flashing white teeth, chattering to each other in their high-pitched voices.

'The woman there has pearls!' said Garcia at Rich's shoulder.

Round each arm above the elbow she wore a rope of pearls, each pearl larger than any they had obtained before.

'Look at them, by God!' said Tarpia.

The Indians noticed their gestures and turned to see what it was which was attracting so much attention; it was obvious enough to them that it was the pearls. They chattered and laughed to each other, the wearer of the pearls – a fine, handsome woman of early middle age – laughing as much as any of them, a little bashfully. The wrinkled old man beside her – husband or father, it was not apparent which – laughed and clapped her on the shoulder, urging her forward. She approached them modestly, eyes cast down. She stripped the pearls from her arms, stood hesitating for a moment, and then thrust one rope into Garcia's hand and the other into Tarpia's, scuttling back to her companions with a laugh. The Spaniards eyed their treasures.

'We must give them something in exchange,' said Rich.

The Admiral's orders had been very strict on the point that all treasure should be bartered for and never taken.

'I know what I should give her,' said Garcia, eyeing her nudity.

Rich tried to ignore him; he sheathed his sword – a simple act which yet caused a new outburst of piping comment from the Indians – and fumbled through his pockets. He had two silver coins and a handful of copper ones, and he walked towards the Indians and dropped a coin into each hand as long as the supply lasted. The Indians looked curiously at the money. One of them suddenly spied the Queen's head on the coin and pointed it out to the others. Instantly they were all laughing again. To them it appeared to be the greatest joke in the world that someone should represent human features on an inanimate object – such an idea had never occurred to them. The wrinkled man presented Rich with his spear – a mere cane with the point charred with fire – and made a gesture embracing all his fellows and the encampment. There was an inquiring look in his face; clearly he was anxious to know if there was anything else the Spaniards would like. It dawned upon Rich, remembering also the interview with the other Indians in the canoe, that the first instinct of these people on meeting strangers was to give them presents. He smiled and nodded pacifically, a little embarrassed.

A fresh idea suddenly struck the wrinkled man, and he turned and cried out to the others. His suggestion was greeted with obvious acclamation. The Indians laughed again and clapped their hands. Some ran towards the huts, some came and took the Spaniards' hands and led them towards the space between the huts and the fire, skipping like children at the new prospect. There was a fallen log near the fire. From the huts the Indians dragged out a few more blocks of wood, and most of the Spaniards found seats in this way. To tempt the others to sit down the Indians patted the earth invitingly. The women ran in and out of the huts, all a-bustle, while the men took sticks and began to open the earth near the fire.

A girl put a big leaf on Rich's lap; another girl brought him a flimsy basket filled with lumps of strange bread and offered it to him.

'Cassava,' she said; Rich remembered the word as occurring in the depositions of survivors returned from the Indies.

The men had by now completed their task. They had laid open a hole beside the fire, and from it arose a savoury steam which smelt deliciously, even to the Spaniards who had eaten only an hour ago; obviously the Spaniards had reached the clearing at a moment when the Indians were about to dine. With sticks the Indians hoisted from the hole what looked at first to be a bundle of dead leaves, and when they peeled the leaves off the smell grew more delicious than ever. The operation was not completed with ease – two of the men contrived to burn their fingers, to the accompaniment of fresh peals of laughter – but at last the unrecognizable roast was laid bare. The wrinkled man took a leaf in each hand and began to break up the meat; the women scurried back and forth with more leaves. Rich found a savoury bit on his lap; he bit cautiously into it. It was a delicious tender meat. Another woman brought him a little gourd; it was only fresh water, for, as Rich knew already, the Indians of these islands knew no other beverage.

'What the devil is this we're eating?' asked Bernardo de Tarpia. 'It's good.'

'What is this?' asked Rich of one of the women. He pointed to the meat and raised his eyebrows inquiringly.

'Iguana,' said the woman. 'Iguana.'

The name meant nothing to any of the Spaniards, as their expression showed. One of the Indian men came to the rescue. He pointed up into the trees, and, going down on his hands and knees, made a pretence of scurrying along a branch.

'Monkey, by God!' said Tarpia.

'Monkey?' asked Acevedo.

He made a series of gestures like a monkey, much to the amusement of everybody. The Indians clung to each other and laughed and laughed. Then one of them wiped the tears from his eyes and began a new pantomime. He went down on all fours. He turned his head this way and that. He put the edge of his hand on the base of his spine and waved it from side to side. He projected two fingers from his face beside his eyes and moved them in different directions.

'Iguana,' he said, rising.

It was a graphic piece of work. There could be no doubt what he meant – he had imitated the lashing of the iguana's tail and the goggling of its strange eyes to perfection.

'He means a lizard,' said Rich, trying to keep a little of the consternation out of his voice.

'Does he?' said Tarpia. 'Well, lizard is good enough for me.'

'My God, yes,' said Garcia. 'Look at this.'

He had drawn one of the girls to his knee, and was caressing her naked body. She stood stock-still, with eyes downcast, trembling a little. Rich looked anxiously round the ring. He saw the smile die away from the face of one of the Indian men. The merriment ceased, it was as if a shadow had come over the sun.

'Remember the Admiral's orders, Don Cristobal,' said Rich, anxiously.

'Oh, to Hell with orders,' expostulated Garcia.

'Don Cristobal's talking treason,' interjected Acevedo. He grinned as he said it, but that did not blunt the point of what he said.

'Oh, very well then,' grumbled Garcia. He clapped the girl on the flank and pushed her from him, and the tension died away from the attitudes of the Indians. The women hastened round, offering more bread; the wrinkled man broke off more meat. There were fruits being offered, too, like pale yellow eggs, faintly aromatic when Rich smelled one, vaguely acid and pleasant when he bit into the pulp.

'Guava,' said the lad who gave it to him, explanatorily.

The shadow had passed from over the sun now; there was giggling and talking again. It dawned upon Rich that these people had given away the meal they had been about to eat themselves; he wondered if they had anything left over, and he realized that he need not let his conscience trouble him too much on the point. Their pleasure in giving was so obvious and unassumed. It was the Spaniards who were conferring the favour by accepting. He felt a sudden wave of melancholy come over him. These laughing, generous people, naked from the day of their birth, with sticks for weapons and houses of leaves, and destined to the damnation awaiting the unenlightened, had no need or desire for gold or jewels. They had no more knowledge of labour than they had of property or of civilized warfare. To try to make an empire out of them, as the Admiral dreamed of doing, meant either suffering for them or weakness in the empire. They would be happier left alone – he caught himself up on the verge of heresy as well as of treason. It was the Christian man's duty to see that their feet were set in the way of God, and it was the sensible Spaniard's duty to seek out the treasures of this land to the increase of the wealth of Spain. Yet he still revolted from all the implications. Weakly, he tried to brush the problem from him as he brushed his hands together and rose. The shadow of the forest stretched from side to side of the clearing; it was late afternoon. Only this morning they had dragged their anchors in the Serpent's Mouth, and it seemed like a month ago.

'Back to the ship!' he called to the others. He was conscious of the invidiousness of his condition of uncertainty as to whether he had to request or could command; more, he knew with a qualm that he was not of the stuff to whom command came naturally. But they rose to obey him. Tarpia and Garcia were arm in arm, muttering to each other with their eyes on the women – he could guess the sort of filth they were saying to each other.

The wrinkled man came with a new question, pointing up to the sky, repeating his question and tapping Rich on the breast and pointing upwards again. He was asking if they were going to return to their habitation in the sky.

'Oh, no, no, no,' laughed Rich.

He thought for a moment of trying to explain all the complexities of ships and sea passages and the kingdom of Spain in sign language, and gave up the notion as soon as he thought of it. Others who might follow him could tackle that task. He shook the old man's hand and he waved good-bye to the women. As he set his feet on the homeward path with his own flock, he looked back at them, standing grouped in the clearing, each with his arm on another's shoulder. The melancholy he had felt before flooded back within him, and he plunged without a word along the narrow path, the others trailing after him.

The journey back to the boat was not as toilsome as the upward climb. At one corner, by the brook, they caught a glimpse of the sea – the ships had drifted a league or more along the coast, but were still within easy reach; from the way their bows were turned to all points of the compass it was obvious that they were quite becalmed. The brook gurgled sleepily, the parrots overhead squawked and fluttered, and all the noises of the forest engulfed them again as they went on down the hill. Far away, Rich heard the faint cry of a strange bird, high and shrill, repeated more than once.

They came out at last into the bright evening sunshine of the beach, where Don Diego Moret dozed on his back and Jorge whittled at a stick with his knife. They looked up as the party approached.

'Is all well?' asked Rich, and then, in the same moment, he knew that all was not well. Gonzalo Acevedo was close behind him. One of the seamen was a little farther back.

Rodrigo Acevedo emerged from the forest as he stood and waited, and after him there came – nobody.

'Where's Don Cristobal? Where's Don Bernardo?' he demanded.

'I thought they were in front with you,' said Acevedo, a little surprised.

'Where's Diego?' asked Jorge of the seaman.

'I thought he was following me.'

'Perhaps they are coming,' said Acevedo. But his eyes met Rich's, and they both knew they were thinking the same thoughts.

'Shall I give them a call?' suggested Jorge.

He lifted up his voice in a loud seaman's bellow. Startled birds rose from the trees; an echo came faintly from above, but no answering cry. He bellowed again, and there was still no answer.

'I shall go back for them,' announced Rich. The unaccustomed exercise in the sweltering heat had tired him out; his legs were stiff and weary already. It had been an effort to cover the last few hundred yards to the beach, and it was only the prospect of resting there which had brought him down to the sea without a halt. His heart sank as he thought of the stiff climb back through the forest.

'It's an hour's march to the village,' said Rodrigo Acevedo warningly, 'and not more than an hour of daylight.'

The sun was dipping towards the horizon.

'They may be coming down another way,' suggested Gonzalo Acevedo. 'You could miss them easily. Wait a few minutes.'

Rich wavered. There was a great deal in both arguments; and if what he suspected was the case, if the missing men had made their way back to the village, they must have already had an hour or more to work their will there, and would have another hour before he got back again. And what was he to do when he got there? And how was he to find his way back to the boat in darkness?

'I'll wait,' he said, bitterly, turning his back on them to hide his feelings.

He had been flattering himself he was learning to command men, and this was the first of his achievements. He sat down on a fallen tree and gnawed at his fists.

'What's all this about a village?' asked Moret, curiously, of the Acevedos.

They began to tell him of their experiences and discoveries; the eager babble went on unheeded by Rich, who sat with his back to them, his joints aching and his heart sick. Suddenly a new recollection came to him, one that set his heart beating fast and increased his feeling of nausea. That wild, high-pitched cry which he had heard repeated, far back in the forest, and which he had thought to be the cry of a strange bird – he knew what it was now. He could guess what bloody work it told of, back in the village. He got to his feet, and paced the sand stiffly, boiling with helpless fury. He found himself gripping his sword hilt, he who had never crossed blades with an enemy in his life, and he snatched his hand away in self-contempt. He started for the forest, and turned back. The sun was setting in a wild glory of scarlet; the lower edge of its disk was almost touching the sea, and the level light strangely illuminated the beach and the boat with the little waves lapping round it.

A dull report reached his ears, and, looking towards the ships, he saw a little puff of smoke at the bows of the *Holy Name*. The great standard at her mainmast-head came slowly down, rose again, descended and rose.

'That's a signal to us, sir,' called Jorge. 'We'll have to go back.'

'Very well,' said Rich, his mind made up. 'The others will be left in the forest.'

They began to put their gear back into the boat, and they made preparations for pushing her out. Rich climbed in and sat in the sternsheets. A shout from the forest made them pause and look round.

'That's Garcia,' said Rodrigo Acevedo.

The three of them came in sight now at the edge of the trees, running over the sand towards the boat. Rich saw their faces in the light of the last of the sun, like a trio of schoolboys caught in a piece of mischief, guilty and yet impudent, meeting his eyes and looking away again.

'Where have you been?' asked Moret as they came up, panting.

'Oh, we missed our way,' said Tarpia, looking sidelong at Rich in the sternsheets.

They followed the example of the others, throwing their weight against the boat and splashing out with her in the shallows. There was no opportunity of talking for a moment, and then they all came tumbling in over the sides. Garcia was on the aftermost thwart beside Jorge and face to face with Rich. He reached for an oar along with the others.

'Shall we have to use these things?' he asked, loudly, dropping the oar clumsily into the rowlock.

Rich was staring at Garcia's hand and Garcia caught sight of his expression and followed his gaze. The hand was stained with dried blood, hand and wrist, black in the light of the fast-dying sunset. Very coolly, Garcia leaned over the side and washed clean his hands in the sea.

'It will be a long pull back to the ships,' he said, and took hold of his oar again. His teeth showed white in his swarthy face as he smiled.

CHAPTER SIX

In the Admiral's cabin, vaguely lit with its two horn lanterns, accusation and denial were hotly exchanged.

'I say we missed our way,' said Garcia. 'You know what the forests in these Indian islands are like, Your Excellency. It is easy enough.'

'And you, Don Narciso?' asked the Admiral. 'You say – ?'

'I say they went back to the village,' said Rich, unhappily. He was beginning to be sorry that the argument had started; if he had worded his report to the Admiral more tactfully it might not have begun at all, and now Garcia and Tarpia had been called in and he had fears as to what the end would be.

'You have no right to say that at all!' burst out Tarpia.

'Gentlemen, moderation, please,' expostulated the Admiral. 'What makes you think so, Don Narciso?'

Rich thought of the way in which they had looked at the women, of the furtive conversation they had held as they started their homeward march, of what he thought was a human cry of fear and agony, and he knew all this was not evidence. He remembered the contempt he had in his own court for people who had no better sort of case than this to present.

'You see, Your Excellency,' sneered Garcia. 'He finds it hard to think of something to say.'

'And what right has he to accuse us?' demanded Tarpia. 'Is he in authority over us?'

'I represent Their Highnesses' interests,' said Rich.

'I have represented Their Highnesses' interests in a dozen battles,' said Tarpia. 'There are twenty soldiers on board this very ship who follow me.'

There was a threat behind that last statement, as anyone could see who caught the glance at the Admiral which accompanied it. Rich looked at the Admiral, hoping against hope that he would take up this challenge to his authority.

'Gentlemen,' said the Admiral. 'We are on a holy mission – a crusade. Must you wrangle like this?'

'The wrangling', said Garcia, haughtily, 'is not the fault of Don Bernardo and me. The blue blood of Spain does not wrangle willingly with the base-born.'

Rich checked himself as he was about to counter hotly with the statement that he was a cabellero de fuero of Catalonia. It would be of no avail. No hidalgo would dream of admitting, even inwardly, any equality between himself and a caballero de fuero – legally a gentleman – and, what was worse (and it was this which sent a little shudder of fear through Rich's plump body) Garcia might take advantage of the statement to challenge him to a duel. In that event Garcia would kill him for certain, and Rich shrank from the imminent prospect of death, as presented harshly to him by his imagination. He had not mentioned to the Admiral the bloodstains he had seen on Garcia's hands because he knew that Garcia would give a flat denial that they had ever existed; now he realized that he had been doubly wise, because if he were given the lie direct the incident could not end until more blood – his own – had been shed.

'Very well, gentlemen,' said the Admiral, when the struggle of emotion in Rich's face had died away and there was clearly no reply to be expected of him. 'I have heard your explanation and of course I accept it. But with regard to the pearls which I understand you received from the Indians?'

Garcia and Tarpia exchanged glances, and then Garcia looked across at Rich with no friendly expression.

'All gold and all treasure', said the Admiral, sharply, 'must be handed to me – to me, the Viceroy. That is the Royal order, as you are aware, gentlemen.'

There was no weakness in his attitude now, that was obvious enough. He was prepared to enforce his will in the matter of money, just as he was not prepared to enforce it in the matter of discipline. Sulkily the two gentlemen produced the pearl armlets and handed them over.

'Thank you, gentlemen. I need take up no more of your time.'

They swaggered out of the cabin with all the dignity the low deck beams over their heads would allow, leaving the Admiral fondling the glistening treasure and Rich staring malignantly after them.

'These hot-blooded gentlemen', said the Admiral, 'are a little unruly. Even unreasonably so, occasionally.'

'Without a doubt,' agreed Rich, bitterly.

What was he to do or say? he wondered bitterly. The moment had clamoured for a sharp example, and had been allowed to pass. In the essential matter of discipline the Admiral had allowed his authority to be challenged successfully. The dissensions and squabbles and final anarchy in the colony of Española were explained by that one incident. He thought of that ludicrous agreement between Their Highnesses and the Admiral, which made the latter Viceroy of all the lands he might discover. The fact that a man was a capable navigator, or even that he had ideas and was tenacious of them, did not imply that he would be an effective governor. The agreement handed over unlimited territory to a man who could not control his subordinates – there was no blinking the fact. Rich wondered to himself how Caesar Borgia, conquering Central Italy, would have treated those two.

'The pearls we have already obtained on this voyage', remarked the Admiral, 'are nearly sufficient to repay the cost of the expedition. There will be much profit.'

'Let us hope so,' said Rich.

He felt himself to be friendless and desolate; he had incurred the hatred of Garcia and Tarpia, which meant that his very life was in danger. He did not dare to risk antagonizing the Admiral as well with untimely criticism. No one would trouble much about the fate of a wretched lawyer, not even Their Highnesses across two thousand miles of sea. He was very sorry he had come.

'And I expect', went on the Admiral, 'that when we reach Española we shall find a shipload of gold awaiting us there. I made arrangements for its collection. The Royal fifth should be a large sum. So should my eighth and tenth!'

That absurd agreement gave Their Highnesses a fifth of all treasure. But to the Admiral it gave a tenth of everything shipped home, not merely of treasure, but of merchandise or spices. And besides that he could claim an eighth share of the gross profit, and an additional one-tenth share of the net profit; of each individual expedition that sailed from Spain. And the agreement itself made the Admiral the judge as to what was or was not merchandise, and what was or was not profit, it made him Admiral and Viceroy with the right to nominate all his officers; and lastly, it empowered him to leave by will all these varied privileges and powers in perpetuity to whomsoever he should think proper. It occurred to Rich that perhaps it was as well for Spain that the Admiral was not the ruthless leader of men he would have liked him to be five minutes back. Such a man could make himself greater than Their Highnesses themselves. If the choice lay between anarchy and independence he would have to choose anarchy for the Admiral's empire.

The consideration had made him forget his own misery for the moment. Outside the cabin awaited him the hatred of the men he feared; he felt like a tale-telling schoolboy, safe for an instant with his teacher, but doomed sooner or later to have to face the resentment of his fellows. He yearned to stay a little longer here in the light and safety. Why, oh why had he ever allowed his restless curiosity to carry him off on that infernal expedition in the longboat?

Antonio Spallanzani came into the cabin and broke the chain of his thoughts.

'Ah, you are in time to lock these away,' said the Admiral in his native Italian, handing over the armlets, and then in Castilian, 'Thank you, Don Narciso.'

There was nothing for it now but to leave. Rich took a deep breath as he set his hand to the door, for he was by nature a timorous man. Then he passed out into the darkness of the after-deck, under the break of the poop. The inky blackness here, even after the dim light of the cabin, left him blind for a second or two. Somebody brushed against him, and he jumped with nervousness, and then breathed with relief as he heard Rodrigo Acevedo's voice.

'Who is that?' asked Acevedo.

'It is I,' said Rich, trying to keep the quaver out of his voice.

'Don Narciso? Our two companions of today have been here breathing fire and murder against you.'

Acevedo's voice was pitched low, and Rich whispered when he replied.

'Where – where are they now?'

'Over on that side, talking with Moret and the others.'

The night was warm, but to Rich the sweat that beaded his face was cold.

'I don't know what to do,' whispered Rich, pathetically, and was promptly startled by hearing Acevedo suddenly start speaking in a normal tone, loud enough to be heard by the dark mass of figures on the far side of the ship.

'Oh, no, Don Narciso,' said Acevedo, speaking with a distinctness which was agony at first to Rich. 'You can hardly do that. I feel for you, and sympathize with you. But you ought to know the rules of shipboard life if anyone on board does.'

'What do you mean?' whispered Rich.

'Brawling on board is terribly punished. The hand that draws a weapon is nailed by it to the mast, and remains nailed there until the owner tears himself free. If you were to kill him you would be tied to his dead body and thrown overboard.'

'Oh, not so loud, not so loud,' whispered Rich, wringing his hands, but Acevedo continued quite calmly.

'So all I can advise is that you swallow your resentment, at least for a time – although I quite appreciate how unpleasant it is for you. Diego de Arana of Cordoba is alguazil mayor – master-at-arms – on board here, and you know his reputation. He holds his commission direct from the crown.'

'But why – ?' began Rich, still too stupid with fright to see the trend of what Acevedo was saying.

'He'd stick at nothing,' continued Acevedo. 'Gentle or simple, seaman or hidalgo, it's all one to him. At the first sound of steel he'd be upon you with his chains and his fetters. Twenty stinking seamen would throw you into the hold, and next morning we'd see you nailed up. You'd never hold a sword again, and I for one would be sorry for that.'

'So would I,' said Rich, taking his cue at last.

'By God!' said Acevedo, striking one fist into the other. 'Do you remember disarming that swash-buckling lout that night outside the Santo Spirito in Florence? If I'd been in your place I should have killed him – he deserved it. With his French sword-play and all, behaving like a boor because he thought he was the best fencer in Florence. Holy Mary, the look on his face as his sword fell on the ground!'

Acevedo laughed, lightly and reminiscently.

'That was 'ninety-two, wasn't it? Or was it 'ninety-three?' said Rich, desperately trying to heap on the local colour, and feeling a fearful joy in doing so.

'It was my second visit, anyway. But as I was saying, we can have nothing like that on board here, Don Narciso. No point of honour can be satisfied if the successful combatant is liable to execution. All courts of heralds are agreed upon that. Any offence given must be passed over in those circumstances – the dishonour is confined to the man who offers the offence.'

'Yes,' said Rich, remembering the frequent teasing he had undergone at the hands of his bedmates of the 'tweendecks.

71

'Yes. I knew that. It was only because I was so angry this evening that I had forgotten it.'

Don Rodrigo yawned elaborately.

'Well,' he said, 'I for one am sleepy. There is little enough to do – shall we go to bed? Or are you still too wrought up to sleep?'

'Oh,' said Rich. 'I think we might as well.'

Perhaps Acevedo sensed the intoxication which Rich felt at that moment, and appreciated the danger of his saying a word too many which might spoil the whole effect so elaborately built up. He slipped his hand under Rich's elbow and guided him firmly to the companionway. As they fumbled their way in the darkness the silence which had overlain the shadowy group against the opposite bulwark was broken by a thin nervous cough.

Rich stripped to his shirt in the cramped 'tweendecks in a wild exultation, hardly knowing what he was doing. The reaction from his earlier terror was profound. He began a jocular remark to Acevedo at the farther end of the tier of chests, but the almost invisible figure there made no reply and offered no encouragement to conversation, so that Rich realized that in a ship anything he said might be overheard if he did not desire it as much as if he did. One of the philosophers had said: 'I have often regretted having spoken, but I have never regretted holding my tongue.' Rich remembered the saying, and got himself into bed with no more speech.

Of course he was not yet asleep when the rest of the party came into the 'tweendecks and prepared for bed, groping about in the puzzling light of the single evil-smelling tallow dip. Don Cristobal Garcia came to his bed beside him, and Rich would not even feign sleep, only sleepiness, opening his eyes and then closing them again as if the sight of Garcia was not enough to discompose him. And Garcia, crouching under the deck beams as he undressed, was much more careful than usual not to discommode his neighbour.

That may have been, decided Rich, thinking tumultuously, because of his new reputation as a swordsman. Or it may have been because Garcia now realized that any squabble might end in disaster for both of them. Or just conceivably he might have taken to heart Acevedo's remark that it was ungentlemanly to offer provocation without the chance of satisfaction. Or it might be because Garcia was in a sober mood. Or it might be just coincidence. In any case, it seemed a lifetime since, some fifteen hours ago, they had first sighted the Serpent's Mouth. Rich's agitated mind began to turn over afresh all the numerous occurrences since then, from the moment of sighting the Island of Grace to that of Garcia's retirement to bed.

CHAPTER SEVEN

THERE was a very marked northerly current along this eastern shore of Trinidad. Hove-to during the night, the squadron was carried steadily northwards, until at last the late-rising moon had revealed such looming masses of land ahead that the Admiral had been roused, and the sleeping men on board had been awakened by the bustle and noise of letting go the anchors. Now, at dawn, everyone could see more clearly what lay ahead. There were several small steep-sided islands in a chain across their course, with narrow passages between, over which soared and wheeled innumerable sea birds. The Admiral beside the taffrail was studying the sea on their quarter towards these passages – Rich was still landsman enough to feel a slight shock at the realization that in an anchored ship one does not necessarily look ahead to examine the course one intends to pursue.

'More dangerous passages, Don Narciso,' announced the Admiral. 'There are currents and eddies there as bad as the Serpent's Mouth yesterday. These channels are narrower, and more dangerous. The Mouths of the Dragon, do you think?'

They both smiled as they remembered their conversation of yesterday.

'A very appropriate name, Your Excellency,' said Rich.

'I am not justified in risking the passage,' announced the Admiral. 'I intend heading eastward along this chain of islands until we find an easier one.'

'It is not for me to discuss questions of navigation with Your Excellency,' said Rich in perfect sincerity; the Admiral was the best practical seaman the world could show.

Orders were bellowed back and forth from the ship to the

caravels; men set to work at the capstan while others loosened the sails.

'It is better if we head eastward in any case,' went on the Admiral, turning back to Rich from the business of getting the squadron under way. 'It cannot be far to the east of here that the Earthly Paradise is to be found. I am convinced of it – the air blows fresher and purer with every league.'

'I had not noticed it, Your Excellency,' said Rich, boldly.

'You are insensitive, and you have not had my experience of this climate. And besides, you were present when Alamo discovered bitumen in the island, weren't you? He told me that there was obviously some undiscovered central source of bitumen in Trinidad. The analogy with the Dead Sea is very close. The Euphrates – only across the desert from the Dead Sea – was one of the four rivers of Eden, and not even the most learned fathers of the Church have been able to identify the other three. They have remained unknown for as long as all our knowledge was derived from the westward. Now we are approaching from the east and shall solve the mystery.'

'But between us and the Euphrates must lie all India, and the Spice Islands, and the empire of the Great Khan, Your Excellency,' protested Rich, bewildered.

'Undoubtedly they must lie to the northward,' admitted the Admiral. 'It would be hard to reconcile the theory with that of a perfectly spherical earth. But remember what I suggested to you before, and assume that in this quarter of the world the sphere is prolonged into a pear-shaped extension. That would then allow room enough to the northward for Asia, and at the same time account for the balminess of this air, and for the fierce ocean currents here – probably, when our knowledge is more advanced, for the existence of sources of bitumen on either side of Eden, and for the steep-sided shape of those islands there.'

'I see, Your Excellency,' said Rich.

The theory was a difficult one, but no more difficult than that of an earth which was not flat, nor than the postulate of the existence of antipodes, and the Admiral and the Portuguese had between them established these firmly enough. Rich began to feel a new excitement at the thought of fresh discoveries and began restlessly to pace the deck, exchanging a courteous formal bow with Garcia as he did so. After Garcia's deeds of yesterday Rich wondered what men of that stamp would be guilty of in the Earthly Paradise, and at the same moment he found himself wondering heretically whether perhaps the Earthly Paradise had not already been discovered, and whether those laughing hospitable folk who entertained them were not dwellers in it, pagans though they were. The thought struck him with sadness, and he turned again to look at the land.

They left the islands of the Dragon's Mouths to starboard and crept slowly before the wind on an easterly course. The north-eastern corner of Trinidad, which they were leaving behind them, had been steeper and loftier than the central part where they had landed yesterday, and this chain of islands appeared to be a continuation of the ridge. The last island of the chain in sight was not quite so bold in outline, but as they drew up to it Rich could see that it was steep enough, all the same, and as wooded and green as the others. Slowly they coasted along it but it was a good deal bigger than the rest of the chain. Rich could see no end to it as he looked along its green flank.

Throughout the ship there was a bustle and an interest in what they were discovering, oddly at variance with the comparative apathy of yesterday. Rich told himself that the enthusiasms of men in a mass ebbed and flowed like the tides of the ocean. They ate their food today with one eye over the ship's side; they stayed voluntarily exposed to the two tremendous rainstorms which swept down on them from Trinidad. Even the hidalgos were interested, talking freely and imperilling their dignity with their pointings and gesticulations. The look-out at the mast-head announced land right ahead, across their course – low green hills again. With land to the west of them now, as well as land to the north and land to the east, and the water shoaling fast, the Admiral ordered a southerly course in his determination to circle round this large island. He had ordered a chair to be brought up to the poop, and sat there with his white beard fluttering and Perez and Spallanzani at his elbow. He feared lest his squadron might be embayed here, where the wind blew always from the east, and it was well before sunset that, as the sea grew shallower and the land ahead was seen to trend farther and farther to the southward, he ordered the anchors to be let go.

'I shall send the longboat tomorrow, Don Narciso,' he announced, 'to discover if there is a passage ahead or to the southward. Would you care for another jaunt?'

'I am no seaman, Your Excellency,' said Rich, taken a little aback. He had not been ready for this question.

'There will be seamen with you to take the soundings and set the course,' said the Admiral. 'I would go myself, but, as you see – '

With a gesture the Admiral indicated his rheumaticky joints. There was a hurt, pleading look in his eyes. Rich had won his trust, and there were few enough people on earth whom the Admiral trusted. Ever since Pinzon had deserted him on his first historic voyage of discovery, and set out to discover new countries for himself, he had been cautious about dispatching expeditions which could make themselves independent. It was dangerous – in his view, at least – to delegate authority either to turbulent and needy hidalgos or to adventurous captains. Rich might be an agent of the King and Queen, but he was an honest one; he could be trusted not to plunder the inhabitants nor – much worse – to conceal treasure, not to go off on expeditions of his own nor (the Admiral's suspicions were unbounded) to bring back false information which might wreck the whole voyage.

'It would please me very much if you would go, Don Narciso,' said the Admiral. Several hidalgos were listening.

'I will come and pull an oar,' said Rodrigo Acevedo.

'I, too,' said his brother.

There was a little ripple of volunteering round the circle. A respite from the cramped conditions of the ship, the chance of fresh food and new sights, the possibility of finding women and pearls and gold – they were all willing to come for the sake of these. They all eyed Rich, with his new reputation as a bold fighting man, and for the sake of that reputation he could not refuse.

'Thank you, Your Excellency,' he said. 'I shall much appreciate the honour.'

Five seconds later Garcia was addressing him as privately as a crowded ship permitted.

'May I be one of the party?' he asked.

Their eyes met – the burly young hidalgo with his bristling beard and his shabby flaunting clothes, and the stout little lawyer with the sharp eye belied by the unobtrusive manner. It was strange for the one to be asking a favour of the other, and yet he undoubtedly was.

'There are others who have not been ashore at all,' Rich temporized.

'Yes,' answered Garcia with a placatory grin, 'but I should like to go again.'

'And you remember what happened?' said Rich. He did not want Garcia in his party; he was afraid.

'I remember. But – '

Rich knew that if he refused him he would offend him. On the other hand there was a chance of loyal service from him now – only a chance, but that was better than making a certain enemy of him.

'Will you stay with me if you come?' he asked.

It was a big effort to screw himself up to talk like a superior to this haughty young man who could wring his neck like a chicken's – who had been on the point of doing so the night before. But it was the only course open to him.

'Yes,' said Garcia.

So Garcia was one of the twenty men who crowded the

longboat at dawn next day when they pushed off from the *Holy Name* and headed for the low green shore while the ones left behind waved farewell. The air was hot and sticky; it had rained heavily during the night and the overcast sky bore promise of more rain still. There was only just enough wind to fill the sail and push them slowly forward; it was fluky and variable, too – twice Osorio at the tiller had to shout an order as the sail flapped heavily over the other side. A flight of pelicans flapped solemnly overhead.

There was no sign of a break in the land to the northward; to the south the hills grew lower and died away into a flat green coast. It was to the south, then, that Rich directed Osorio to steer the boat. The sun broke through the clouds and glared upon them with a terrible eye, illuminating the shore to which they were trending; a seaman standing in the bows cried out that he could see a break in the coast. Rich climbed to his feet and stood precariously balancing in the sternsheets – he had no faith in his own judgement, and yet, as commander of the expedition, he had to make some pretence at employing it. So low and flat was the shore that it was hard to distinguish where the sea ended and the land began, but Rich thought he saw what the seaman indicated – there was at least an arm of the sea running up into the land there.

With the dying wind they were compelled to take in the sail and set to work with the oars, and they took an occasional cast of the lead as they headed in. Three fathoms – two and a half fathoms – three fathoms again.

'Hardly enough for the flagship,' commented Osorio, spitting loudly over the side.

They were close to the shore now; the trees that fringed the sea were a sad grey, not the bright green of Trinidad, and they seemed to have their roots set actually in the water. Osorio put the tiller over until the boat was close in, and the men rested on their oars while she drifted, the gurgle and bubble at the bows dying away along with her motion.

'Look there!' said somebody, pointing to the trees.

On the bare grey stems close to the surface of the water there were oysters clustered thick. Osorio reached out and snapped off a brittle branch – the tip that trailed in the water bore four of them.

'We know now where those pearls come from,' commented Rich.

Osorio eagerly prised an oyster open with his knife, and poked a gnarled forefinger into its interior.

'None there,' he said, hesitated a moment, and then swallowed it noisily.

The boat lurched as everyone tried to grab for oysters; there was an interval as oysters were gathered and knives were borrowed. Food and pearls were sought with equal eagerness, but no pearls were found. Osorio turned over the shell he held in his hand and examined it curiously.

'They are nothing like our oysters at home,' he said, with his mouth full, and then, looking across at the birds wheeling over the sea, 'It is more than pearls that they make. No wonder there are so many sea birds here.'

'So the birds eat oysters, then?' asked Rich.

'No,' said Osorio, 'the oysters grow into birds.'

He opened a fresh specimen for the purpose of his lecture.

'These half-tide shellfish always do that. Many's the goose I've eaten which was a barnacle once. I expect these become pelicans. See here, sir. You can see the wings starting to sprout. And this must be the head – the long beak must grow later, when they are fledglings. Every spring tide brings them out in thousands, the same as butterflies come from chrysalises.'

It was an interesting point in natural history, and an apt comparison. Rich told himself that it was no more marvellous that a pelican should develop from a half-tide oyster than that a butterfly should emerge from a dull chrysalis, and yet somehow it did appear so; the one was a wonder to which he had been accustomed all his life, and the other was new. He supposed that when at last the expedition reached the Asiatic plains he would experience the same sensations on seeing the unicorns that only a virgin could tame, and the upas tree which destroyed all animal life within half a mile.

They took to the oars again, and the boat crept along up the inlet. Monkeys appeared on the shore, chattering loudly at them from the tree-tops; gaudy birds flew over their heads, and the steaming heat closed in upon them. The inlet was no more than half a mile broad when it divided, one portion continuing easterly and the other trending off to the south. Osorio at the tiller looked to Rich for orders.

'Which do you think looks more promising?' asked Rich as casually as he could manage.

Osorio shrugged enormously and spat again.

'Go to the right, then,' said Rich; if one way appeared as good as another to Osorio it was no use for himself to try to judge by appearances. Southward lay the Isle of Grace, opposite to Trinidad across the Serpent's Mouth; that was one solid bit of knowledge. The best chance of finding a passage was to keep to the northward of Gracia.

Now it began to rain, the usual relentless downpour to which they had grown accustomed in these latitudes. The roar of it drowned the noise of the oars in the rowlocks and the squeaking of the stretchers. The nearby land was almost blotted from sight, and the jesting conversation in the longboat came to an untimely end. The men at the oars rowed in dogged silence, and the rest sat patiently suffering. The channel divided again, and Rich again took the northern arm, but this immediately divided once more, and he took the southern arm this time in the hope of preserving as direct an easterly course as possible. And these were only the main channels; peering through the rain Rich fancied that there were plenty of minor waterways, mere threads of water by comparison, diverging from the wide channels. It was bewildering.

Then at last the rain stopped, and the sun shone once more. The forest beside them steamed, and they could hear again the innumerable sounds of the life within it. The men at the oars were relieved by their companions, and the longboat pushed on along the channel. And here they were balked; the channel split into two channels, at right angles to each other, and each was barely wide enough – the oars caught against the vegetation on either side.

'There's no way through here for the flagship,' said Osorio.

'No,' agreed Rich, hoarsely.

At Osorio's orders they backed water again until they could turn the boat, and they retraced their course; there was a resentful murmur at this wasted labour.

'We must try again,' said Rich, loudly. 'The Admiral relies on us to discover a passage.'

But the mention of the Admiral had small effect – he did not command these men's devotion.

The bank where the nose of the boat touched it in turning was soft and oozy; this was an amphibious sort of island, plainly; the distinction between land and water was not a sharp one. Still they rowed along winding channels, turning now south and now north, yet in general holding steadily eastward, rowing interminably.

'We must be three leagues from the sea,' said Osorio.

'That at least,' agreed Rich.

'And no sign of a spring yet.'

Everyone on board would be glad of fresh water to drink, instead of the flat and unpalatable reserve carried in the two casks. In these salt marshes there would be no chance of finding drinking water. Rich wondered what the birds and the monkeys drank – presumably these torrential rains made pools among the greenery. Anything was possible here; yet it was strange to find a marshy island surviving in the midst of the ocean, where one would expect the great waves to wash it away. To the east Trinidad gave it protection, but what of the north, and the west, and the south? It was puzzling.

The channel in which they found themselves now was wider than several they had previously traversed. And here the vegetation did not come quite to the water's edge. There was rock – pebbles – in sight. The same idea seemed to strike Osorio and Rich at the same moment. Osorio moved restlessly in his seat, staring at the bank. Rich cautiously put one hand into the water and tasted the drops which he lifted out. It was palatable water, almost fresh.

'We're in a river, by God!' said Osorio.

'Yes. The water is drinkable,' said Rich.

The rowers rested on their oars at the announcement, mopping their sweat. Two or three men leaned dangerously over the side and sucked up water like horses. There was a babble of talk.

'Under that bank', mused Osorio, 'there's quite an eddy. Look! There is a current running here. And it's a big river.'

A river a quarter of a mile wide, thought Rich. And those innumerable marshy channels through which they had struggled! Rich thought of Padua, of the innumerable arms of the Po, embanked by the labour of centuries. And there were all the mouths of the Ebro, too, in the dreary marshland beyond Tarragona. He had seen the mouths of the Rhône, too, and he had heard of the mouths of the Rhine and of the Nile. This must be a delta, too; and the deductions to be drawn from that simply staggered the imagination. It could be no small island which they were exploring; a river the size of the Ebro implied a land the size of Arragon at least. Larger still, most probably. Perhaps – perhaps it was the mainland of Asia at last.

But then again there were difficulties. Rich remembered the description by the Venetian, Marco Polo, of the Asiatic countries and of the court of the Grand Khan, its wealth and its fleets and armies. If this were the mainland those armies must have pushed hither to conquer this productive country, and those fleets must have coasted along these shores. Certainly the land would not be sparsely peopled by naked

Indians with no knowledge of metals – and wearing pearls worth a king's ransom. If the Grand Khan's fleets had not come here, it must be because it was not part of the mainland of Asia at all, but a mere island – a large island – and far enough from Asia not to have been discovered from that side. That implied a wide stretch of ocean to the westward of it, as large a stretch, perhaps, as the ocean they had already traversed on their way from Spain. And this in turn implied that the world was far larger than anyone thought, that the Admiral's calculations were vastly at fault, and that they had not reached the Indies at all. That was as nonsensical as the other theory.

It was a dangerous thought, too. There had been doubters before, on the Admiral's second voyage, and the Admiral had not only compelled everyone to swear a solemn oath that they believed Cuba to be part of the mainland of Asia, but also had publicly threatened to cut out the tongue of any man who affirmed the contrary – very right and proper treatment for dangerous sceptics, thought Rich, involuntarily, until he came back with a shock to the thought that it would take very little more to push him himself over into the abyss of scepticism as well. And he had never yet been a sceptic in his life.

Osorio was addressing him – apparently had been trying to attract his attention for some time.

'Shall we land and eat our food?' asked Osorio.

'No,' said Rich, after a moment's thought. 'Let's push a mile or two more up the river first.'

As far as he was concerned, he would have no appetite for food while consumed by his present doubts. There was just a chance that the theories were all wrong, that this was not a river at all, current and fresh water notwithstanding. A little further effort might resolve all doubts, might carry them to a place where all was clear – might even take them again to the open sea on the farther side of this mysterious island.

The oars groaned in the rowlocks, the blades splashed monotonously alongside, and the boat crawled steadily up the channel round a vast bend. Another bend succeeded that, the banks here lined with a wide stretch of golden sand. Some vast dull-coloured creatures lay sunning themselves there; at the sound of the oars they bestirred themselves and wallowed down into the water.

'Iguanas,' said Garcia, in reply to a question from a companion. 'Lizards.'

They certainly looked like lizards, like large specimens of the kind of creature they had seen scuttling along the branches in Trinidad, and of which they had eaten at the Indians' invitation.

'Tender and sweet as chicken,' said Tarpia, with a smacking of his lips. All hands stared over at the sandbank, now quite deserted.

Round the next bend the character of the river changed. A long way upstream they could see rocks, and a sparkling of wavelets, and a hint of white water.

'Rapids,' said Osorio.

'I fancy so,' agreed Rich. At that rate they had reached the limit of their expedition in this direction; no sensible purpose could be served by dragging the boat over the rapids, even if it were possible. Yet Rich was conscious of a feeling of disappointment; he did not want to turn back. He wanted to push on and on into the depths of this new and mysterious island. But the men were hungry and tired, and already the current was running faster.

'We'll land,' said Rich, curtly.

A narrow deep channel ran aimlessly up between a sandbank and the sand of the shore, and Osorio guided the longboat into it. The sharp shelving edge made a suitable landing place; while the oarsmen scratched ineffectively at the sand with their blades a seaman in the bow took a grip with the boathook and drew the heavy boat in, so that Rich was able to step ashore almost dry-shot. The heat and glare from the sand came up into his face like a fountain of fire, and he hurried forward to the shade of the trees with the rest of them capering and chattering after him. A little crowd of monkeys overhead peeped through the branches at them and chattered more shrilly back until misgivings overcame them and they fled over the tops of the trees like thistledown over a field before they stopped again to peep.

'That would be meat for our dinner,' roared Tarpia, pointing. 'Better than mouldy olives.'

They all looked eagerly to Rich for permission, and he gave it after a glance at Osorio's expressionless countenance.

'Bring your crossbow this way, Pepe. We can cut them off,' said Tarpia. 'Will you go along the shore, Cristobal? Take Estaban with you. Try round there, Acevedo.'

They clattered and crashed off into the forest, leaving Osorio and Rich standing in the edge of the shade, the food bags at their feet and the river shining in front of them beyond the glaring sand. Shouts and cries came from the hunting party. They heard the sudden clatter of a discharged crossbow, a burst of laughter, and more cries. Birds were fluttering over the tree-tops in panic.

'The gentlemen are full of life,' said Osorio, philosophically. 'Let us hope St Hubert will favour them.'

St Hubert apparently did, for they came back soon along the sand dragging their spoils with them.

'These little men', said Garcia, exultantly, 'have never seen a crossbow before. That is plain. They squeaked with surprise when a bolt reached them at the top of a tree – that was a good shot of yours, Estaban.'

He turned over with his foot one of the limp bodies on the sand; the greyish brown fur was clotted with blood.

'Pepe got these two with one shot,' said Tarpia. 'It broke this one's leg and hit that one in the belly.'

'Pedro got a parrot,' said someone else, displaying the dead bird.

Garcia drew his dagger and knelt by the dead animals.

'Who'll light a fire?' he asked over his shoulder. 'Holy Mary, the last game I gutted was a seven-point stag in the forest of St Ildefonso.'

CHAPTER EIGHT

EVERYONE had eaten; everyone had swallowed at least a mouthful or two of monkey's flesh despite the brutal jokes which were passed; everyone had decided that parrot's meat tasted of tough carrion and was not food for Christians. Two or three of the more phlegmatic were asleep in the shade; most of the men, too excited with their run ashore to wish for a siesta, were lying talking in low tones. Rich was too restless even to lie still; he heaved himself to his feet and asked Osorio to walk with him, and the boatswain obeyed even though he would clearly have preferred to continue to take his ease in the shade.

'I want your opinion on the rapid there,' said Rich.

With notable self-control Osorio refrained from pointing out that whether the rapid were easy or difficult its mere existence made it impossible for the *Holy Name* to pass it, even if, unlike all the other rivers which Osorio knew, this particular one ran from sea to sea. They plodded doggedly side by side over the blazing sand, which scorched their feet through their boots.

'I have the Admiral's order', said Rich, 'to spend four days if necessary seeking a passage.'

'We will need every minute of four days,' said Osorio in an elaborately neutral tone. 'Four weeks or four months. You do not find rivers this size on a small island.'

'I am afraid so,' said Rich. 'But we can at least report to the Admiral whether it is possible for a force to get up into the interior of the island this way.'

'Yes, sir,' said Osorio, non-committally, and they plodded on in silence.

The rapid when they reached it was clearly a difficult one.

Flat grey rocks showed everywhere above the surface of the water, which swirled sullenly round them. Upstream, as far as their vision extended, the rocks were to be seen scattered over the river. Here and there they were so thick that the water came tumbling through the gaps in cataracts.

'M'm,' said Osorio. 'A league of broken water. I can tell you this, sir. It would take the twenty men we have with us now a week at least to drag the longboat up there.'

'Thank you,' said Rich, 'that was what I had to find out. We must go back and look for another passage.'

'We must,' said Osorio.

Yet Rich lingered for a while longer beside the rushing water, reluctant to turn back; he was surprised at himself, both for this unexpected yearning to push on, to explore, to make discoveries, and at his disappointment at having to retrace his steps. Osorio waited patiently until at last he made up his mind to return to the boat. Rich was silent as they walked back, puzzling over this unexpected development in himself, and Osorio's sudden remark roused him with a jerk from his brown study.

'The gentlemen are hunting again,' he said.

Half-way between them and the boat lay three bulky shapes sunning themselves on the sand – iguanas like the ones they had disturbed on their passage up the river in the boat. Half a dozen gentlemen were stealthily approaching them over the sand, Garcia, conspicuous in his glittering helmet, in the lead. Their cautious movements brought them to within a score of yards of the creatures while Rich and Osorio were still a hundred yards away in the opposite direction. Rich watched one of the men kneel down and aim with a crossbow; the faint clatter of the released steel reached Rich's ears over the heated sand.

From then on events moved rapidly. Two of the creatures vanished into the river; Garcia, leaping forward with a rope, noosed the third before it could escape. A whirl of the brute's tail sent him flying, but the others grabbed the end of the rope and hauled manfully, while the one with the crossbow was frantically working his windlass. The iguana, oddly agile for a thing so deformed, made at the prostrate Garcia with open mouth, but the drag of the rope just deflected him and Garcia was barely able to roll out of reach of the snapping jaws.

Rich and Osorio came running up to see the fun, but Rich stopped, appalled at the spectacle of mad ferocity exhibited by the iguana. This was no harmless tree lizard to fall a victim to the sticks and stones of naked savages; it was a ton weight of hideous strength. Its jaws were frightening and its lashing tail a formidable weapon. Coursing through Rich's mind, like a river in spate, came a torrent of recollections of what he had heard and read of the crocodile of the Nile. This was more like a crocodile than anything he had imagined. Its left foreleg was crippled by the crossbow bolt driven deeply into it, to which perhaps Garcia owed his life, but it was still lively enough and fierce enough to face eight men with every chance of success, despite the noose round its neck.

With a whirl of oaths Osorio snatched the knife from his belt and sprang forward into the fray while Rich stood rooted to the sand, his hand clutching the hilt of his undrawn sword. As he slowly pulled out the weapon a sudden swerve on the lizard's part swept off their feet the men at the end of the rope. They tumbled in the sand, and the beast, after a futile snap at the rope, caught sight of Rich and rushed straight at him. Rich stood still fascinated for a second by its little dead eyes which yet were so malignant; the shouts of the others reached his ears so faintly that he hardly heard them. Yet his mind was racing; he knew in that moment that if he ran away, as his every instinct dictated, he would forfeit any regard which the others, thanks to Acevedo, might feel for him. He changed his movement for flight into a clumsy evasion of the rush, and swung his sword frantically at the brute's head; he felt and heard the blade ring loudly on the bone. Three times he slashed; it seemed like a long minute that he was at grips with the thing. A crossbow bolt whizzed harshly past him

– apparently the gentleman with the crossbow had taken a hurried and ineffective aim for his second shot.

Then suddenly and unexpectedly the brute, as it swung round, turned over on to its back, revealing its whitish belly; the others had grabbed the rope again, which, passing under its body, had twisted round its right foreleg. The thing squirmed insanely for a second or two while Rich slashed again; Garcia was beside him now, slashing too. Rich saw the pale green-grey belly gape widely in a red wound. As it righted itself, the creature's tail knocked Garcia violently against him, but in an instant of time, as he reeled, he saw a hindleg within the sweep of his sword, as he slashed once more. There was a thrill as the blade bit deep; Rich had the gratifying feeling that the muscles of his back and loins – all his strength – had been behind that blow. Red blood spouted in a dark trail over the sand from beneath the animal. The rush the thing was about to make at Osorio was crippled and disjointed, and a fresh drag upon the rope flung it on its side.

Moret was here now, sword in hand, too. He plunged the weapon deep into the thing's side behind the foreleg, and the other men dropped the rope and came running in, plucking out their swords. The thing died under the sword blades, its huge jaws still snapping together with a ringing sound, and the mad yelling – they had all apparently been shouting at the tops of their voices – died away as they looked at each other across the corpse.

'Holy Mary, Mother of God,' said Osorio, solemnly. He stood dagger in hand and looked round at the sweating gentlemen, at the torn-up sand with its bloodstains, and the dead lizard.

'Did you say the Indians kill these things?' asked João de Setubal of Garcia; the latter was cautiously feeling the bruises on his thigh.

'Smaller ones. I said smaller ones before we attacked it.'

'I should well think so,' said João.

'And you say you have eaten their flesh?' asked another. 'Jesus, how the thing stinks!'

It stank indeed; their nostrils were assailed with the foul musky stench which arose from the corpse.

'This is more like a crocodile of the Nile,' said Rich, and there was a murmur of agreement as they recognized the likeness.

'The brute is armoured with scales,' said Garcia by way of diversion. 'Is the armour proof against a sword blade?'

He thrust with all his strength at the armoured back; the sword point pierced the hide with difficulty and sank into the flesh below. At the prick of the steel the dead thing twitched convulsively, causing a roar of laughter. They all hastened to prick at the brute with their swords, but the life of the thing – the half-life of the dead organism – was ebbing fast and hardly a movement rewarded their efforts. Alfonso de Avila came up with the crossbow and shot it off into the soft underpart of the tail, but the only response was a languid flap.

'That's a better shot than your last one,' said Garcia, rounding on him. 'I'll swear it went within a yard of me – and Don Narciso, here, it must have gone past his ear. It did, Don Narciso, did it not?'

'Maybe so,' said Rich as indifferently as he could manage. He had no wish to be involved in any controversy.

'I hit the brute well enough with my first shot,' retorted Avila, hotly. 'Look, you can see the bolt still in the bone. I was the first of us to wound it.'

There might have been a quarrel if Moret had not intervened.

'It was Don Narciso who first struck it with steel,' he said.

'By God, that is so!' said Osorio. 'I heard the sword ring against the thing's head.'

'It is for Don Narciso to claim the kill, then,' said Moret.

In the tradition of the chase the honour of the kill in the

case of dangerous game went to the man who first set steel in the quarry.

'Yes,' said João de Setubal in his half-intelligible Portuguese. 'And look at that hind leg! I saw him strike that blow myself.'

The creature's left hind leg was cut nearly through close to the body, hanging merely by a bit of hide.

'A good blow that,' said Osorio.

They all looked at Rich; he felt himself blushing in the hot sunlight.

'Gentlemen,' he said, feebly, and then experience in court loosened his tongue and found him words to say, despite his embarrassment. 'It was the efforts of all of us that killed this crocodile. There was the crossbow bolt which crippled its foreleg. There was the skill and courage of Don Cristobal, who dropped the noose over its head. There was our worthy boatswain, who came rushing into battle with no more than a dagger. There were the intelligent men who dragged at the rope at exactly the right moment. Why, gentlemen, there is no need for us to dispute for honour.'

They murmured in pleased agreement at that; they all had a better opinion of themselves now, and there were no hard feelings. It was odd, the influence trifles had over these hot-blooded gentlemen.

CHAPTER NINE

A FRESH distraction came when one of the seamen cried out that a canoe was approaching. Every eye turned down the river; they could see the canoe paddling briskly against the current towards them. The sun flashed on the paddle blades. Rich walked to the water's edge and waved a welcome, and the canoe came steadily on towards them until it grated on the sand and the five Indians in it stepped out and lifted it – it was a tiny, cranky thing – beyond the water. The Indians wore cloaks of white cotton, and aprons of the same material. They were handsome, of the palest copper colour, and with long straight hair hanging to their shoulders.

What Rich noticed specially was their lack of surprise at finding the white men here; he decided immediately that they had been watching them for some time probably from across the river. The initial shyness displayed by the Indians of Trinidad was wanting; immediately after salutations with raised hands they came forward and examined the Spaniards as curiously as the Spaniards examined them. The Spaniards' clothing and armour and beards came in for specially close study; the two older Indians displayed a curious tendency to smell at the things that excited their curiosity, lifting the sleeve of Rich's coat to their noses in turn. They all fingered Garcia's polished steel helmet – Rich guessed that the sight of it, glittering across the water, had been the cause of considerable argument among them. They stood in a group and admired the longboat, marvelling at its size and its accessories and at the cunning way in which the planks were joined together – their own wretched boat was made of a single piece of wood and had hardly three inches of freeboard.

Three of them wore thin metal collars – half the Spaniards

hurriedly called Rich's attention to them – which seemed to be of pale gold, but Rich forbore to offer to barter for them until their curiosity might be satisfied. With inquiring looks and beckoning gestures they walked away from the longboat towards the dead lizard, confirming Rich's theory that they had been studying the Spaniards' actions from across the water, and they stood and stared at the dead body with ejaculations of wonder. Garcia approached them and pointed to it.

'Iguana?' he said inquiringly, and, when they only looked puzzled, he repeated the word, varying the intonation. 'Iguana? Iguana?'

A look of understanding came over their faces and they made emphatic gestures of negation.

'Caiman,' said one, and then, pointing to the trees, 'Iguana.'

He helped his meaning out with more gestures; clearly the iguanas who lived in trees were vastly different creatures from the caimans that lived in rivers.

'Eat caiman?' asked Garcia. He pointed to the body and then to his mouth and then rubbed his belly.

The gestures of dissent were still more emphatic now; they made wry faces and held their noses. One of them, too, made all the gestures of fear, pretending to run away, and holding his hands to represent the snapping jaws of the caiman. That brought them back to their wonder that this ferocious animal had been killed at all. They marvelled loudly at the severed hind leg, and one of them turned to Garcia in an attempt to discover the magic means by which such a blow had been dealt. Politely he put out his hand to Garcia's sword hilt – he must have seen swords drawn already. Garcia pulled the weapon from its sheath.

'Hey! Careful!' said Garcia; the Indian had grasped the blade with his bare hand. Garcia's involuntary gesture and the Indian's withdrawal between them gashed the palm – fortunately not deeply; the Indian looked with amazement at the blood, while Garcia was voluble in apology and prodigal of gesture. But the Indian only smiled and shut his fist upon the cut; from the chattering that went on it was apparent that they were explaining to each other that a weapon which could cut at a touch could sever a caiman's leg at a blow.

Rich judged it to be as well to be conciliatory. He produced some of the trade goods with which the longboat had been supplied, and jingled a hawk's bell enticingly. There was just the same awe and delight displayed at the gifts as Rich had seen on the first occasion. He tapped at one of the collars of gold, and without a moment's hesitation the Indian unsnapped it from his neck and thrust it into his hand. It was harder and tougher than pure gold would have been; it was clearly an alloy, but its weight demonstrated that it must contain a large proportion of gold. Rich tried to display in dumb show great affection for the gold, and pointed inquiringly to the horizon. Instantly the Indian pointed south, with many words and gestures. Rich caught one word – 'Guanin.'

'Guanin?' he said.

'Guanin,' said the Indian, tapping the collar.

They knew now the Indian word for gold. The two other collars were put into Rich's hands without his even asking for them. These uncultured folk clearly were possessed of the instinct to present strangers with whatever they desired. One of them began a new pantomime, pointing to his mouth, pointing to the whole group of Spaniards, and then, in a wide gesture, away across the river.

'He's inviting us to dinner,' said Garcia.

'I fancy so,' said Rich. 'He wants to take us to his village.'

He nodded in acceptance, and with little more ado the matter was settled satisfactorily. They pushed the longboat out from its mooring place and pulled after the canoe, which preceded them down the river with the Indian in the stern looking anxiously back at them and calling to see that they understood what they had to do. His gesture towards the setting sun indicated his wish to arrive at their destination before nightfall.

The current bore them down the river, while they quartered steadily across. Down where the delta began the canoe turned abruptly into a side channel which led them into a broader arm again, where trees grew with their feet in the water. It was not very far up here; the forest receded from the river bank leaving a wide clearing. Four more canoes floated moored to the bank, and a little crowd of Indians stood at the landing place to welcome them, men, women, and children, some in cotton aprons, many of them naked, and all of them chattering and laughing with pleasure at the success of their embassy in inducing these strangers to visit them.

Everything was on a much larger scale here than in Trinidad, as Rich saw when he mounted the bank with the others bustling like schoolboys behind him. The clearing was wider, and there were obvious patches of cultivated crops; Rich's attention was caught by the yellow hue of corn – presumably that strange golden Indian corn which he had heard about from Spaniards returned from Española. The Indians were laughing and chattering around them, leading them towards the leaf-built huts grouped to one side. It was a sort of triumphal procession, the naked children scampering in front of them, the adults leading the Spaniards by the hand, the original party which had found them talking loudly to everyone, apparently telling of all the extraordinary things these strangers could do. There was plenty of laughter, shouts of it – the Indians had to stop in the progress more than once while they all clasped midriffs and doubled up with mirth.

'You left no guard on the boat, sir,' muttered Osorio to Rich. He made a strange spectacle when Rich looked at him, his hat pulled awry and a naked girl clasping each arm; they had stuffed a handful of scarlet flowers into the breast of his leather coat. It was with a shock that Rich remembered that he had indeed neglected the precaution suggested by Osorio – nothing of the sort had occurred to him at all.

'No guard is necessary,' he said; he meant it, and yet he would have posted a guard if it had occurred to him.

'They might steal the boat's gear,' suggested Osorio.

'No,' said Rich. 'Oh, no.'

He was absolutely certain that these people would not steal; when the matter was presented to him as bluntly as that he realized that there was certainly no need to leave a guard with the boat.

'Very well, then, sir,' said Osorio, clearly washing his hands of the whole business. Nor could he have continued the conversation, for another girl was distracting him. She was presenting him with a small live parrot – a gorgeous green bird, with touches of yellow and red – which perched on her forefinger and looked at him with its head on one side in the most comical fashion. Laughing, she put the bird on his breast; it clung to his leather coat with beak and claws, pecked for a moment at the red flowers, and then, climbing desperately, reached the summit of his shoulder, from which it squawked into Osorio's ear its own contribution to the din around them.

A dignified Indian, taller than his fellows, met them at the huts, and for the moment chatter ceased. The speech he made was obviously one of welcome.

'Thank you,' said Rich. He said something about Their Highnesses, and about His Excellency the Admiral. He mentioned the Church of Christ, and to all of this they listened with grave attention. The chief tapped his own chest.

'Malalé,' he said.

Rich tried to reproduce the name. The chief listened courteously, and repeated it.

'Malalé,' said Rich.

The chief clapped his hands with pleasure, and all the mob round clapped as well. Yet the chief still waited for a second or two, and then with extreme deference he began again.

'Malalé,' he said, pointing to himself, and then pointed to Rich, who grasped his meaning at last.

'Rich,' he said, touching his breast.

Malalé hesitated.

'Rich,' said Rich again, encouragingly.

'Lish,' said Malalé with an effort.

'Rich,' said Rich.

'Lish,' said Malalé.

It was too much for anybody's gravity, certainly too much for the very precarious gravity of the Indians. Everybody laughed, including the chief. Everybody was saying 'Lish' in a hundred different intonations. The harsh 'r' and 'ch' were clearly beyond their powers of articulation.

'Lish,' said the girls on Osorio's arms.

'Lish,' said a pot-bellied little boy, laughing with his head thrown back and his stomach protruding.

'Lish,' said everyone else; it was like the wind rustling in a grove of willows.

The chief waved his arms to terminate the seance; Rich was irresistibly reminded of the kindly young teaching friar in his first school breaking off the chorused repetition when it grew too riotous. Everyone remembered the real business of the meeting, and the Spaniards were led by their chattering escorts up to the leafy huts. There were hammocks in there, standing on the earthen floors; a few gourds; a headless spear; some fantastic shells – practically nothing. Rich was led into the main hut, and seated on a couch of trellised creeper beside the doorway. It wobbled under his weight; it was as impermanent as the hut in which it stood. Osorio was given a block of wood on which to sit at Rich's side, and Garcia another – apparently these two were singled out to share the place of honour, the one because he had been seen much in Rich's company and the other because of his glittering helmet.

It was almost dark by now. Someone stirred the two fires into a bright blaze, and the rest of the Spaniards were led to seats by them. Then came the food, a prodigal display. There was fish and there was fruit, yellow cornbread, and grey cassava bread. There was roast meat of a nature quite unidentifiable, all served by the women and young men, while the older men stood by anxiously watchful that their guests should want for nothing.

'A cup of wine, now –' said Garcia. 'Hey, Don Malalé.'

He made a gesture of drinking, and in obedience to Malalé's request a girl approached him, carrying under each arm a bulky gourd. Another girl followed her with a couple of small drinking gourds. She put one in each of Garcia's hands. The first girl filled one of them, and stood by while Garcia tasted it.

'Queer,' said Garcia, savouring it on his palate. 'Sickly. I can't say that I like it.'

The expression on his face was sufficient indication for the girl to stoop and fill the other cup from the other gourd.

'Sour,' said Garcia. 'But still – Drinkable, at any rate.'

He drained the cup, and it was refilled for him. When Rich came to taste the drink he found it sour, as Garcia had said. The flavour was indefinable, and he simply could not guess whether it was fermented or not.

Malalé was standing ready to make polite conversation. It called for a good deal of effort to make him understand that he wanted to know the name of this little town.

'Paria,' said Malalé at length. He pointed all about him into the surrounding darkness. 'Paria.'

So this country was called Paria. Rich could remember no geographical name that resembled it, in the way that Cibao resembled Cipangu.

'Guanin?' asked Rich, and the chief evinced a little surprise at Rich's knowing a word of his language. One of the Indians who had been in the canoe interposed with a voluble explanation in which Rich heard the word repeated more than once. Malalé called to his subjects. There was a good deal of bustling about, and people brought Rich ornaments of gold and put them at his feet – two more collars, and several shapeless lumps, the largest the size of a walnut.

'This wench here has pearls on,' said Osorio.

'I was going to ask about them next,' said Rich.

He reached out and touched the armlet, and at his touch the girl stood stock-still, quivering a little like a frightened horse. At a word from Malalé she stripped off the armlet and put it in his hand, still stood for a second, and then, presumably deciding that it was only the pearls that interested Rich, quietly withdrew. More pearls were brought; a little pile of wealth lay at Rich's feet.

Beyond the ring of light round the fires something was happening in the darkness. The circle of Spaniards had grown thin. The din and chatter had died away into a more secretive murmur. Uneasily Rich guessed what was going on, and felt a little sick both with apprehension and disgust. He himself had lived celibate for nearly twenty years, ever since he had said good-bye to Paoletta in Padua after he had received his doctorate, and he had not been conscious of missing anything, thanks to his interest in his work and in the minor pleasures of life. He could feel only small sympathy with the animal grossness of these hot-blooded Castilians; he was a dozen years older than the eldest of the hidalgos, and he felt as if it were more like thirty or forty. Nothing, not even gold, could cause quarrelling and bloodshed so easily as could women, but that was only a practical point. Morally, Rich felt an uneasy sensation of sin at the thought of condonation of promiscuousness. He had his own immortal soul to think about.

But a casuist might argue that there was no sin in promiscuousness with these simple pagans who knew nothing of God, who gave so gladly and who submitted so willingly. Their souls were put in no further peril by it: the devil, although he wished to entrap Christian souls, would not assume the guise of these girls whose simple nakedness stripped the glamour – to Rich's mind – from the act and reduced it to a mere function of brutish nature. Rich found himself lapsing into heresy again; it was perilous to try and distinguish between deliberate sin and instinctive sin. And no thief would ever be hanged and no heretic would ever be burned if it were once admitted that inability to resist temptation constituted an excuse. That way lay chaos and anarchy. Natural instincts were in themselves suspect.

All the same, it was dangerous to interfere, physically dangerous. To take a girl from these men was like taking a kill from a wild cat. They would challenge him, perhaps. Any of these brawny louts could kill him five seconds after crossing swords. Rich vividly pictured to himself a sword blade slicing through his soft flesh, and his red blood flowing; the thought made him sick, and decided him instantly to take no action. After all, he did not know – he was not certain – what was going on. That was sufficient excuse, although he despised himself for his weakness at the same time as he yielded to it.

Somewhere in the darkness a woman screamed sharply, and Rich felt his heart sink. He tried to act as if he had not heard, and the cry came again. Garcia was eyeing him curiously in the firelight, and Osorio was looking at him sidelong, to see what he would do. The Indians were tense; everything seemed to be waiting on his decision. In a few moments there might be a bloody massacre, he realized now. He got slowly to his feet, and as he did so an Indian girl came running into the firelight. She made straight for one of the men and threw herself into his arms; she pointed back into the darkness with tearful explanations as he stood with an arm round her shoulders.

As she pointed, two figures came into sight, blinking a little sheepishly in the firelight, João de Setubal and Diego Moret. They saw everyone on their feet, and they felt the tension, and they were self-conscious with every eye on them.

'What is this?' asked Rich. Every word was a torment to utter.

'I found the girl first,' said Moret, sullenly.

'You found her first? *You* found her?' protested Setubal in his slobbering Portuguese. 'She promised me an hour ago.'

'Can you talk this monkey-talk, then?' Moret was a fat and lazy man, but he was thoroughly roused now.

'No. But she knew what I meant, well enough,' said Setubal. 'She promised me.'

'Nonsense. She was willing enough for me, or would have been if you had not interfered and frightened her.'

'You had no right to her.'

'Nor had you!'

'I claimed her first!'

'That's a lie!'

Their hands went to their sword hilts at those words. To give the lie was as much an invitation to bloodshed as to give a blow. Someone was at Setubal's elbow in the half-light, and someone else at Moret's. In a moment there would be a dozen swords drawn. Everyone's life would be in peril, with these Indians uneasily looking on, and Rich had to plunge in, lest worse befall.

'Don Diego! Don João!' he cried, hurrying forward from the hut between the two fires.

His words barely sufficed to check the men as they stood with their swords half drawn. They looked round at him, their bodies turned towards each other, right feet advanced, left shoulders thrown back. In the tenth part of a second those blades could cross.

'Take your hands from your swords!' roared Rich. The desperate urgency of the moment gave power to his voice – it was like shouting at a child who was about to touch unwittingly a brazier of burning charcoal. They hesitated, and then, as Rich strode between them, they dropped their melodramatic poses; their right hands left their sword hilts, even if their left still retained their grasp on the scabbards.

'Are you fools enough to want to fight with a hundred Indians looking on?' spluttered Rich. 'They may think us gods now, but how long will they think it if one of you has a yard of steel in his belly?'

A training in rhetoric may have enabled his tongue to move

more freely, but he had never before been so desperately anxious to win a cause, and the idiom he used and the tactics he employed were the proof of the inspiration of necessity. The sound of the quarrel had called back to the firelight the other Spaniards who were out in the shadow; they were coming back to the ring one by one, and taking their places in it, while the Indian women were grouping together in the background behind the screen of their menfolk – Rich was conscious out of the tail of his eye of this byplay.

'Will the women be so easy for you if they see you think 'em worth squabbling about?' he asked, wondering, as he said it, whether his tone of self-confident coarse good-fellowship rang true. 'Twenty of you came with me in the longboat, and I've got to take twenty of you back, or there'll be the devil to pay when I make my report to the Admiral.'

He ran his eyes round the ring; every Spaniard was present now. Somebody damned the Admiral in an undertone, but low enough for Rich to be able to pretend he had not heard.

'If it comes to that,' he went on, amplifying his earlier speech, 'what'll these women think of us anyway if you go on as you do? With our clothes on, and our helmets, and our sword belts, and our white skins we're gods to them now. There's gold and there's pearls for the asking. But with our breeches off we're men. Aren't we, now? And you've been taking the surest way of making the men angry and dangerous. Think of your own case. If an archangel visited you in Spain you'd give him dinner, wouldn't you? But if you caught that archangel with your wife? What then?'

He got a laugh at that – a most encouraging sound.

'Let's have no more of this nonsense,' he said, taking the bull by the horns at last, and assuming the attitude of authority which he dreaded. 'It's time for sleep, and we'll sleep close together for safety's sake. I'm not going to take chances with my eyes shut. Seamen can sleep by the fire here. Gentlemen here. Don Diego, you can make yourself obeyed by these hot-headed lads. See that nobody wanders off in the night and gets his throat cut. Boatswain, you can do the same with your seamen.'

To delegate the responsibility to Garcia was a bold and successful move. Garcia would not like it to be demonstrated that he could not make himself obeyed after Rich had assumed he could, and he certainly could fight if necessary, which was more than Rich could do. And the simple assumption of authority and of Garcia's support worked a miracle, too. The young men were impressed by it – and perhaps Rich did not realize that they were the less ready to resent his authority after he had withstood sword in hand the first mad charge of the wounded caiman. Nor was the hint that their lives might be in peril, here in this unknown land, without its weight.

CHAPTER TEN

FOR the four full days which the Admiral had allotted as a maximum Rich explored this new coast in the longboat. Southward they went, and southward again, finding the land continuous. The marshy delta-formation continued for miles – more than one big river contributed to its formation. There was a fresh water lagoon where flocked countless white aigrettes, beautiful in the sunshine. There were cranes and monkeys and parrots, while each sand bank bore its two or three caimans – the sight of them always raised a laugh in the longboat, at the memory of Garcia's temerity in attempting to kill one with a noose and the bare steel. There were Indians in little groups everywhere, each group with a hospitable welcome, and ready to accompany them to the next group even though it was impossible to explain to them by sign language that they were seeking an easterly passage to the open sea – they were never able to make them understand this. The Spaniards' gesticulations were met with a wooden lack of understanding which their utmost efforts could not enlighten. The Indians knew of no sea to the east, but the evidence was not convincing, seeing that it appeared unlikely that any one of them had ever been more than ten miles from his birthplace.

One little piece of useful information they acquired, however. They were eating some of the little half-tide oysters which grew on trees, and Rich, showing pearls, was able to make it clear to one of their guides that he wanted to know if these oysters produced them. The suggestion met with an emphatic negative. By signs the guide was able to indicate that pearls were found in another kind of oyster, one with a much bigger shell, for which one had to dive deep, and which was only found in certain places to the north. It was a useful confirmation of Rich's already well-developed theory that these little oysters would be quite fully occupied in developing into pelicans without wasting further strength on producing pearls, and it agreed with what he knew vaguely of the pearl fisheries of the east. Rich wondered how extensive these new fisheries were. Certainly there were pearls in plenty to be seen in this country, but these Indians had lived here for countless generations undisturbed, and the pearls they wore might be the accumulation of centuries. With no idea of barter or trade, and wearing the things purely for ornament, it might easily be the case that the pearls they owned might represent the annual produce of the fisheries a hundred times over.

Of the Indians' ignorance of barter, or their utter improvidence, the longboat bore ample proof. She was laden deep with gifts; every village had stripped itself bare to supply the strangers with anything they might require – bread and fruit and strange edible roots in addition to gold and pearls. The weary crews of the ships would experience a welcome change of diet on the longboat's return, but Rich wondered a little about how the Indians were going to live until their next crops ripened. Hawk's bells and red caps and steel mirrors would not fill empty bellies, but the Indians seemed to have no qualms on the subject. There might be a word in their limited vocabulary for 'tomorrow' – although he doubted even that – but there certainly was none for 'the future'. He felt a little pang of sympathy for them each time the longboat pushed away from the creek-side landing places. Southward, through the lagoons and waterways, the longboat sought for the passage to an eastern sea. Then westward as well as southward, as the trend of the land forced them that way. The sun roasted them, and the rain saturated them, and insects bit them. There were tiny creatures, some flat and some cylindrical, which found their way under their clothes when they were on land and sank their jaws so deeply into their skin that their heads parted company from their bodies sooner than loose their holds when the Spaniards tried to pull them off. Next day there was an itching sore where the head had been left in the wound, and each day the soreness and irritation grew worse. Wrists and faces swelled with the bites of the mosquitoes.

In the sweltering nights there were things even worse than mosquitoes to be dreaded. On the third night they slept in an abandoned Indian clearing at the water's edge, under the crude shelter of the boat's sails spread to protect them from the rainstorms, and Rich found himself awakened at dawn by Osorio shaking his shoulder. Rich was stupid with sleep – it was not until the early morning that he had been able to lose consciousness in the heavy heat – and it was with bleared eyes that he followed the line of Osorio's pointing forefinger. From under the shelter of the mainsail two yards away projected the naked leg and foot of one of the seamen, thrust out, Rich presumed, in search of coolness during the night. And resting on the foot was a greyish lump, which moved a little as Rich looked. There was hardly light to see, for the faint dawn could as yet barely penetrate the forest around them, and the thing was too vague to be seen clearly, but it was ugly, menacing, obscene.

Bernardo de Tarpia had shared the shelter of the mizzensail with Rich and Osorio, and he, too, was awake and staring at the thing, crossing himself and breathing hard. Then the leg moved and the thing dropped off the foot to the ground with a flutter of wings; it made towards them. There was something vile about it and they all three flinched back. The wings fluttered again in the short undergrowth; it was trying to fly and yet was unable to rise, and its course brought it close to Rich. His hand was on the hilt of his sword, which he had grasped instinctively at the first alarm, and he whirled the sheathed weapon and struck at the thing, shuddering. Again and again he struck, but Tarpia had his sword out by now, and with a cry, half prayer and half blasphemy, he slashed at the thing and the flutterings ended abruptly.

It was a bat, a furry thing, brownish above and greyish below, with widespread leathery wings, dead with its open mouth revealing a gleam of sharp white teeth. The revolting ugliness of the face made Rich shudder again, and the spreading pool of blood in which the creature lay disclosed the work it had been at; it had gorged itself until it was unable to rise in the air. The occupants of the other tent had awakened, and were on their feet and out now; one of them was bare-legged and pale under his tan. At Rich's order, he showed his foot. A patch of skin the size of a finger-nail had been shaved from off it at the root of the great toe, and a broad stream of blood still flowed from the wound, even though the seaman was ignorant of its existence until his attention was called to it. He paled still further when he learned what had happened, and during that day they waited for him to die of the poison they thought the bat had injected into the wound. But he did not die, and the flow from the wound ceased after it had soaked the cloth in which they bound it. On their return to the ships the surgeon bled him from the right elbow, as was of course necessary after a wound in the left foot, and he recovered some days later with the help of purges. But they did not foresee his recovery at the time. During the exploration of that day Rich was thinking of the wretched man with pity, and watching him as he lay in the bottom of the boat with the oars creaking over him.

A shallow exit from a lagoon brought them out into open water again; there lay Trinidad to the westward, well up over the horizon, while to the eastward and the southward was the land they had been exploring. There was only a narrow gap between the two – the Serpent's Mouth. The Admiral's Isle of Grace, as he had named the land across the Serpent's Mouth from Trinidad, was something more than an island, then. It was a part of the big island whose innumerable river mouths they had been examining.

'That settles it, sir, I should think,' said Osorio, peering round under his hand. 'If the Admiral wants to find a passage to the eastward he'll have to come back through here first. And I don't expect he'll want to do that – not with that current running.'

'Perhaps not,' said Rich, looking at the green slopes of Trinidad and of what he had thought of so far as the Isle of Grace. But now they had circumnavigated the whole of this sea of Paria and there were only the two exits – the Serpent's Mouth to the south and the Dragon's Mouths, which they had hardly examined, to the north; if the Admiral would not use the one, he would have to use the other. Yet Rich was reluctant to give up the search for another way round. He had a strange feeling that this land of Paria held the secret of the Indies. He wanted to know how far it extended, and what ocean lay beyond it. He felt a little thrill of pleasure – at which he was inclined to smile – at the thought that his foot had been the first from Europe to be set upon it. Trinidad was a mere small island, but Paria – no one knew the limits of Paria yet.

'Take the boat in again,' he said, hoarsely, and Osorio swung the tiller over and they headed in towards the flat delta once more.

There was a bigger river mouth even than usual here; Osorio tasted the water which he lifted in his hand from over-side.

'Fresh,' he said laconically – it meant that the volume of water coming down the river was considerable, if here at the edge of the sea there was no taste of salt.

But save in the matter of size, this channel was like the others they had explored; mud and jungle, mosquitoes and aigrettes. Rich wondered whether he would be able to persuade the Admiral to bring the squadron back to here and push a strong expedition, equipped for weeks of exploration, up this river. He felt a sudden yearning to head such an expedition – he felt in his bones, ridiculous though he knew such an idea to be, that this river drained no mere island, but a new unguessed-at continent. A mad theory, contrary to all the ideas held by the Admiral, a dangerous, almost a heretical theory. If only there was some means of ascertaining how far round this revolving globe they had sailed, whether it was one-third the way round, as the Admiral's theories demanded, or one-eighth the way, as Rich saw would have to be the case if his own mad guesses were correct! If only some miracle would let them know, even just for once, what time of day it was at that moment in Cadiz!

Sand glasses turned half-hourly for a ten-week's voyage could be as much as a week out in their record at the end of that time, he knew. Ingenious mechanics were constructing engines in Germany which could tell the time with an error of not more than an hour a day. If some remarkable man could devise one accurate to a second a day, and able to withstand the shocks of a sea voyage, the problem would be solved, but no such miraculous workmanship could ever be hoped for. Wilder and more chimerical ideas flowed through Rich's brain. Supposing a string were to be laid by a ship on the bottom of the ocean from Cadiz to the Indies, so that a twitch from one end would announce the hour of noon to the other end! Supposing some vast explosion, some flash of light, could be contrived at Cadiz at noon which could be observed in the Indies! That was plain madness, said Rich to himself, terminating his meditations with a jerk. Three thousand miles of ocean sundered Spain from the Indies. It was a gap which no wild theories could bridge and no one – at least no one without the help of magical powers – would ever be able to tell at one place what was the time at another; neither the Greek philosophers nor the Fathers of the Church held out any hope of the contrary.

'Another Indian boat, sir,' announced a seaman in the bow. 'See! He's gone up that creek over there to starboard.'

They turned the longboat and headed across the river to the creek, and sharp eyes detected the canoe hiding among the trees whose feet stood in the water. The two young Indian men who were in her had no concrete fears for their personal safety, just like all the other Indians they had encountered. They had merely taken flight before the unknown, and their confidence had only to be won for them to begin to smile broadly, with white teeth showing in contrast with their pale copper skins. The technique of handling them so as to reassure them was being acquired rapidly. Jingling hawk's bells, bright red caps – the young men were soon enraptured by the acquisition of treasures whose very possibility had been unguessed at by them an hour ago. But they had no treasures to give in exchange; the canoe contained nothing save a few fibre fishing lines with fish-bone hooks attached.

'Guanin?' said Tarpia to them; as they showed no understanding a dozen voices repeated the word in a dozen different intonations. One of them understood at last, saying the word over again. It was the initial sound which troubled these Castilians and Andalusians, noted Rich. The 'gu-' pronunciation which they used did not exactly reproduce the real sound because the latter had no place in their language. It was more like the beginning of a good many Arabic words – 'Wadi', for instance – which was reminiscent of the way in which he himself, speaking Catalan, or the Provençals speaking their native tongue, pronounced an initial 'v'.

'Guanin?' repeated everybody eagerly.

The Indian spread his hands deprecatingly. He had no gold.

'Where can we find guanin?' asked Acevedo; he went through the motions of someone seeking something, steadily repeating the word meanwhile.

The Indian grinned and pointed south. It was always to some other quarter that these Indians pointed, south or north or west; they knew no mines of gold close to them.

Rich was trying to question the other Indian about the geography of the neighbourhood – a heartbreaking task in dumb show, but the Indian paid courteous attention to his strained gesticulations. He partly understood at last and replied in a long speech, pointing round about him. Twice in the rapid sentences Rich caught the name 'Paria', and he knew already that was the name of this country. He pointed to the river, and peered along it under his hand, pointed back to the sea, and then inland again, in a desperate effort to inquire about the existence of a westward passage. The Indian grasped some of his meaning. He smiled and nodded his head; he spread his arms wide, striving with all his body to convey the impression of something big – big – big. Did that mean there was a big sea beyond? wondered Rich. The other Indian joined in. He, too, pointed to the river and spread his arms.

'Orinoco,' he said, and the other eagerly echoed the word, 'Orinoco.'

'Orinoco?' asked Rich.

The Indians were delighted, and gesticulated more vehemently than ever. This Orinoco, whatever it was, was something very big, and was somehow connected with the river by which they were. One of the Indians hissed and shushed, swinging his arms horizontally with twittering fingers – the Orinoco must be a rushing river, and, judging by the way the other Indian pointed and spread his arms, far wider somewhere in the interior than this arm of it. The Indians chattered together and then one of them turned back to Rich; he was clearly faced with a difficult explanation, but that could not account for the reverent solemnity of their expressions. He was about to try to describe something which they considered very important, perhaps connected with some god of theirs. He held his hands high, the fingers dancing, and moved slowly along – this was the steady course of a wavelet-capped river.

'Whoosh!' he said, and his hands dropped suddenly to the level of his knees. 'Whoosh!'

His hands indicated a turmoil in the water at a lower level.

'A waterfall!' said Osorio.

'Of course,' said Rich. 'How far?'

He made a gesture of walking towards this Orinoco waterfall, and the Indian dissented emphatically. The Indian closed his eyes and inclined his head sideways against his folded hands in a gesture of sleep. Then he held up his finger. He slept again, and held up his finger again, and then again. After that repetition he gave up the effort of trying to convey the exact number, and spread all his fingers, over and over again. A man would have to sleep many nights before he penetrated as far as this waterfall. Two more vivid gestures disclosed the fact that he had himself seen this marvellous phenomenon, while his companion had not.

'Are there people to be found on the way?' asked Rich. 'Many people?'

The Indians presumably grasped the meaning of his signs, and dissented doubtfully. There were some people, a few people, apparently, along the river – but apparently these Indians had no notion of an uneven distribution of population.

'Guanin?' asked Rich.

The Indians were puzzled. There might be gold there, a little, but clearly they were not interested in gold, and could not understand this persistent questioning about the existence of gold. Rich tried to work by analogy in his effort to understand their mentality. Supposing a Negro of unknown tongue landed in Catalonia, and was not interested in the service of God or in money, and yet persistently asked about the existence of, say, sandstone – or even birds' nests – something of no special appeal, his questions might be received with the same blank lack of sympathy.

One of the Indians was examining Pedro's crossbow with more interest. Pedro was always glad of the opportunity of demonstrating the effectiveness of his weapon. He wound the thing up, making great play of the amount of strength necessary to turn the windlass, while the Indians looked on, deeply interested but entirely without understanding. When the cord clicked over the catch and the windlass spun free they actually thought the demonstration was complete, and smiled politely.

'No,' said Pedro; he was one of the school which believed that people who did not understand good Spanish might understand bad Spanish. 'Big shooting. Look. See.'

He laid a heavy bolt into the groove against the string and looked round for a target. A few score yards away, out on the broad surface of the river, a sea bird drifted with the current. Pedro called their attention to it, raised his heavy weapon, took careful aim, and shot. The bolt splashed into the water not more than a couple of yards from the bird, which squawked with surprise. Such an amazing result naturally impressed the Indians as much as did the clatter of the released bow. They looked with reverence upon the man who could do such extraordinary things, and these Spaniards who manned the longboat took a childish delight in displaying their powers – the sharpness of their heavy swords, and the impenetrability of their armour, and the way their clothes fastened with brooches and buttons. Rich allowed them plenty of time for it before he suggested a move.

They would have to turn back and seek the ships now, and it was with a curious sinking of heart that he directed the longboat's course away from the mouth of the Orinoco, and northward, with the easterly wind just fair enough to enable them to proceed under sail. As they coasted along, leaving on their left the flat delta which they had explored, Rich looked across at the land with this persistent feeling of unhappiness. He might never return here, to this land of the laughing Indians, he might never explore the vast Orinoco, and he felt that it was this that he wanted to do, despite the heat, and the rain, and the insect pests, and the vampire bats. Whatever might be the wonders awaiting him in Española, he felt as if this vast new land where he had been the first Spaniard to set foot was peculiarly his own. He hardly paid attention when Osorio announced, after cautious experiments, that even out here the water was hardly brackish.

CHAPTER ELEVEN

THE Admiral listened courteously to Rich's report. His eyes brightened at the sight of the gold and the pearls which Rich handed over, and he seemed pleased at the news that the longboat was full of fresh food. The Admiral had no interest in food himself – his bad teeth alone would have limited it – and with him it was an article of faith, not of knowledge, that weaker men found benefit in a varied diet. He laughed at Rich's account of how they had attacked a caiman under the impression that it was an iguana.

'It is a pity you had no men with you with experience of the Indies,' he said, and then his face hardened as he realized what he said. When the squadron sailed from Spain no inducement offered had been great enough to tempt a single one of those survivors of the previous expedition who had returned to Spain to sail again for the Indies.

Rich noticed the Admiral's hurt expression, and went on hastily with his report so as to smooth over the difficulty.

'It is a vast land, Your Excellency,' he said, and the Admiral nodded doubtfully. 'The rivers are huge.'

'You mean the channels between the islands?'

'Rivers, Your Excellency. Vast rivers of fresh water. So vast that they freshen the water far out in this inland sea.'

'That freshness is interesting – we have noticed it here, near the ships, while you have been away. I have decided on the cause.'

'It is caused by these big rivers, Your Excellency.'

'Oh no. There is no land near which could support a river of that size. It is far more likely that – '

'We found a river the Indians called Orinoco, Your

Excellency,' said Rich. He was desperate enough to interrupt in his anxiety not to hear the theory. 'They said one could ascend it for many days' journey, as far as a great waterfall.'

'There is nothing so easy to misunderstand as the signs these Indians make,' said the Admiral, kindly. 'Believe me on that point; I have had sufficient experience to know.'

Rich remembered the Admiral's early reports and their frequent mentions of the consequences of such misunderstandings, and yet he was sure that on this occasion there had been no misunderstanding.

'Their gestures left me in no doubt,' he said.

'That is often enough the case, believe me. Could they have been referring to a fountain, perhaps? The fountain of youth – what did you say this river was called?'

'Orinoco, Your Excellency.'

'There were four rivers in Eden. Euphrates, Hiddekel, Pishon, and Gihon.' The Admiral thought for a while; Rich could see the struggle in his face as he gave up the attempt to reconcile one of the last three names with 'Orinoco'. 'No matter. These Indians often have several different names for their rivers. Let us hear more.'

Rich told of the oysters which grew upon trees.

'Ah, that is the source of these pearls. Pliny has a passage on the subject. Did you notice any clinging with their shells open?'

'No, Your Excellency.'

'Pliny tells that oysters exposed by the tide open their shells to receive drops of dew from the skies, and then solidify these drops into pearls. It is natural to meet with confirmation here.'

Rich kept his mouth tight shut. He was not going to risk a further snub by advancing the further information given him by the Indians about the pearls. And then with a shock he realized that the Admiral was right. He remembered perfectly plainly now the passage in *De Rerum Natura* that dealt with the point. He certainly must have mistaken the Indians' gestures in this case, at least. Pliny could not be wrong; Rich withdrew in horror from the brink of the abyss of free-thinking into which he had been about to plunge.

'What is the matter, Don Narciso?' asked the Admiral, politely. 'You look unwell.'

'Oh no, Your Excellency, thank you,' said Rich, hastily. Not for worlds would he confess to a proximity to heretical unbelief. 'I am perfectly well.'

'Then let us hear more.'

Rich told of the endless marshy channels, of the vampire bat, of their eventual recognition of the Isle of Grace as they emerged beside the Dragon's Mouths.

'So that between here and the Isle of Grace you think the channels impracticable for the squadron, then?'

'Yes, Your Excellency.'

That was one way of saying that he thought the Isle of Grace a peninsula jutting out from a vast continent, and it was one which saved argument. Besides, after the incident of Pliny and the pearls Rich was in a bewilderment of doubt again.

'Then we shall have to risk the passage of the Dragon's Mouths. We have no more time to spare at the moment – my presence is probably urgently needed in Española. We shall make the passage tomorrow morning.'

'Yes, Your Excellency.'

Rich had foreseen this development some time back – he was coming to know the Admiral so well and to anticipate his reactions. It was the Admiral's way to touch lightly upon one subject of investigation and then dash on to the next, to formulate a theory and neglect the confirmation of it, to find the distant prospect always more alluring than the present – an extraordinary trait in a man with the obstinacy and firmness of character to pursue, as the Admiral had done, a single aim through eighteen early years of rebuffs and poverty. It was as if that effort had drained him of all his single-purposedness.

'My brother, I hope, will have reduced the colony to order, and will have several shiploads of treasure awaiting us. As Adelantado I left him full powers.'

'Yes, Your Excellency.'

Bartholomew Columbus was one of the few men whom the Admiral trusted – but these clannish Genoese could be, of course, expected to trust their brothers. And Bartholomew had sailed with Diaz to the Cape of Good Hope, and was generally reputed to be a man of parts. With the powers of Adelantado – deputy to the Viceroy – he certainly might by now have effected a change in the colony since the date of the last depressing reports; but Rich was aware that it would call for a man of vast ability and courage to enforce an orderly government on the adventurers and gaolbirds who had accompanied the Admiral to Española on his second voyage. He hoped it had been done.

'If all is well in Española, Your Excellency,' ventured Rich, 'I hope you will consider it advisable to dispatch a new expedition to explore these parts.'

'I hope I shall,' said the Admiral. 'But there is so much to explore – there is so much to do.'

The Admiral sighed, and his heavy lids drooped over his blue eyes; the man was weary.

'But here there is so much to discover,' said Rich.

'Yes, indeed,' agreed the Admiral with more animation; his face brightened as he spoke. 'I have written it all in the report I am sending to Their Highnesses. The Earthly Paradise, the mines of Ophir, the Fountain of Youth – I am glad that you are with me, Don Narciso, to confirm me in all these matters.'

Rich had not the least intention of affirming to King Ferdinand the presence of any such phenomena in these parts; he wanted a great deal more evidence before he could do that, even though he knew that the counter theories at the back of his mind were ridiculous and dangerous enough to call for instant repression with nothing to replace them. But he had to swallow twice before his innate honesty forced him to hint as much to the Admiral.

'The gold and the pearls which you will send will be better evidence of the wealth of the country, perhaps, Your Excellency,' he said, 'and I am not geographer enough to venture an opinion on the other points.'

The straight deep line reappeared between the Admiral's eyebrows at the suggestion of an opinion contrary to his own.

'The ultimate exploration of this group of islands', he said finally, 'will reveal many wonders. I should be accustomed by now to having my ideas mocked at by those unqualified to judge.'

'At least, Your Excellency,' pleaded Rich, 'I am aware of my lack of qualification.'

For the first time in his life Rich was feeling sympathy towards heretics faced with a demand for a recantation. Someone, who should know, spoke of a group of islands where he considered lay a mass of land, and in the face of superior experience Rich could not help but cling to his own opinion, despite himself. Whether he would go to the stake for it or not Rich could not decide; certainly he would face a good deal of unpleasantness, and he was decidedly glad that it was a geographical point, and only distantly a theological one, which was at issue.

'Then you need not continue to weary me with argument,' said the Admiral, dismissing him.

Rich went on deck again depressed and unhappy, to watch the sun descend slowly towards this unknown land – or islands.

A little group of canoes came stealing out to the squadron over the glassy waters of the Gulf of Paria; they were the usual cranky craft of which Rich had seen a good many specimens during the longboat's voyage, mere strips of bark two or three feet wide. The two ends were tied into thin bundles and bent upwards, so as to accentuate the natural trough-like curve of the bark, thus making a boat which a venturesome boy might use on a millpond, but which would roll over at the first incentive and which buckled about, snake-like in its lack of rigidity, under the impulse of the paddles. Two or three such groups had already visited the squadron during the longboat's absence, and the ships' companies watched the approach of this one without excitement; Rich was too deeply sunk in his own thoughts to pay any attention at all.

It was Acevedo who raised him from his depression.

'Don Narciso,' he said, crossing the deck. 'A friend of yours is hailing you.'

A small canoe was creeping alongside the ship, propelled slowly by the paddles of two boys, and in the middle a naked Indian half stood, half crouched on his precarious foothold.

'Lish!' he was calling. 'Lish!'

He saw Rich's head and shoulders appear over the bulwark, and nearly capsized the canoe in the enthusiasm of his arm waving. It was Malalé, the chief of the first village which Rich had visited here; he smiled wildly and stooped to seek something down by his feet as the boys brought the canoe to the ship's side.

'Perhaps it is a royal collar of gold and pearls which he has brought you,' suggested Acevedo – someone was throwing a rope for Malalé to climb into the waist.

The Indian swung himself up over the bulwarks; he blinked for a moment, like a man emerging into strong sunlight, at the proximity of all the massive wonders about him, but he had confidence in Rich and was still smiling with the pleasure of seeing him again.

'No, it's a parrot, by God,' said Acevedo; perched on Malalé's hand was a big blood-red bird, which, as it moved, betrayed bewildering markings of a vivid blue – it was an extraordinarily stimulating combination of colours.

Malalé approached, talking volubly but deferentially; it was not hard to guess that he was employing formal phrases which for once had a real meaning. He stopped, and waited for Rich to speak.

'I am delighted to see you again, Malalé,' said Rich. 'I hope you are well.'

He might as well say that as anything else, and it was all true. Malalé lifted the red parrot and offered it to Rich, and at the latter's hesitation burst into voluble pleading; Rich held out his hand and Malalé set the parrot upon it. Rich was about to utter formal thanks, but was checked by a new outburst of speech from Malalé. He was chattering to the parrot, stroking its feathers and rubbing the back of its head, and the parrot contorted its neck and goggled up at Rich with beady eyes. Still Malalé chattered and caressed; the parrot put its head on the other side and said something in reply – but evidently not the right thing, for Malalé continued to address it, coaxingly. Suddenly the parrot seemed to realize what was expected of it.

'Lish,' it said, clearly and unmistakably. 'Lish, Lish, Lish.'

Everybody laughed, and Malalé stood by with modest pride while the parrot looked round the ring with its inhuman eyes and ruffled its blood-red feathers and repeated 'Lish' half a dozen more times before it trailed off again first into Indian speech and then into silence, with its long claws gripping Rich's finger.

'They must have started teaching the bird to say that the moment we left the village,' commented Acevedo.

Rich did not need Acevedo's friendly comment to call his attention to the forethought that contributed to the gift. He was inexpressibly moved by it – foolishly, he told himself – and he was surprised to find such a strong emotion in him, impeding his utterance and blurring his vision for a second or two. Not many people had ever made gifts to the learned Narciso Rich save in payment for his professional services. He found it hard to stammer his thanks, and it moved him still more to see Malalé's obvious delight in the pleasure he had given.

The parrot flapped impotent wings and began to sidle along his sleeve with beak and claws.

'Lish,' it said, peering up at him.

Malalé's visit and the gift he bore drew some at least of the sting from out of the necessity of saying farewell to the Gulf of Paria.

CHAPTER TWELVE

THEY sailed next morning by the central channel of the Dragon's Mouths. It was reassuring to see the drastic change which came over the Admiral when he was confronted with a problem in seamanship. He was no longer a touchy old gentleman rather set in his ideas; his very rheumatism seemed to leave him, and he paced the deck like a young man, his high clear voice as he called his orders to the captains of the caravels reaching easily across the intervening sea.

Rich stood beside him and watched the manoeuvre; there was a fascination about seeing the actual practice of an art with which he was theoretically well acquainted. Close-hauled, they reached to the southward – that was obviously to avoid the necessity of having to go about when they were at the point of entering the straits. Rich had to look up at the mast-head, where the red-cross pennant flapped, to make sure of the direction of the wind, but the Admiral was under no such necessity. Presumably he based his judgement on a whole host of trivial indications to which Rich was insensitive – the wind upon his cheek, the heel of the deck, the action of the sails, and the general behaviour of the ship.

Osorio was out in the longboat at the entrance to the strait; he had to be allowed plenty of time to make the passage, because he had to sound carefully every yard of the way, lest there might be a hidden transverse reef which would allow the passage of the longboat and yet would rip the bottom out of the ships; when the latter came hurtling down with the wind on their quarter and the current behind them there would be no chance of changing their minds – and yet the longboat must be kept in sight for her signals to be seen. The Admiral gauged the force of the wind and measured the distance to the straits with a considering eye. He gave a quiet order to Carvajal and turned to hail the caravels again. Round came the *Holy Name,* her canvas flapping and her rigging rattling while the crew scuttled round in the flurry of going about. She steadied on her new course, the caravels in her wake and her bows pointing to the passage. Far ahead the longboat danced in the turbulent race – they could see the flash of her oars as her crew strove to hold her on a steady course in the eddies.

They ran down towards the islands; a brief order from the Admiral corrected the course a trifle to allow for the leeway the clumsy ship was making and which was carrying her a trifle away from the exact centre of the passage. The lofty green hills of the north-western corner of Trinidad approached them nearer and nearer on their right hand – Rich guessed from the glances the Admiral darted at them that he was wondering what effect they would have on the wind as the ships came under their lee. The longboat was through – Osorio was standing in the sternsheets waving the white flag which indicated an absence of shoals. But the wind was growing fluky, thanks to the hills of Trinidad. Twice the sails flapped angrily; Carvajal was pulling at his beard and watching the man at the tiller. The steep-sided island that rose midway between Trinidad and the land of Paria was close upon them now; that, too, would have its effect on the wind. Rich saw the island swing round in relation to the foremast. Carvajal snapped angrily at the steersman and was answered with excuses – the dying wind was leaving the ship at the mercy of the eddies. But another puff came to steady her on her course, and the island was drawing up beside them.

Now they were through, and the longboat was waiting to come alongside. The wind, the eternal east wind, was blowing again here more freshly after an unimpeded course over three thousand miles of sea, and the long ocean swell was waiting for them – Rich felt the *Holy Name*'s bows lift to it, and heard its music, strangely welcome, under her stern.

Behind them now lay Trinidad and Paria, the islands of the Dragon's Mouths ringed with white where the swell burst against their feet. To his right hand, as he looked aft, Rich saw the green coast of Paria stretching until it was lost in the faint haze; whatever the Admiral might think, it was certainly a much larger country than Trinidad.

But curiously enough, that question was not so urgent in Rich's mind now. An hour ago his memories of Paria had been sharp and distinct – Malalé, and the rivers, and the caimans, and the myriad fireflies at night, and the croaking frogs, but now they were already vague. Ahead lay the open sea, and beyond it, Española. The lift and surge of the *Holy Name,* the fresh wind, the prospect of a new voyage – all these things distracted him. The relief from tension after the passage of the Dragon's Mouths helped as well. Rich found himself all a-bubble with pleasurable anticipation, and for the life of him he could not tell why. Bernardo de Tarpia's crossbowmen seemed to have caught the infection; they were strutting a measure on the fore-deck to the rhythmical thumping of a tambourine, while Antonio Spallanzani looked on smiling, his lute across his knees.

The Admiral was giving the man at the tiller a new course to steer, and that recalled Rich a little to reality. He wondered by what process the Admiral had reached his conclusions as to the correct course. Española lay at least two hundred leagues away, and he was approaching it from a point as to whose exact whereabouts (Rich knew only too well) the Admiral could be none too certain. Even the compass was no longer the steadfast friend which they knew in the Mediterranean – in these waters it pointed for some unknown reason a little east of north instead of west of north, and allowance would have to be made for its variation, even though that variation were unknown. Vaguely – very vaguely – they knew their distance from Spain, and the distance of Española from Spain. Within ten leagues or so they knew the distance of each point from the equinoctial line, but all that gave only small data for a calculation as to the direction of the one from the other. And in these waters they had already had proof of the existence of currents which might confound all calculations, and even when the calculations were made and the currents allowed for there was still the variation of the compass; all this in addition to the normal mariners' problems of leeway and drift – and in the dark hours, in these unknown seas, they would have to lie-to for fear of shoals, thus doubling the effect of the currents and of their leeway.

'I shall spend the rest of today, Don Narciso,' explained the Admiral, 'in examining the northern coast of this island of Paria, as you say it is called. But it would be inadvisable for us to proceed westward after that – it would carry us too far to leeward of our destination. Tomorrow we shall head for San Domingo; I think that will be the best point in Española to make for.'

'Whatever Your Excellency decides,' said Rich.

He would be quite content if they reached Española at all, without any conditions as to which bay or inlet they should sight first. He could well imagine themselves lost altogether when they left Paria and headed north-westward in search of Española across an uncharted ocean. They might blunder about for days – for weeks – seeking the island; provisions and water might fail; disease might break out among them even if they struck no reef or shoal. He certainly did not share the Admiral's bland confidence regarding what landfall they would make, and he felt a great deal more sober now than half an hour ago when they had passed through the Dragon's Mouths. The antics of the dancers on the forecastle were not at all to his taste.

'There is more land there, right to windward,' said the Admiral, staring with narrowed eyes.

Rich's sight was not as good. Stare as he would, he could see nothing on the horizon resembling land, but Osorio, called into consultation, confirmed the Admiral's opinion.

'Two islands, Your Excellency,' he said. 'One much to the northward.'

'They must be the end of the chain I explored last voyage,' said the Admiral. 'Dominica, Matinino, and the rest. That is the Cannibal region – these islands to windward have a different people from those of Española and Cuba and here in Trinidad. They are anthropophagous – they raid the other islands for human prey. Caribs, Canibs, Cannibals, or some such name they bear. We shall root them out, extirpate them. They are magicians as well as eaters of human flesh. And I cannot permit them to put my own people in fear of their lives.'

Rich pondered that expression 'my own people'. It was fit and right that cannibals with magical powers should be rooted out – that was a Christian duty – but it was hardly fit and right that the Admiral should speak of 'my own people'. That was an expression emphatically reserved for royalty; Their Highnesses might see treason in it. Yet on the other hand the Indians, as pagans, might be considered the Admiral's property, after deduction of the Royal percentage. In that case the expression might pass, drawing a nice distinction between slaves and subjects. Legally, as the wielder of the Royal power, the Admiral was entitled to treat as slaves any of his Indians who were not expressly protected by charter – and no charter had yet been, or would ever be, granted to the naked and illiterate. Morally and ethically the position might be different; at the time Rich left Spain the Church there was trying to decide whether the Admiral was justified in sending shiploads of slaves – as he had begun to do in default of other cargo – for sale in Spain. It was a nice point, Rich would have liked to have heard it argued, even though he was no theological expert; but Aristotle and the Institutes would have no authority in an ecclesiastical court, and equity would stand little chance against the law (or the absence of law) – unless indeed Queen Isabella should intervene. Rich wished he knew what decision had been reached, yet with his worldly knowledge of judges he could guess that men who had been encouraged to expect cargoes of gold would not look with favour on the arrival of cargoes of slaves which would have to be paid for. That might give the slaves a chance.

The Admiral had left his side while he had been allowing his thoughts to digress in this fashion; the coast of Paria was still unfolding itself as the *Holy Name* ran along it before the wind. It was a coast of steep green hills, and every hour that the ship progressed demonstrated it to be five or six miles longer; a big island, therefore, if it were not the coast of Asia, or – the continent Rich dared not think about. At nightfall the coast was still close to the south of them, and at dawn next morning, after a dozen miles of drifting while lying-to, it was still there. The first break they saw was at noon, and when they came up to it they found that it was only a channel between the Parian coast and an island lying off it. A nearer approach revealed two islands instead of one, but Paria still continued beyond them.

And in these islands there were Indians – Indians who fled as the vast ships came sailing in, and who soon lost their shyness when they were approached with gifts. And they were Indians who wore pearls, great strings of them, which they were glad to give to the bearded white men who seemed to want them. Rich watched the bartering going on; the squadron, as it lay at anchor in the lagoon, was surrounded by canoes and the decks were thick with Indians while treasures which could have ransomed a prince were being handed over in exchange for broken fragments of painted earthenware.

The Admiral was trying to discover by means of signs whence came all these pearls, and the Indians, when they understood him, pointed over-side, to the lagoon whereon the *Holy Name* floated. The Admiral pressed for details, and two of the Indians swung themselves over-side into their canoe and pushed off to a short distance away. The younger Indian crept forward into the bows and rose cautiously to his feet.

He was young and tall and slender – a handsome figure of a man. He poised himself with a foot on either gunwale, the twisted stempiece of the canoe rising to his waist, and then he dived with a sideways wrench of his body which took him clear of the stempiece and yet, miraculously, did not capsize the canoe. He went straight down – for several feet they could watch his progress through the clear water – and it seemed a long time before he rose again, shaking the water from his eyes, and with his hands full of grey objects which he dropped into the bottom of the canoe without troubling to climb in. He swam back to the *Holy Name* as quickly as his companion could paddle, and, running up on deck again, he laid the oysters at the Admiral's feet. An upward gesture showed that he expected to wait until the sun caused them to open, but Osorio's dagger did it at once, to the chattered amazement of the Indians. There were no pearls in the half-dozen oysters he had brought up, but it was clear enough to everybody that they were to be found, and the Indians pointed here and there over most of the lagoon to indicate the presence of oyster beds.

'God!' said Garcia. 'If we could set a thousand men diving here – there must be a thousand men to be caught – we should have pearls by the bushel. Don Narciso, can't you suggest it to the Admiral?'

'We have pearls by the quart, at least,' commented Acevedo. The Admiral was measuring the takings into a leathern cup.

Rich had not heard Garcia's suggestion, for his thoughts were digressing again. Those vast flat oysters were far different from the little ones which grew on the trees above low water in Paria, and they lived always under the sea. They would never have a chance of catching a falling dewdrop and converting it into a pearl, and yet they produced pearls – pearls by the quart, as Acevedo said. So Pliny was wrong – was more ignorant than a naked Indian.

It was an appalling discovery, shaking Rich's faith to its foundations. With Pliny proved incorrect, where was the thing to end? Rich stood stock-still, while the pearls poured in a milky cascade from the leathern measure into a canvas bag before his unseeing eyes. The structure of his world was rocking unstably.

There was a loud squawk in his ear as the red parrot launched itself, with a fluttering of almost ineffectual wings, from the rigging beside him and just managed to reach his shoulder, retaining its balance there with a vigorous use of beak and claws.

'Lish,' it said. 'Lish.'

It nibbled at his ear with a gentle beak, and maundered off, like an old man, into unintelligible Indian speech. Rich smoothed the ruffled feathers and felt in his pocket for the bit of weevilly ship's biscuit which he had already begun to carry there for the parrot's benefit – to the parrot this new kind of food appeared to be a supreme delicacy. Rodrigo Acevedo came along; he carried the jesses and the swivel and leash of the unhappy hawk which had died on the voyage out, and with long, busy fingers he quickly looped the jesses round the parrot's legs and attached the leash.

'There will be no need to cut his wing feathers now,' he remarked; he rubbed the parrot under the beak, and the parrot dug his claws into Rich's shoulder in an ecstasy.

'It is very generous of you, sir,' said Rich.

'Oh, a mere nothing, Don Narciso,' answered Acevedo.

'And I am in your debt for more than that,' went on Rich.

It was to Acevedo that he owed his baseless reputation as a swordsman, perhaps life itself as well, and certainly the satisfactory settlement of an incident which might have caused the gravest possible trouble. There had never yet been an opportunity, in the crowded ship, for Rich to express his gratitude, and Rich had never attempted to make an opportunity, even though he had repeatedly told himself that he ought to. Shyness had held him back – he was blushing now as he spoke.

'That was a mere nothing, sir,' said Acevedo. His handsome face wore a smile, but he was as much embarrassed as Rich was.

'Nothing to you, perhaps,' said Rich.

'I think it is going to rain,' said Acevedo; Garcia had drifted within earshot from the crowd round the pearls. Acevedo petted the parrot, which squawked and flapped and dug its claws with delight. Garcia came and joined in. The fantastic blue and red – a colour combination so bold as to be on the verge of the unpleasing – played under his hands.

CHAPTER THIRTEEN

THEY had left behind them the Pearl Islands and the coast of Paria, and had turned boldly to the north-west towards Española. The wind blew steadily from the east – sometimes backing towards the north so that the ships could hardly hold their course, sometimes veering southerly so that, with the wind over her quarter, the *Holy Name* put on her best speed, the spray flying from her bluff bows in gorgeous rainbows. Dolphins accompanied them, leaping in the waves of the wake like children playing a game. At the mast-heads the look-outs kept keen watch over these seas which no ship had ever sailed before, but they saw no shoals, no land, only the blue, clear water with the white wave crests in dazzling contrast. At noon the sun passed over their heads, so that a man's shadow lay round his feet; at evening it sank into the sea, leaving the eastward sky already dark with night even while the glows of sunset still coloured the west.

Every hour they measured the speed of the ship through the water, chalking the figure on the board; at noontide, the Admiral, balanced stiffly on the heaving deck, took the altitude of the sun as best he could with his astrolabe, and at night that of the Pole Star as it peeped over the horizon, while the ship, hove-to, pitched steadily over the regular swell. In his great cabin the Admiral had a grubby parchment, cracked along its folds, on which some German philosopher had inscribed, with coloured pigments, the signs of the zodiac and the corresponding heights of the sun – the sun was in Leo now, and it should have been easy to calculate their distance from the equator. But Rich, observing the pendulum of the astrolabe, swinging uncontrollably with the heave of the ship, was not so sure; and even in those clear, vivid nights the vagueness of the horizon – as he discovered when he timidly handled the quadrant – made the altitude of the Pole Star an equally vague figure.

He mentioned his doubts in conversation with the Admiral; in his opinion they could not be certain of their latitude within five or six degrees, a hundred leagues or so. As for the other coordinate which would help them to fix their position – the longitude about which the Greek philosophers argued so glibly – he already knew the difficulty regarding that. With a compass of unknown variation, and with unknown currents deflecting them from their course, it seemed to Rich quite unlikely that they would ever see Española – they might miss even San Juan Bautista or Cuba, and arrive in China or some new undiscovered land. But so diplomatically did he express his doubts that the Admiral hardly guessed at them.

'In five days,' he said, 'if the wind holds and no undiscovered land lies on our course, we shall sight Española.'

He looked up from the chart, in the dim light of the lanterns, and Rich could see the calm certainty of his expression. The Admiral had no doubt at all regarding his own ability in the practice of his art. But it was the same certainty which he had displayed regarding the proximity of the Earthly Paradise, or regarding the transmutation of dewdrops into pearls. Rich did not know what to believe; but one thing only was certain, and that was that nothing he could do would make any difference. At sea one was never one's own master unless in command. He tried to compose himself to wait in patience.

And five days later at noon the look-out, hailing from the mast-head, announced land. The Admiral was summoned, and came limping on deck; right ahead lay the land like a chalk mark of a different blue on the horizon where the blue of the sky met the blue of the sea.

'You see, we have sighted land within five days, as I foretold, Don Narciso,' said the Admiral.

'And it is Española, Your Excellency?' ventured Rich. The question brought the Admiral's brows together.

'Naturally!' he said, but there was more surprise than anger in his voice. He had not thought Rich such a fool as still to have doubts on that score.

Yet as the squadron drew closer, and the land acquired definition, Rich saw him looking more anxiously towards it under his shaggy white eyebrows. The deep-set blue eyes strained in their effort to make out the details. He consulted with Alonso Perez, his servant and the only other man in the squadron who had sailed these waters before.

'Don Narciso,' said the Admiral at length, 'my navigation has been faulty.'

'It gives me pain to hear Your Excellency say that,' said Rich, and waited to hear whether they had sighted Cuba.

'It must be that the currents are stronger than I have allowed for,' said the Admiral. 'Or perhaps it is the needle – yet I think it must have been the currents. We are not in sight of San Domingo, as I intended to be, That point there is the island of Beata, five full leagues to leeward.'

'Only five leagues!' exclaimed Rich.

He could only marvel; it was miraculous to him.

'Five leagues to leeward!' snapped the Admiral. 'Thirty leagues to windward would have caused less delay.'

He stumped about the deck on his rheumaticky legs in irritation.

'But, Your Excellency,' protested Rich. 'It is seven weeks to the day since we left Cape Verdes, and that was the last known land which we sighted. An error of five leagues in a voyage of seven weeks! It is amazing – extraordinary.'

The enthusiasm and astonishment in his voice were so obviously genuine that the Admiral could not help but be touched by them.

'It is kind of you to say so, Don Narciso,' he said, a little flush of pleasure showing in his cheekbones above his white beard. 'But I am all impatience. I wish to reach San Domingo. There is my brother, the Adelantado – I want to hear an account of his viceroyalty. And the gold mines of Hana;

they should be in full bearing by now. And the three ships we sent on from Ferro – I want to know if they have arrived yet. I am worried, Don Narciso.'

The Admiral had reason to be, as Rich knew, judging by the year-old reports which had reached Spain regarding the conditions in the colony. Rich looked about the crowded deck, at Garcia, fleshy and arrogant, swaggering at Tarpia's side; at the uncouth soldiers, who were plaguing Alonso Perez for information regarding this new land. It would not be many hours now before this fresh horde would be poured into the island. Now that he had had experience of Trinidad and Paria, Rich could visualize better the conditions prevailing here on the Admiral's first landing – it had been an Earthly Paradise, too, a pagan paradise of few wants and all of them satisfied, and he could guess what a hell the first settlers had made of it; he had learned much since he had sailed from Spain. It would be his duty to advise the Admiral on how to repair the damage, how to render the island peaceful and productive again, and the instruments for the work would be this undisciplined mob. Rich felt a sinking at heart.

The hidalgos were grouped near him now, all talking together, the fresh wind ruffling their beards, for the squadron was now close-hauled, trying to claw up to windward towards San Domingo. They drew him into their conversation, and he stood among them a little awkwardly, for he never felt at ease among these men of war with their hundred and twenty-eight quarterings of nobility apiece.

'What is the delay?' fumed Bernardo de Tarpia. 'We are coming no nearer to the land.'

'Look, by God!' said Avila. 'We are turning away from the land now!'

'We are going on the other tack,' explained Rich. 'San Domingo lies to windward.'

They looked at him without understanding. Despite the length of the voyage none of them had acquired any knowledge of how a ship is worked. Horses and hawks and hounds, they understood, because they had been taught about them from boyhood, but none of them was possessed with the lively curiosity that urged Rich to learn about everything that came under his notice.

'How far is this San Domingo?' asked Garcia.

'Five leagues.'

'And we shall not reach there tonight?'

'Perhaps not. But after dark there may be a wind off the land which would help us. There usually is.'

'Did the Admiral say so?'

'No.'

Rich could not explain that he had learned about land and sea-breezes by night and day from simple observations while fishing in Barcelona roadstead.

'But how will a wind off the land help us to reach the land?' asked Avila; his contorted features showed how hard he was trying to think.

'We shall have it on our beam and can get well to windward of San Domingo tonight, so that in the morning we can go straight in with the first of the sea-breeze,' said Rich.

'You're as good a pilot as the Admiral, Don Narciso,' said Garcia, looking at him curiously.

'Not a bit of it,' said Rich.

'At least it is not *your* fault that we have arrived the wrong side of San Domingo,' put in Acevedo. Rich rounded on him.

'You don't appreciate what a marvellous navigator the Admiral is,' he said. 'There is no other sailor living who could have brought the squadron so directly here. That is true, believe me. With ordinary piloting we might have been a hundred leagues away instead of five.'

'You must never say a word against the Admiral in Don Narciso's presence,' said Garcia, half bantering and half serious; perhaps he was remembering the occasions when Rich had conscientiously reported the acquisition of treasure.

'Hullo, we're chasing our tails again,' said Tarpia.

The ship was going about again and standing in to the shore, and Rich was for a moment puzzled as to the motive for this manoeuvre. But he guessed it when he saw the Admiral looking keenly shorewards and followed his gaze.

'There's a canoe coming out to us,' he said.

There it was, a dark spot bobbing on the waves; the sinking sun lit up a white speck in motion on it – somebody was waving to the ships from it.

'We'll get news of our friends now!' exclaimed Tarpia, eagerly.

Everybody rushed to the side of the ship and watched the canoe as it danced over the glittering water towards them. It was an Indian who paddled it, but not a naked one. He wore a shirt of coarse towcloth, as everyone could see when he scrambled up the side, but it was not that which specially caught Rich's notice – and the Admiral's notice, too. In his hand he carried a crossbow; it was rusted, and the cord was frayed, and the winding handle was bent lopsided, but it was a crossbow for all that, and in the Indian's belt of creeper was a single bolt. Before the Indian, blinking round at the ring of Spaniards, had time to collect himself the Admiral was demanding where he had obtained the weapon. The serious-ness of natives of the island possessing such weapons of precision was apparent to all.

'Loldan gave it me,' said the Indian; he could speak Spanish after a fashion.

'Roldan!' exclaimed the Admiral. 'The Alcalde Mayor?'

'Yes. We friends,' said the Indian, proudly. 'I shoot bad Indians. Christian I am.'

He bent his head and made the sign of the cross, and intoned something in a weird sing-song, which was just recognizable as the Pater Noster. Some of the group round him laughed, as they might at the antics of a performing ape.

'Where is my brother, His Excellency the Adelantado?' asked the Admiral.

'In the town,' said the Indian, pointing down the coast

with an appearance of indifference. 'He not Loldan's friend.'

'Not Roldan's friend?' repeated the Admiral, blankly.

'No. He fight. Loldan fight. Indian fight.'

The Indian grinned a simpleton's grin. A gesture more eloquent than his bad Spanish called up a picture of bloody confusion throughout the island. Someone in the background whistled in amazement at his words.

'But why? *Why?*' groaned the Admiral. The Indian grinned again and tried to explain. There was no sense in his words. Spanish quarrels meant nothing to him. Rich suspected him of being mentally sub-normal, even when allowance was made for the difficulties of language.

At least the Admiral was prepared to waste no more time on him.

'Take that crossbow away from him,' he ordered, curtly. 'Put him over the side. Captain, lay the ship on the other tack.'

This was decision, activity. Only a few seconds were necessary to bundle the protesting Indian back into his canoe and to begin to claw seaward again away from the lee shore. Rich admired the Admiral as he stood on the high poop rapping out his orders. Firmness and decision of this sort would soon stamp out any disloyalty when they reached San Domingo.

The wind blew briskly past them as the *Holy Name* ploughed along, lying as close to the wind as she could; it set Rich's clothes flapping and blew the Admiral's white hair out in horizontal streamers as he stood, staring forward. If intensity of desire could carry the *Holy Name* along, the clumsy ship would fly, thought Rich, watching the Admiral's face. The Admiral did not take his eyes from the ship's course as he began to speak.

'It was bad news that Indian bore, Don Narciso,' he said.

'We know nothing of the truth of the matter yet, Your Excellency.'

'No. I find it hard to believe that Roldan would oppose

himself to my brother, the Adelantado whom I myself appointed.'

'Who is this Roldan, Your Excellency?'

'The Alcalde Mayor – the Chief Magistrate. He owes that position to me.'

'Naturally,' said Rich. There was no appointment in the Indies which was not in the Admiral's direct gift. 'But who is he, Your Excellency? I do not know the name. Is he a gentleman? What rank did he hold before this appointment?'

'He was my servant,' said the Admiral. 'But I thought he was honest. I thought he was loyal. I thought – '

The Admiral checked himself with a sigh.

'Perhaps he is,' said Rich, with cheerful optimism. 'We cannot condemn him without knowing the facts.'

'If he has been fighting my brother he must be disloyal,' said the Admiral, conclusively. Rich was not so sure; it may have been mere professional sympathy, but he felt that a Chief Justice might easily find himself at odds with a Columbus and still have right on his side.

'Is he learned in the law, Your Excellency?' he asked. 'As I said, I am not acquainted with his name.'

'Of course he is not,' said the Admiral, petulantly. 'Did I not say he was my servant? He was my body-servant, my valet.'

After that, Rich felt there was nothing more to be said. A Chief Justice who had been a valet would certainly be as great a source of trouble as any Columbus. Rich could only gaze forward as anxiously as the Admiral himself, wondering what would be the situation he would find awaiting him when at last he reached San Domingo.

CHAPTER FOURTEEN

THEY entered the river mouth in the late afternoon, after two weary days of beating against headwinds. The Spaniards on board were pleased and excited at the thought that at last their voyaging was really at an end, and at the prospect of seeing new white faces. The details grew clearer under their eager gaze as the sea breeze pushed them briskly into the inlet; there was the wooden church with its square tower, and beside it the fort – only the simplest arrangement of ditch, palisade, and parapet, but quite impregnable to the simple unarmed folk who were its only possible assailants. At the Admiral's order the *Holy Name* swung round the point of the shoal and headed across to the anchorage, where there was deep water up to the foot of the church. Close on their left hand they opened up a clearing in the wild tangle of trees that came down to the water's edge, and there, starkly visible to all the interior, stood a gallows, from which dangled two corpses.

'Holy Mary!' said Moret, with genuine sincerity. 'It is good to be in a Christian country again!'

He pointed to the gallows.

'Are they Indians or Spaniards?' asked Garcia, shading his eyes with his hands, but no one could answer that question. Rich read a moral lesson in the fact that death and putrefaction made the European indistinguishable from the Indian.

Cannon thundered with wreaths of white smoke from the citadel in salute to the Admiral's flag; the Admiral was standing proudly on the poop looking across at his town; armour winked and glittered in the setting sun over the citadel walls. A small crowd of people were already launching boats and canoes to come out and welcome them.

The leading boat was distinguished by a flag held up in the bows, displaying the Admiral's arms within a white bordure to indicate the presence of the Admiral's deputy, the Adelantado. Bartholomew Columbus, when he came on board, looked round him with piercing blue eyes which at first glance gave him a striking resemblance to his brother, but he was more heavily built – a stoop-shouldered, burly man whose dense beard did not disguise the heavy jaw and the thick lips. An Indian woman mounted next after him; there were pearls in her ears, round her neck, and in her long loose hair. She was cloaked in blue velvet, but she made no effort to keep the cloak about her to conceal the slender naked body beneath. She was smiling and chattering excitedly, white teeth flashing, with her hand laid on the Adelantado's arm. Not even the harsh contrast between the blue velvet and her nudity could mar her beauty.

The brothers kissed, under the gaze of every eye in the ship; the Admiral had a brief word for the woman before he received the bows of the Adelantado's escort. Rich watched the little ceremony keenly from a distance, anxious to form his opinion of the Adelantado – the latter's undoubted influence with the Admiral would count for so much in the future of the New World. He saw Bartholomew pluck at Christopher's sleeve; he pointed ashore and glanced anxiously at the sun – clearly there was work to be done ashore that demanded the Admiral's immediate attention. The Admiral nodded distractedly; Carvajal and Osorio and Tarpia were all asking for his attention, and the decks were crowding with people from the shore, so that there was hardly room to stand. The din and bustle were tremendous. Carvajal wanted instructions regarding the ship and crew, Osorio regarding the stores, Tarpia permission to take his soldiers ashore. Each had a brief unsatisfactory word in reply, and continually Bartholomew plucked at the Admiral's sleeve and begged him to come ashore.

'Yes,' said the Admiral, 'I will come. One moment – '

He caught Rich's eye and beckoned to him.

'Bartholomew, I want to present the learned Don Narciso Rich. Their Highnesses have lent me his services to help on the legal side of the administration.'

'A lawyer, eh?' said the Adelantado, turning a coldly belligerent eye upon him.

'Yes, Your Excellency.'

'We need men of action more than men of law.'

'I expect so, Your Excellency. But I am here at Their Highnesses' express command.'

That scored the first point for Rich; he had no intention of being browbeaten, and though his reply was in a humble tone it made a clear statement of the strength of his position. As long as no one knew that his mission was to find a means of curtailing the Admiral's cherished power, he would have all the prestige of a court favourite and there would be no reason for anyone to dislike him. He was a long way from home, and he wished to see Barcelona again.

'It is as a man of law that I welcome Don Narciso here,' interposed the Admiral. 'What you have told me about what you want to do this afternoon – '

'I will have no interference in that,' said Bartholomew, loudly.

The tall Dominican friar at his shoulder broke into the conversation.

'Indeed not. The Crown itself – Queen Isabella in person – could not interfere there. The Holy See long ago decided that matter. The secular arm has only to do its duty after the Church has reached its decision.'

'I beg your pardon, but I do not understand,' said Rich. 'What is the point at issue?'

'It is not at issue,' said Bartholomew, loudly. 'Brother, please come. Soon night will fall and make an excuse for the Indians to steal away. It has been hard enough assembling them.'

'Come with me, Don Narciso,' said the Admiral hastily.

The boat in which they rowed to shore was loaded to the water's edge – it had been full enough on its way to the ship, but now it held the Admiral and his squire and Rich in addition. Rich was crowded in the bow, wedged so tight that he could not even turn his head to see the approaching shore as the boat moved sluggishly over the little waves, so different from the big rollers outside. He could make a guess at the point under consideration – some heretic had been detected and was about to make solemn recantation. He would lose his goods and would vanish into the dungeons of the Inquisition. Certainly it was a matter in which he could not interfere, nor would he if he could.

The boat took the ground with a jerk – it was strange that no pier had as yet been built – and Rich swung himself, with the others, over the side. He might perhaps have stayed and kept his feet dry, as did the Admiral and the Adelantado and the Dominican, but he judged that it might be better if he remained inconspicuous. He splashed ashore, the Indian woman, her cloak held high, beside him. She gabbled something to him, hastily.

'I beg your pardon?' he asked.

The queer Spanish which she spoke suddenly took shape as she repeated herself.

'Save them, sir. Please try and save them.'

There was a frightful anxiety in her face as she spoke – her features were working with the stress of her emotion.

'I will try,' said Rich, cautiously, and puzzled.

'Try. Speak to *him*. Speak to the Admiral.'

Next moment her face had resumed its earlier animated interest, and she was smiling at the Adelantado as he stepped out of the boat.

'This is where the pier will be built,' said the Adelantado to his brother.

'I expected to find it built already,' said the Admiral in a tone of mild expostulation.

'It would have been, if the lazy dogs of Indians would only

work. But they would sooner die. I have seen them die under my very eyes, in the quarries, sooner than labour. It was all I could do to get in the quotas of gold and cotton and build the church and the citadel. We put a hundred corpses a week into the sea, even before the present troubles began.'

They were at the summit of the beach now, with the town before them – a hundred or so of brown huts built of timber and leaves.

'Where are all the people?' asked the Admiral.

'They are awaiting, Your Excellency.'

Someone in the Adelantado's following had run on ahead, up one of the straight narrow lanes between the houses. They could see him wave his arm as he reached the farther corner, and they followed him. Pigs and fowls were rooting among the filth underfoot, but no human creature was to be seen. Now they emerged from the lane into a wide open space. The houses were on three sides, on the fourth was the forest. Two trumpets brayed in the heated air; there was a long roll of drums.

It took the sun-dazzled eye some time to note all the details. The three sides of the square other than the one in the middle of which they stood were lined with naked Indians, packed in dense masses; there must have been thousands of them, five or six thousand. At intervals before and behind the crowd stood Spaniards, conspicuous in their armour, all at the salute while the trumpets blew and while the Admiral returned the compliment.

'There is a pavilion for Your Excellency,' said the Adelantado – close beside where they had emerged was a flat-roofed, open-fronted shed of leaves, in which stood a row of chairs, and beside which the colours of Spain and of the Admiral drooped in the heat. But that was not all which the eye slowly took in. Standing in the square were a whole series of lofty stakes, on which hung chains. And round the foot of every stake was a pile of wood. Rich counted them; there were sixteen stakes, each with its chains and faggots. He felt a little chill, for he had an irrational dislike of burnings – he had witnessed very few. The Indian woman was trembling, he could see. There was appeal in her eyes as they met his.

'The ceremony will begin now,' said the Adelantado, ushering his brother to the central chair with the utmost formality. 'Have I Your Excellency's permission to sit?'

'I don't like this business, Bartholomew,' said the Admiral. 'I used to think them very harmless people. Must it go on?'

'They are relapsed heretics,' said the Dominican. 'It is God's law that they should burn.'

'I've kept five thousand Indians herded here all day', said the Adelantado, 'expressly to see this. What would be the effect if I let them go?'

'But if it were I who pardoned them,' said the Admiral. 'What have they done? Is their guilt certain?'

'They are blasphemers as well as relapsed heretics,' explained the Dominican. 'After they had accepted baptism they not merely relapsed into idolatry. They burned down a chapel, and they broke the holy vessels and images to pieces.'

'Did they know what they were doing?'

'Having listened once to our teaching they must have known. But even if they did not it makes no difference to their guilt.'

'But why?' asked the Admiral. 'Why did they do it?'

'The devil prompted them,' said the Dominican.

'They were in rebellion over the gold quota,' said Bartholomew behind his hand.

'They are like children,' said the Admiral. 'Trying to do the wickedest thing they can think of.'

'And they succeeded,' said the Dominican. 'Children can be guilty of heresy and relapse.'

That was perfectly true, as Rich knew well. With his training in Roman law he found it hard to hear of condemnation for a crime committed without guilty intent – this was one of the points over which Roman law and the Church law disagreed – but at the same time it was heresy to question the principles of the Church, and he had no intention of being guilty of heresy himself. He simply could not argue on this point, and he resolutely kept his eyes from meeting the pleading glance of the Indian woman's.

'It is a golden opportunity', said the Adelantado, 'of teaching these people a real lesson. I have given instructions that the heretics are not to be strangled at the stake. Perhaps then those that see them die will learn what it means to incur our wrath.'

'You misunderstand the intentions of the Church, Don Bartholomew,' said the Dominican, sternly. 'This is not intended as a punishment. It is to save these poor people's souls that they must pass through the fire.'

'It coincides all the same with the needs of government,' said the Adelantado, complacently.

'We are saving sixteen souls today,' returned the Dominican. 'We are not trying to make the collection of the gold quota easier.'

A drum was beating in a measured tone up at the citadel. The victims were about to be brought down. Rich realized that any intervention in his power must be made at once.

'There are sixteen souls to be saved,' he said, 'but as a matter of pure expediency in God's cause, Reverend Sir, might it not be better to risk the loss of these sixteen in the hope of winning many more?'

'How do you mean?' asked the Dominican; his black brows approached each other, and his eyes narrowed as he turned his gaze on Rich.

'Perhaps if the lives of these sixteen were spared the rejoicing would be so great that many more souls would be won to God.'

'Perhaps – and perhaps there would be many doomed to Hell. These thousands who witness this act of faith will take care in future to keep heretical thoughts out of their minds.

146

They will pay closer attention to the teaching of the Church. They will have a glimpse of what Hell is like. No, sir, there is no substance in your argument. And it is an evil thing to gamble in human salvation.'

'Don't you think there is something in what the learned doctor says?' asked the Admiral.

'No, Your Excellency. A thousand times no. They must burn, so that their souls may be saved and that a thousand other souls may not be imperilled.'

The procession was filing into the square. A friar bore a crucifix at the head of it, and following him a dozen Spaniards herded the victims along, pricking them with their swords' points to force them to walk. The resources of the island had been sufficient to provide yellow fools' coats, gaudily daubed with red symbols, for the victims, whose hands were tied behind them. One of them screamed at the sight of the stakes; two of them collapsed into the dust of the square, writhing there until the escort kicked them to their feet again. The Indian woman beside Rich screamed, too. She ran round between the Admiral and his deputy and flung herself on the earth before them, one hand on the knee of each of them, frantically jabbering the while.

'What does she say?' asked the Admiral.

'She wants us to spare these people,' explained his brother. 'Anacaona, don't be a fool.'

Anacaona lifted a face slobbered with tears, her beautiful mouth all distorted. She was trying to talk Spanish, but Indian words tumbled from her lips as well.

'She says some of these men are her brothers,' went on Bartholomew. 'She means cousins by that – it is the same word to them. But every Indian is everyone else's cousin thanks to their mothers' habits.'

Anacaona bowed her head in the dust before them, her shoulders shaking under the blue velvet, before she lifted face and hands again to beg for mercy. There was a low moaning from all round the square, through which could be heard the rattle of chains as one man after another was fastened to the stakes.

'Can we not commute the punishment, as an act of grace, by virtue of the powers I hold from Their Highnesses?' said the Admiral. 'The dungeons, or the quarries? Would not that be sufficient?'

'Does not your heart tell you it would not, Your Excellency?' retorted the Dominican. 'And I must remind you that not even Their Highnesses can interfere with an act of faith.'

'Stop that noise, Anacaona,' said Bartholomew. 'Here, you two, here. Take this woman to my house and keep her there.'

Two Spaniards of the guard beside the pavilion dragged Anacaona away. To every stake now a victim was chained, fourteen men and two women. Already the torch was being borne from pile to pile; the man who had screamed was still screaming – they could hear his chains rattle as he strove against them.

'*Laetabitur justus cum viderit vindicatam,*' said the Dominican, solemnly. 'The righteous shall rejoice when he seeth the vengeance.'

That quotation from the Psalms had been given its full weight by St Thomas Aquinas, the greatest of Dominicans. But Rich thought that St Thomas must have given it too much weight – or else he himself was not of the just who could rejoice. Smoke was issuing from the piles of wood now; in one or two of them the sticks were already crackling and banging with the flames. Rich, looking against his will, saw one of the women try to move her feet away from the heat that burned them. He tore his glance away, staring up at the blue evening sky as he stood behind the Admiral's chair. But he could not shut his nostrils to the stench that drifted to them, nor close his ears to the horrible sounds that filled the square. He felt faint and ill and oppressed with guilt. St Bernardino of Siena had pointed out that just as harmonious singing demands deep voices as well as high, so

God's harmony demands the bellowings of the damned to complete it. But these bellowings and screams caused him no pleasure, and even did very much the reverse. He feared lest his faith were shaken, lest his Christianity were unsound and this weakness of his should be a proof of it.

He tried to tell himself of St Gregory's comment upon a text of St Ambrose, pointing out that as St Peter cut off a man's ear, which Christ restored, so must the Church smite off the ear of those who will not hear, for Christ to restore them. But his fiercest concentrations upon his authorities did not relieve his senses of the assaults made upon them, did not give strength to his weak legs nor solidity to his watery bowels. He feared for his soul.

CHAPTER FIFTEEN

NEXT morning Rich was desperately weary. There had been long debate the night before in the Adelantado's house within the citadel walls – and even here they were not quite free from whiffs of stinking smoke from the square – while through the town the newly landed Spaniards rioted as if they had taken it by storm. One of Bernardo de Tarpia's handgunmen had allowed his spirits to rise so high that he had twice let off his weapon to the peril of passers-by, sadly interrupting the anxious argument regarding the treason of Francisco Roldan. Nothing had been settled then; this morning the debate was to continue, and yet in the meanwhile he had not slept a moment, what with the strangeness of his new surroundings, the hideous events of the evening, and the plague of mosquitoes which had hung round him in a cloud all through the night – and Antonio Spallanzani, who had shared a leaf hut with him, had snored fantastically. Rich's head ached and he felt numb and stupid as he made his way past the sentry at the citadel gate up to the governor's house again.

The debate began afresh, with all the Columbus clan present – the Admiral in his best clothes, and Bartholomew the Adelantado, and James, rather weak and foolish, and John Antony, more weak and foolish still. But hardly had the session opened when something happened to terminate it. The man who entered wore spurs which jingled as he strode in over the earthen floor; his face was yellow with fever – like most of the new faces Rich had seen lately – but he wore an expression of unruffled gravity. The Adelantado checked himself to hear what he had to say.

'The Indians are in rebellion again, Your Excellency,' he announced. 'Seriously, this time.'

'Where?'

'In the Llanos. By tonight there'll be twenty thousand of them at Soco.'

'How do you know this?'

'One of my Indian girls told me. I was the only Spaniard with a horse, so I left the others gathering at the fort and rode here through the night. At dawn five hundred or so tried to stop me at the ford, but they were too frightened of my horse, and I broke through. Were those Indians burned yesterday, Your Excellency?'

'Yes.'

'That explains it, then. The rising depended on that, and the news has spread already.'

'You are not speaking with proper deference. Don't you recognize the Admiral here?'

'Your pardon, Admiral,' said the newcomer. 'But I was trying to tell my news in the shortest way possible.'

'What is your name?' asked the Admiral.

'Juan Ruiz, Excellency.'

'I remember you now. Go on with what you have to say.'

'I have said all that is necessary, Excellency. The Indians all have their sticks and stones. Some of those at the ford this morning were painted. They seem more bent on fighting than I have ever known them there last four years.'

'Is this Roldan's doing?' asked James Columbus; the words were no sooner out of his mouth than he received an angry look from Bartholomew.

'No,' replied Ruiz.

'Thank you. You may leave us now,' said Bartholomew, and the moment Ruiz was out of the room he turned on James. 'Will you never learn sense? Do you want the whole island to know we are afraid of Roldan? Over in the Vega Real how can he influence the Indians of the Llanos? You only open your mouth to utter idiocies.'

James shrank abashed before his brother's anger.

'We must send at once,' said the Admiral, 'and pacify

these poor wretches. I know they have grievances. I wish I could go myself – they would listen to me.'

'Pacify them?' asked Bartholomew.

'That is what I said.'

'Brother, leave the pacification to me. *I* will pacify them as they ought to be pacified. This is the moment I've been waiting for. A sharp lesson is what they need.'

'I know your sharp lessons, Bartholomew,' said the Admiral, sadly.

'By God,' said Bartholomew, 'I'm glad I have your two hundred men. Without them I would hardly have two hundred men to take out against them. If only the ships with the horses had come! I've barely fifty horses, and in those plains it's horses we need.'

'Bartholomew,' said the Admiral. 'I forbid you to be cruel. You must show them all the mercy possible.'

'That is what I will do,' said Bartholomew, grimly. 'Brother, you are too good for this world. And supposing I did what you think you want? Supposing I encouraged them to think they can rebel against our authority with impunity? What would happen to the gold quota? How much cotton do you think they'd grow for us? What would you say then, brother? Who was it who was complaining at the shortage of gold only five minutes ago? Kind words won't make these people work, as you know. Only the fear of death'll do that – and even then half of 'em prefer to die.'

'I suppose you've been promising them in Spain gold by the ton, as usual,' put in James, taking the side of his younger brother against the elder, who sat shaken and helpless before the double attack.

'I never expected my own brothers to turn against me,' he said, pitifully.

'We haven't turned against you,' snapped Bartholomew. 'We're doing your work for you. And there's no time to lose unless we want the whole island in a blaze. We'll march this afternoon. James, set the drums beating and the church bells ringing.'

The room was in an immediate bustle. Bartholomew flung open the door and began to shout orders through it to the guard at the gate. The three Dominican friars – Brother Bernard who had supervised yesterday's act of faith and the two who had just arrived – were whispering together in one corner.

'Don Narciso,' said the Admiral, and Rich went across to him. 'You must go with my brother. With this cursed gout I can neither walk nor sit a horse. And there are so few I can trust.'

Rich contemplated with some distaste the prospect of marching out with four hundred men to fight ten thousand painted savages.

'I doubt if Don Bartholomew will welcome my presence,' he said.

'You must go. You must. Bartholomew told me last night he had a horse of mine in his stables. Bartholomew, I am giving Don Narciso my horse so that he can ride with you.'

'Come if you like,' said the Adelantado after a momentary grimace. 'I'd rather put a man-at-arms on that horse. Have you armour as well as that long robe?'

'I have,' said Rich.

Bartholomew was a man of action. It took him no more than two hours to assemble every European round, to select his expeditionary force, and to detail the fifty men he was leaving behind to their duties as garrison. The few stores which had been brought up out of the ships he divided out among his army.

'There'll be food to be got in the villages,' he explained, 'but with savages to fight, the whole secret lies in being able to march without a halt and give them no time to rally.'

Four hundred men marched out of San Domingo in the blazing heat of the day. Juan Ruiz rode ahead with six horsemen as an advanced guard in case of an ambush. Then came the long column of leather coats and dull armour, Bernardo de Tarpia with his handgunmen, and Moret's cross-bowmen, the spearmen and handgunmen led by Juan Antonio Columbus – four years in Española had made these last familiar with the island, even to the extent of calling it by its native name of Hayti – and forty sailors from the ships under Carvajal's command, armed with pikes and swords. Bartholomew Columbus rode with forty horsemen, Cristobal Garcia and Rodrigo and Gonzalo Acevedo among them. Rich had his place with these, a little uneasy even astride the grey horse with which he had been provided, spiritless nag though it was.

The sun roasted him in his half-armour, but he was determined to utter no complaint until his companions should, and they were full of high spirits at being mounted again and faced with the imminent prospect of action. On their right was the blue, blue sea, and on their left the high mountains, vivid green from base to summit, towering to the sky. Ahead of them lay a wide, rolling plain, stretching from the mountains to the sea, green and luxuriant, broken only here and there by thickets and woodland. There were herds of cattle to be seen here – in four years the few beasts brought by the second expedition had multiplied beyond all count – and scattered patches of cultivated land where the Indians grew their roots and their corn. This was the famous plain of the Llanos, which the Admiral had compared, in extent and fertility, with the valley of Guadalquivir.

But at the moment there was not a soul to be seen, save the long column of Spaniards trudging along the faint track. Ruiz and his horsemen turned aside repeatedly to examine the hamlets which lay in sight, but each in turn was found to be deserted, and from each in turn rose the smoke of their burning as the torch was applied to the frail structures.

'Where are these Indians?' grumbled Avila. His visored helmet was at his saddlebow, his painted shield at his back, his long lance at his elbow, as if he was on his way to joust at a king's court.

'Perhaps you may see some,' said the veteran Robion. 'They may perhaps stand to fight here in the plains. They fight like sheep – you will be able to spike six of them at once on that skewer of yours. I doubt if they have learned even yet that they are safer from us in the mountains.'

'They are not worthy enemies, then?'

Robion gave a short harsh laugh.

'Not worthy of a knight errant like you. They know nothing of war, nothing at all. One might as well fight with children.'

'With children?' broke in someone else. 'A Spanish shepherd boy would be more dangerous than ten of their grown men. They had never fought in all their lives until we came among them – they didn't know what fighting was!'

'And I came here to gain honour!' said Avila, drawing a fresh laugh from the old hands.

Rich was pondering over what he had heard. In a land in which there was no tradition of violence at all, how long would it take to develop the art of war afresh? How long would it be before its people learned the axioms which even to a man of peace like himself were as natural as the air he breathed – the value of discipline and of order, the efficacy of surprise, the importance of a position. Why, he himself had read the foremost military treatise in history, Vegetius's *Epitoma rei militaris*, and was conversant with the principles of war, even if he would not be able to put them into practice. The laughing, thoughtless people of the islands, who had never had even to avoid a flung stone or dodge a blow, would not learn them in a generation.

'I expect they are all howling round the fort at Soco,' said Robion. 'Twice I've stood a siege like that. They howl until they are tired, and then you can go out and drive them back to work. But this is the first time I've ever known so many of them unite together, all the same.'

They were filing over a ford now, and everybody eagerly slipped out of their saddles to drink from the dark water; Rich found himself, after two hours' riding, already so stiff that he could hardly swing his leg over, but fortunately no one noticed. The column halted to rest in the shade along the banks, the sweating infantry lying stretched out flat with their weapons beside them until the Adelantado set the trumpet blowing to call them to their feet again. Rich scrambled somehow back into the saddle – he was already sore and his body shrank from contact with the harsh leather. By the end of the day he was in misery. The chatter went on unnoticed round him, blended with the squeaking of leather and the occasional ringing of hoofs or accoutrements. The final order to halt found him quite stupid with fatigue. He tried vainly to make some pretence to attending to the sorry grey horse, and experienced unfathomable relief and gratitude when Rodrigo Acevedo relieved him of the task unobtrusively.

'I can't thank you,' was all Rich was able to say, white-faced.

Ruiz and his companions had driven a small herd of cattle up to the encampment, and fires were lighted for roasting the meat. There was cheerful chatter round the fires, where the meat was roasted upon huge grids of green boughs – 'barbecues' or 'boucans', strange Haytian words which the old-timers used naturally and at which the newcomers made tentative attempts with as realistic an appearance of habit as possible. No more than five sentries were necessary to protect the camp while the others slept.

That had been a day of sunshine; the next was a day of rain, perpetual rain falling in torrents from a grey sky. It soaked everyone to the skin, finding its way remorselessly down inside the necks of leather coats and from there into the leather breeches, so that the horsemen had wet, squelching bags of water round their thighs. The men on foot sank to their ankles in the mud, the horses to their fetlocks. The little streams from the mountains became broad rivers bordered by knee-deep marsh; armour and weapons rusted almost perceptibly under their very eyes, and every man was daubed and streaked with mud. In those conditions not nearly so prolonged a march could be made as the Adelantado had wished – it had been his plan to camp that night so near to Soco as to make it possible to surprise the besiegers at dawn. With ten miles of slippery ground and three water courses still between his army and the fort the Adelantado was forced to give up the project.

'But marching at dawn we shall be at Soco by noon,' he said to the disgruntled group of hidalgos round him. 'Time enough then for the lesson I want to teach them.'

It rained until dawn, men and horses suffering miserably under the continued drenching, but with morning came a fiery sun which put new life into them – into all save a score or so of the earlier colonists who lay shuddering and with chattering teeth despite the heat. They were in the grip of malaria – everyone who lived long in the island went down with it in course of time, apparently, and exposure to wet and to night air was certain to bring on an attack. One of the shivering victims begged with blue lips to be left with his companions where they lay.

'So that when we have gone the Indians can beat you to death with their clubs, I suppose,' commented the Adelantado. 'You could not raise a finger to stop them if they did. No. You must come with us. There are horses enough until we reach Soco.'

So Rich completed the march on foot, leading the grey horse and with another man on the other side to help him keep one of the invalids in the saddle. Nor was he specially sorry, for two days of riding, even at foot pace, had rubbed his flesh raw. He trudged along with his sword tapping against his leg, while the sick man on his horse blasphemed wearily about the island and the Indians and the fate which had led him thither. Rich tried to make himself listen, because unguarded speech of this sort would be a valuable source of evidence for the report he would later have to make to His Highness, but it was hard to concentrate on the business with the imminent prospect of a battle before him. The handgunmen had their pieces loaded, and two of them had their matches smouldering whereby a light could quickly be given to their companions; the Adelantado was riding along the column reminding his subordinates of his orders of the line of battle. With every step he took, Rich knew that he was coming nearer to his first battlefield; it was a strange sensation. Once a false alarm ran down the column, and swords were drawn as they halted, but the mounted hidalgos reassured them and they plodded on.

And then they came over a low rise to open up a fresh vista of the plain. Two miles ahead stood a low, grey building with a black speck fluttering over it – the fortress of Soco with its flag; evidently the dozen colonists who had taken refuge there had made good their defence.

'Here they come!' said the Adelantado. 'Form your square, men.'

Rich had no time to see more during the bustle of forming up.

'Invalids here in the centre!' called the Adelantado. 'Gentlemen, mount your horses. Pikemen! Crossbowmen!'

Rich helped his invalid to the ground. There were a dozen helpless men lying there already, but his own invalid was convalescent by now and, with one more curse, lurched away to join the ranks of his fellows. Ruiz and the advanced guard came clattering up as Rich climbed on the grey horse. Other horses cannoned into him and he lost a stirrup and nearly lost his helmet before he found himself in the mass of cavalry grouped round the invalids. The foot soldiers had formed a square round the calvary, facing outwards, the handgunmen with their matches alight, the crossbowmen with their bows wound up.

Pouring up towards them was an enormous crowd of naked Indians. It was like a brown sea rolling upon them, thousands and thousands of them – not merely men, Rich saw as they approached, but women and children as well, all shrieking and yelling, as they waved their arms over their heads, with a noise like surf on the beach.

'Please God they charge,' said the Adelantado, and then, raising his voice: 'Remember, no man is to fire a shot until I give the word. Don Bernardo, see to it.'

Rich, fidgeting with his reins and his sword, marvelled at the Adelantado's sentiments. It seemed to him the most necessary thing in the world that the guns should start firing at once. Through his muddled brain coursed a sudden desire to wheel his horse round and break through the ranks and gallop away; panic was making his heart beat painfully fast and clouding his intellect, and it was only with difficulty that he restrained himself from acting on the impulse.

'If we shoot one now the whole lot'll run away,' explained the Adelantado to the hidalgos round him. 'I want to close with them.'

The huge crowd poured up towards the square. Then it halted a hundred yards from the nearest face, came on again, halted again in the centre, while at the side it still poured forward until in the end the whole square was surrounded at a discreet distance. A few more daring of the Indians ran closer still and, with frantic gestures, flung stones which fell to earth far in front of the waiting Spaniards.

'No shooting!' said the Adelantado loudly again.

The crowd eddied round the square like mist, forward here and back there. The din was tremendous. Then at last came the rush, as some indetectable impulse carried the whole mob inwards towards the square.

'Fire!' yelled the Adelantado.

The crash of the handguns drowned the noise of the discharge of the crossbows. Rich saw no Indian fall, and next moment the two nations were at grips. The Indians carried heavy sticks for the most part, with which they struck clumsily at the helmets in front of them, clumsily, like clowns in a comedy. Perched up on his horse Rich caught vivid glimpses of brown faces, some of them striped with red paint, distorted with passion. He saw the expression on one turn to mild dismay as a Spaniard drove his sword home. Rich's horse was chafing at the bit as the smell of blood reached his nostrils; close in front of him a crossbowman was winding frantically at his moulinet. There came a loud bang as one of the re-charged handguns went off, and then another and another. The brown masses began to hesitate, and ceased to crowd up against the sword-points.

'They're going to break!' said the Adelantado. 'Gentlemen, are you ready?'

The crossbowman thrust his loaded weapon forward between the two swordsmen who were protecting him, and released the bolt with a whizz and a clatter.

'Open out when you charge, gentlemen. Ride them down and show no mercy,' said the Adelantado. 'There! They're breaking! Sailors, make way! Open your ranks, sailors! Come on, gentlemen!'

The sailors who formed one face of the square huddled off to either side, making a gap for the horsemen who poured through it in a torrent, the maddened horses jostling each other. Rich kept his seat with difficulty as his horse dashed out along with his fellows; reins and sword seemed to have become mixed in his grip. Avila was riding in front of him, his horse stretched to a gallop and his lance, with its fluttering banderol, in rest before him. The point caught a flying Indian in the back below the ribs, and lifted him forward in a great leap before he dropped spreadeagled on the ground and Avila rode forward to free his point. The swords were wheeling in great arcs of fire under the sun. There was an Indian running madly close by Rich's right knee, his hands crossed over his head to ward off the impending blow. Rich had his sword hand free now, and he swung and struck at the hands, and the Indian fell with a dull shriek.

This was madly exciting, this wild pursuit on a horse

galloping at top speed with Indians scurrying in all directions before him. Behind him the handguns were still banging and faint shouts indicated that the infantry were in pursuit as well. Rich struck again and again. He found himself leaning far out of the saddle, like any accomplished cavalier, to get a fairer sweep, and the discovery delighted him. He was carried away by the violence of his reaction from his previous panic; there were enemies all about him, running like rabbits. He yelled with excitement and slashed again. An Indian, crazed with panic, ran blindly across his course, and fell with a scream under the forelegs of the grey horse. The grey horse came down with a crash, and Rich found himself sailing through the air. The earth which received him was soft, and he was not stunned by the fall, but the breath was driven from his body as if he were a burst bladder. Dazed and winded, sword and helmet gone, he grovelled about on the ground trying to recover himself. An Indian woman saw his plight; she still had her club in her hand, and apparently she was not as affected by panic as most of her companions. She ran up and struck at Rich, screaming the while for assistance. Two more women arrived, one with a pointed cane which she stuck painfully into Rich's left arm, overbalancing him just as he was on the point of regaining his feet. The club clanged on his breast-plate, the sharpened cane scraped over it. But then the screams of the women changed from excitement to fright. A horse's head loomed hugely over them; one woman fell across Rich, deluging him with blood from her half-severed neck, the others disappeared. Garcia was there riding a maddened chestnut stallion with graceful dexterity; the blood slowly dripped from his reddened sword and his white teeth flashed in a smile.

'Wounded? Hurt?' he asked.

'No,' said Rich, sliding disgustedly from under the woman's corpse.

'I'll catch your horse,' said Garcia, wheeling the chestnut towards where the grey was standing, his reins over his head and his sides heaving.

Rich picked up his sword and helmet and received the reins which Garcia handed him.

'All well?' asked Garcia. 'Right!'

Garcia uttered some inarticulate yell and urged his horse into a gallop again, wheeling his sword in circles; Rich stood with the reins in his hand and watched him catch an Indian and strike him down.

Rich had to sheathe his bloody sword in order to mount. It was an effort to raise his foot to the stirrup, a worse effort to swing himself up into the saddle even though the blown horse stood stock-still for him; he gathered up the reins and wondered what to do next. Behind him the scattered infantry were chasing Indians with small chance of catching them – a few Indians were still running towards him from the direction of the battlefield and swerving frantically away when they caught sight of him. Far ahead the cavalry were still on the fringe of the great mass of flying Indians; the shouts came back to Rich's ears like the distant cry of gulls at sea. He shook his horse into activity and rode forward towards Soco at a ponderous trot – he passed dead and wounded Indians scattered here and there over the plain as witness of the efficacy of the pursuit. The shouting and screaming ahead suddenly redoubled; the distant crowd wavered and hesitated and then broke up into two halves, one flying to the right and one to the left amid the loud reports of gunfire.

The firing enabled Rich to guess what had happened; the garrison of Soco had come charging out across the line of retreat of the Indians, a dozen men against ten thousand and yet sufficient to check their speed enough to give the horse-men's swords a fresh opportunity. There were plenty of Indians even near him, stragglers whom the pursuit had left behind ungleaned – exhausted Indians squatting gasping for breath, crippled Indians limping over the plain, and Indians running madly back towards him from the slaughter ahead. Rich put his hand to his sword-hilt and then found himself, rather to his own surprise, leaving the weapon where it was. He did not want to kill any more.

He rode slowly up towards the fort of Soco, where the horsemen were rallying, breathing their horses and tightening their girths. A dozen men on foot – the garrison of Soco, presumably – were standing with them, everyone talking and laughing excitedly. Dead Indians lay in swathes all about them, marking the area wherein their retreat had been cut off by the garrison's sally.

'Mount again, gentlemen,' said the Adelantado, as Rich came within earshot. 'We can beat back over the ground. Plenty of game broke back and the foot are there to head them off for us.'

The Spaniards who had dismounted got back into their saddles. They were like men who had been drinking – some were giggling like schoolboys with the excitement of slaughter.

'One long line,' said the Adelantado. 'Fifty yards apart. My standard is the centre. Spread yourselves out, gentlemen.'

The Adelantado ran an interested eye over Rich as he trotted up – Rich was conscious of the blood and mud with which he was smeared. He bore clear enough proof that he had played his part in the battle.

'Don Cristobal said you had a fall,' said the Adelantado.

'I had,' said Rich, 'but nothing serious.'

'Are you wounded?'

'Nothing serious again,' answered Rich.

'You can have your revenge now.'

'Do you really mean what you say, Don Bartholomew? Are you going on with this killing?'

'Why, of course. There are four hours more of daylight.'

'Haven't enough been killed?'

'No, by God. I mean this to be a lesson that they will never forget.'

'But they are your brother's subjects – your subjects, Your Excellency. Don't you want them to earn revenue for you?'

'They'll breed again. And we've had no chance of sport like this for months. Don't be mealy-mouthed, Doctor. Trumpeter!'

The trumpet set the long line in motion again in its sweep back across the plain. It was sport for the infantry, too; crossbows and handguns found plenty of targets as the frantic Indians were driven within range. The spearmen and swordsmen, even, hampered though they were with clothes and equipment, were often able to run down on foot the naked Indians who were already exhausted. Some of them showed a pretty wit in their choice of the place in which to plant their weapons when they caught their victims – the same idea had occurred to the horsemen, and shouts of laughter and approval ran along the line as each man vied with the others in displaying his dexterity or strength of arm. Rich followed fascinated.

CHAPTER SIXTEEN

'TORTURE?' said Don Bartholomew surprisingly that night in reply to a question from Garcia. 'There's no need for torture with these miserable wretches. Just keeping 'em in one place and preventing 'em from wandering about is torture for 'em. I'll guarantee that tomorrow morning every one of the fifty in the corral will blab all we want 'em to. Three days of it, and they die, like fish in a bucket. But if they won't talk tomorrow morning they will in the afternoon, after a morning in the sun without food or water. And if not, even then, the slow match that these handguns use will find tongues for 'em. But mark my words, Don Cristobal, by two hours after dawn we'll know all we want to know and we'll be on our way.'

They were discussing the next move in the suppression of the rebellion. The Adelantado had announced his intention of ascertaining from the prisoners who was the ringleader in the affair and whither he was likely to have fled; he was going to hunt him down, him and every other rebel he could catch, even if he had hidden in the heart of the unexplored mountains.

'Are these people likely to have a ringleader?' asked Rich. 'They don't appear to me to have enough sense.'

The Adelantado turned a cold eye upon him, and Rich was conscious of an uneasy feeling of being in a decided minority. It was by no means the first time since his arrival in the island that he had made suggestions in favour of moderation, and he was aware of the danger of being looked upon as a persistent wet blanket.

'Could ten thousand people rise in rebellion *without* a ringleader?' asked the Adelantado, sarcastically.

'With these people I should say it was more likely in the case of ten thousand than in the case of ten,' said Rich.

It was a sweltering hot night, and all those present were feeling trickles of sweat running down inside their clothes, and were moving uneasily on their wooden benches inside the bare room with its earthen walls.

'I don't believe', went on Rich, as the others remained silent, 'that there's an Indian alive in this island who could imagine a rebellion of ten thousand people, let alone organize one.'

'Perhaps', said the Adelantado with elaborate irony, 'the learned doctor will explain to these assembled gentlemen the events of today. I fancied I saw ten thousand Indians armed and in rebellion. Did my imagination deceive me? Were there really only ten?'

'I think they took up arms spontaneously,' said Rich. 'Rebellion grows in misery, like maggots in putrid meat.'

'Misery?' said the Adelantado, genuinely surprised.

'Yes, misery,' said Rich. This was a different argument altogether from the one he had begun, but he was equally ready to debate it now that it had arisen. 'The Indians work now when they never worked before. They see their friends burned alive, and hanged. Their women are raped. They believe that there will be no end to all this unless the Spaniards are all killed – and until the Spaniards came the Indians did not know what it meant to kill people!'

'So!' said the Adelantado. 'They work. How else would we have the gold and the cotton we need? Of course they must work. Men work, relapsed heretics are burned, and rebels are hanged, as in any Christian country. Rape? To an Indian woman there is no such thing. And if an Indian intends to kill me, I intend to kill him first. The learned doctor would not, I suppose. He would have us submit to being killed. No, of course, I know what he would advise. We ought all to get on board our ships and sail home again, leaving the gold in the earth and the pagans in their ignorance.'

Most of the men present were smiling now, even Acevedo, to whom Rich looked for sympathy. There was nobody present who could see his point of view, or understand what he was trying to say. Because the Indians were weaker than the Spaniards, because they were pagans, the Spaniards assumed it to be quite natural that they should be forced to work at unaccustomed labour to provide gold and cotton. The Spaniards could see no injustice in that. To them it was a natural law that the weaker should labour for the stronger. And as regards the question of cruelty, these countrymen of his had a tradition of centuries of warfare behind them; the shedding of human blood was a feat that redounded to a man's credit. The man who killed was performing a natural function of a gentleman; justice in the abstract had no meaning for them. Rich remembered the reminiscent grins which had accompanied their comments on the day's work, and was forced to a further conclusion; these were men who found pleasure in cruelty, apart from considering it merely as means to an end. They liked it.

Suetonius had written the lives of the twelve Caesars of Rome, and had shown how each in turn had been maddened by absolute power; their lust and their bloodthirstiness had grown with indulgence, like a wine-bibber's thirst, until no crime was too monstrous for them. These Spaniards in Española found themselves each in the position of a Caesar towards the feeble Indians. They were intoxicated with the power of life and death, and it was as hopeless to argue with them as it would be with drunken men. He could only sigh and remain silent while the discussion of the plans went on.

So Rich remained a witness of the taming of the Llanos, of all the great plain which stretched between the mountains and the sea in the south-east of the island. He saw the hangings and the floggings. He saw the great troops of Indians rounded up and driven back, after a sufficient number of examples had been made, to their labours. In the foothills of the mountains there ran little streams, in the sands of whose beds there were rare specks of gold; a hundred gourdfuls of sand, washed and painfully picked over, might contain one such speck. Every adult Indian had to produce, every three months, a hawk's bell full of gold – the hawk's bells which had once been so coveted in the island were now symbols of servitude.

Up in the mountains there hid little groups of Indians, those rare ones who had sufficient inventiveness to realize that there they had the best chance of evading their oppressors. Every day little detachments marched out from Soco in pursuit. They were fierce men, trained in every ruse of war. They climbed the passes in the foothills, they hacked their way through the mountain forests; they moved by night to surprise their quarry at dawn, or spread out to make a wide drive that pinned the helpless refugees against impassable declivities. The hardships of the campaign were great, the exertions enormous. The nights spent in the drenching tropical rains brought on ague; not only the two hundred original colonists who followed the Adelantado's banner, but the two hundred newcomers began to show a high proportion of fever victims in their ranks. Food was short; the little patches of roots and corn which the Indians cultivated soon went wild again with lack of attention. Everything, in fact, was short. There was no leather to repair the shoes which the forced marches wore out – no one could tan the hides of the slaughtered cattle, and the rawhide slippers which the men wore lasted only a few days. Clothing wore out, and there was only the flimsy cotton cloth of native weaving to replace it – and not much of that. Every luxury was missing, and every necessity was scarce.

Discontent began to show itself among the Spaniards. The gentlemen wearied of inglorious hardship in the end; the common soldiers and sailors wearied of their exertions even sooner. There was death as well as disease. One Spaniard only died of his wounds – a deep stab by a sharpened cane in his thigh mortified and turned black – but two died of snake bite, several of fever. The survivors began to murmur a little; they even began to come to Rich with their grievances. The old colonists wanted to be allowed to return to their estates and their harems of Indian girls; the new arrivals wanted to be allowed the chance to set up similar establishments. For these latter three weeks of violent activity on land was quite long enough following their months at sea. They yearned for debauch and for ease. Bartholomew Columbus had led them when they had first arrived; now he had to drive, and he was a tactless taskmaster.

Rich was not present at the quarrel between the Adelantado and Bernardo de Tarpia, but he could picture it easily when it was described to him – the bitter words, the challenge given and insolently declined, the smouldering ill-temper badly hidden. And two days after he was gone, and his handgunmen with him, and Cristobal Garcia and half a dozen more gentlemen, half the sailors, and a score of soldiers. It was the Adelantado himself who told Rich about the defection.

'Gone? But where has he gone to?'

'To join Roldan. God blast the souls of both of them!' said the Adelantado. 'And I know whose doing it is. You remember that crop-eared blackguard with a squint? Martinez, he called himself. He lost his ears when someone forbore to hang him in Spain. I ought to have hanged him myself. He came to San Domingo weeks back from Roldan. He said he wanted to resume his allegiance – he was a spy all the time for Roldan.'

'Roldan?' said Rich. 'Always Roldan. Who is this Roldan, Excellency?'

The subject of Roldan had been dexterously side-stepped by everyone from whom Rich had attempted to find out anything; it had been (so he had said to himself) like trying to discuss rope with a man whose father had been hanged. It was only now that he was able to hear the truth, and that thanks to the Adelantado.

'Roldan was once my brother's valet,' said Bartholomew.

'He was given the position of Chief Magistrate. After my brother had left for Spain he began to act as if he was not merely Chief Magistrate, but Adelantado as well. You lawyers are infernal nuisances enough, but a valet with a judge's authority – !'

'You could have deprived him.'

'No, I could not, by God,' said Bartholomew. He was lapsing into Italian in the excitement of the moment. 'He held his post from the Admiral. The mere Adelantado could not revoke an appointment by the Viceroy!'

That was obvious enough; Rich ought to have seen it for himself. And with a flash of insight he could guess at more than the obvious. The Admiral returning to Spain would not trust even his own brother with the full powers he himself held. Fearful for his own authority, he had divided the power between his deputy and the chief magistrate.

'And what happened?'

'You can guess,' said the Adelantado with a shrug. 'I did not put him in gaol when I had the chance. All the shiftless men of the colony, all the lazy ones who grew tired of trying to screw gold out of the Indians, all the men who wanted to snore in the sun with fifty women to wait on them, they all joined him.'

All the men with whom the hot-tempered Adelantado happened to quarrel, in other words, thought Rich, but he did not say so. He remained tactfully silent and allowed the Adelantado to run on.

'Most of them were out in the Vera – the open valley to the north of the island. There they have all settled; they have left off seeking gold, and live idly, with a hundred miles of mountains between us and them. Roldan is a little king among them. I was going to march on them, now that I have tamed the Llanos. With four hundred men I would have been too strong for them. Roldan would have hanged. But now Tarpia has joined him with sixty men at least, all able-bodied, and I have fifty sick and another hundred whom

I can't trust. Roldan has a new lease of life. But not for long.'

'What are you going to do?'

'There are other ships still to come. Any day they may arrive – the ships under my cousin's command. They sailed from Spain with you, and they ought to have arrived weeks ago, while you were exploring, but I suppose they have lost their way among the islands – my cousin was always a poor fool. But sooner or later they will come. Those ships bear a hundred horses. There will be two hundred men. Tarpia took no more than ten horses – Roldan has no more than five, thank God. In the Vera the horseman reigns supreme, the same as in these plains here. Once I get those horses landed, and the two hundred men, Roldan's little hour is finished. I shall hang him on my gallows at San Domingo, and Tarpia and Garcia and half a dozen others beside him.'

That was the right way to treat rebellion, thought Rich, although it occurred to him that the axe would be more fitting than the gallows for men of such blue blood as Tarpia. He found his dislike for the Adelantado diminishing. Rich was heart and soul on the side of orderly government and decent respect for authority, even though it was a shock to him to find himself approving of the execution of Spaniards when he had spent days in silent protest against the killing of heathen Indians. A man who could speak lightly of hanging a terrible man like Tarpia won his admiration for such daring. Rich was a little ashamed of his pity for the Indians; this bold talk of suppressing rebellion was much more the sort of thing he felt he ought to like. All his life so far he had lived as a spectator, and there was something peculiarly gratifying in being at last behind the scenes, in being at least a potential actor. It was better than splitting legal hairs and wrapping up the result in pages of Latin.

CHAPTER SEVENTEEN

In San Domingo, when the Adelantado returned from his chastising of the Llanos, there was nothing new. The fifty men of the garrison who had remained there with the Admiral had done nothing, heard nothing. Most of them were fever-ridden and asked nothing more than to stay tranquil. Apparently the Admiral had made some attempt to persuade them to heave up the three ships which lay in the harbour and make them ready for sea again, but they had vehemently refused to do such heavy work, and the Admiral had abandoned his attempt. Those sailors who had not deserted to Roldan took more kindly to the suggestion when it was put to them on their return with the conquering army. The ships would sail for Spain when they were ready, with messages and treasure, and the sailors were sure of a passage home.

'There are two hundredweights of gold,' said Diego Alamo the assayer – Rich had had hardly a word with him since they had left Trinidad, and it was delightful to encounter him again and hear the results of his observations.

'That sounds enormous to me,' said Rich.

'Large enough,' said Alamo with a shrug. 'Their Highnesses do not receive that amount of gold in a year's revenue. And there are pearls beside, of more value still, I should fancy, if the market is not too hurriedly flooded with them.'

'This one island, then, is worth more than all Spain?' said Rich, eagerly. Solid facts of this sort were reassuring, especially when retailed by someone as hard-headed and learned as Alamo. But Alamo shrugged again in dampening fashion.

'Perhaps,' he said. 'But part of that gold is what the Indians have saved for generations. And nowhere does the earth breed gold rapidly. A speck here, a grain there, in the sand. One gathers them, and it is years before another speck is formed. During the last few years most of the grains available have been gathered, and in my opinion the annual amount of gold found in the island will diminish rapidly.'

'Oh,' said Rich, disappointed. 'Does everyone think that?'

'No. They know nothing about the subject. Nor have they read the ancients. You, doctor, you have read your Livy, your Polybius? Don't you remember how our own Spain was conquered by the Romans and Carthaginians? They found gold there, quantities of gold. Spain was to Carthage what these islands are to Spain. But what gold is there now to be found in Spain? A vein or two in the Asturias. A vein or two in the south. No more.'

'And how do you account for that?'

'Spain was a new country. The simple Iberians had little use for the gold which had been breeding there since the creation. From the rivers and valleys all the gold was soon cleared out when the Carthaginians came. Even the seeds of the gold were taken away, so that the country became barren of the metal. I can predict the same of this island.'

'The gold breeds from seeds, you think?'

Alamo shrugged yet once more.

'If I knew how gold breeds I should be as rich as Midas,' he said. 'But every philosopher knows that, however it is, the process is slow.'

'So that the value of this island will diminish, year by year?'

Alamo pulled at his beard and looked at Rich, considering deeply. He hesitated before he spoke, and when at last he allowed the words to come he glanced over his shoulder nervously lest anyone should overhear the appalling heresies he was about to utter.

'Perhaps', he said, 'gold is not the most important merchandise this island can produce. I have often wondered whether a country is the richer for possessing gold. We may find the other products of this island far more valuable.'

'The spices, you mean? But I thought – '

'The spices are unimportant compared with those which reach Spain via the Levant. The cinnamon which the Admiral thought grew here so freely is poor stuff. There are no real spices here – no cloves, no nutmegs. The pepper is not true pepper, even though one can acquire a taste for it quickly enough.'

Rich found all this a little frightening. If the gold returns were to diminish, as Alamo predicted, and the spice trade were to prove valueless, as Rich had long ago suspected, the colony of Española would not be worth having discovered. The three thousand Spanish lives which had already been expended were quite wasted. But Alamo was ready to reassure him.

'The island has treasures beside gold and spices,' he said. 'It has a soil fifty times more fruitful than Andalusia. The rain and the sun give it a fertility which it is hard to estimate. One man's labour will grow food for ten – see how these wretched Indians have always contrived to live in abundance. Cattle multiply here amazingly. My calculations go to prove that by breeding cattle here a handsome profit would be shown merely by selling the hides in Spain – and I know well enough the cost of sailing a ship from here to there.'

'Cattle? Hides?' said Rich. There was a queer sense of disappointment. A prosaic trade in hides was not nearly as interesting as a deal in hundredweights of gold.

'Oh, there are other possibilities,' said Alamo, hastily. 'Have you ever tasted sugar?'

'Yes. It is a brown powder beneficent in cases of chills and colds. There is a white variety, too, in crystals. I have had packets sent me as presents occasionally. It has a sweet taste, like honey, or even sweeter. Why, is there sugar to be found in this island?'

'Not as yet. But it could grow here – it is expressed from a cane exactly like the canes we see growing everywhere in this country. The sugar cane is grown in Malaga a little, and in Sicily. My friend Patino retails it at five hundred *maravedis* an ounce. Once start the cultivation here and in a few years we might be exporting sugar not by the ounce, but by the ton.'

That was a more alluring prospect than chaffering in hides. A spark of enthusiasm lit in Rich's breast, and then died away to nothing again as he began to consider details.

'It means husbandry,' he said, despondingly.

'It means hard work,' agreed Alamo, a smile flickering over his lips.

Each knew what the other was thinking about. Knight-errants and adventurers like Garcia, or like Avila, would never reconcile themselves to labouring in the cultivation of sugar, or even in the breeding of cattle. They had come to seek gold and spices, and for those they were willing to risk their lives or undergo hardship. It would be far below the dignity of a hidalgo to settle down to prosaic labour. Nor would the lower-class Spaniards who had reached Hayti – the gaol-birds – the bankrupts – take kindly to arduous work.

'There is no labour to be got out of the Indians,' said Rich, despairingly.

'That is so,' agreed Alamo. 'They die rather than work. And pestilences sweep them away even when they are not killed for sport. There were two millions when the Admiral first landed. Now there is not more than half that number, after six years. Perhaps soon there will not be a single Indian left alive in Española.'

'Impossible!' said Rich.

'Possible enough,' said Alamo, gravely.

'But what then?' asked Rich, wildly. The thought of the blotting out of a population of two million left him a little dizzy. Their Highnesses of Spain had no more than ten million subjects in all their dominions. And he was appalled at the thought both of this green land of Española reduced to an unpeopled desert and of the extinction of a pleasant useless race of mankind. This discovery of the Indies was a Dead Sea fruit – alluring to the sight and yet turning to ashes in the mouth.

'There is another possibility,' said Alamo.

'What?'

'It was João de Setubal who put it in my mind,' said Alamo.

It was a queer world in which a cultured man like Alamo could be indebted for ideas to a clumsy barbarian like the Portuguese knight; Rich must have looked his surprise, because Alamo hastened to explain.

'He was complaining of the uselessness of the Indians, just as everyone else does,' said Alamo. 'And then he went on to say how in Lisbon they have Negro slaves nowadays. Stout, dependable labourers, brought from the African coast. I had heard about that before, but it had slipped my memory until Don João reminded me of it. They breed freely, do the Negroes. If Their Highnesses could arrange with the King of Portugal for a supply of Negroes to be sent here – '

'You are right, by God!' said Rich.

'This hot climate would be native to them,' said Alamo. 'They could do the heavy work and our Spanish gentlemen fresh out of the gaols would not think it beneath them to supervise.'

'And the Indians could be spared,' said Rich, with kindly enthusiasm. 'Perhaps part of the island could be set aside for them to live without interference. Save for Christian teaching, of course.'

This last was a hurried addition.

'The Church would give her blessing,' went on Alamo. 'The Negroes would be brought out of heathen darkness in Africa to lead a Christian life here.'

They eyed each other, a little flushed and excited.

'Sir,' said Rich, solemnly. 'I think that today you have

made a suggestion which may change the history of Spain. In my report to His Highness – '

'I would rather, if possible, that His Highness was not reminded of my existence,' said Alamo. 'Torquemada – '

'I understand,' said Rich, sadly.

But this was the most cheerful thing which had been brought to his notice since his arrival in Española. Rich had been worrying about the report he had to write, and which would go to Spain as soon as the *Holy Name* was ready for sea again. It would have been a cheerless thing without this creative suggestion added to it – merely a sweeping condemnation of the Admiral's administrative system, and of the methods of the colonists, combined with the gloomiest prophecies regarding the future of the island. Rich knew quite well what favour was given to those advisers of the Crown who brought nothing but unpalatable truths to the council board. If he could sketch out a future of plenteous cargoes of sugar at five hundred *maravedis* an ounce, and suggest a profitable trade in Negro slaves, his state paper would be a great deal more acceptable and would not prejudice his own future – would not imperil his own life – nearly as much.

'But', said Rich, half to himself, 'there's a lot to be done before that.'

He was thinking of the disorder in the island – of Roldan's passive rebellion, the vague property laws, the muddled policies.

'That is not my concern, thank God,' said Alamo, guessing – as was not difficult – what was in Rich's mind. 'You will have to settle all that with the Admiral. I am no more than assayer and naturalist. Politics are not my province.'

Rich thought how lucky Alamo was. There had been a time when he himself had been delighted at the thought of taking part in the administration of a new empire, but there was no pleasure in it now for him. Those endless conferences in the citadel of San Domingo only left him with an exasperated sense of frustration. It was hard for any decision to be reached – at least, it was hard for the Admiral to reach a decision. There was the pitiful difficulty that Roldan, thanks to his appointment as Alcalde Mayor, could claim a legal justification for his actions.

'Why not revoke the appointment, Your Excellency?' asked Rich. 'Any disobedience then would be treason and could be punished as such.'

'That would drive him to desperate measures,' said the Admiral. 'God knows what he would do then.'

'But what *could* he do?'

'He could march on San Domingo. He could fight us.'

Rich looked at Bartholomew Columbus. This was clearly his cue.

'He *might*,' said Bartholomew. 'But I doubt it.'

'What force has he got?'

'As many men as we have. More perhaps,' interposed the Admiral. 'And – and – perhaps all our men would not fight for us.'

That was perfectly possible, at least in a few cases.

'But would all Roldan's men fight for him?' asked Rich. He was wondering what he himself would do in such a case. Certainly he would think long before he appeared in arms, an obvious rebel.

Bartholomew glanced at him for once with approval. 'Now you're on the right road,' he said. 'Treason is treason either side of the ocean. Some would fear for their necks, and would wait to see what would happen. Proclaim Roldan dismissed. Give him a month to come in and submit. If he does not, march against him. Half his men would not fight.'

'But what would they say in Spain?' said the Admiral, pathetically.

That was the trouble. Once let the Court of Spain know that there was rebellion in her new colony, that the Admiral could not control his subordinates, and Their Highnesses would have every justification for removing their Viceroy from office. There was suspicion in the old man's eyes as he looked round the room. Who would be his successor in that case? Bartholomew, the hero of the Indian rebellion? Rich, who had been sent out for no obvious good purpose? Rich could see the struggle in the Admiral's face. His position, his power – even such as it was – were very dear to him. After a lifetime of unimportance, he now found himself Admiral and Viceroy, and he did not want to lose the splendid position his genius had won for him, even though his genius was not of the kind to make his position supportable. He was bound to regard with suspicion any advice which came from those who might hope to succeed him. He felt alone and friendless, and his first instinct was to temporize.

And Rich, knowing quite well what sort of secret report was awaiting transmission by the *Holy Name* to Their Highnesses, could hardly blame him. But Rich's sense of justice and order, quite apart from his sympathy for the poor old man, urged him to try and make some sort of settlement of this disastrous state of affairs. He wanted to be able to add a postscript to his report, saying that he hoped that shortly the situation would be in hand.

'But something ought to be done,' he said.

'What do you suggest?' asked Bartholomew, curiously.

'Proclaiming Roldan's dismissal would deprive him of the support of some of his people,' said Rich. 'Isn't it possible to split his party still further? Can't we make offers which would bring over a large number? Garcia might come back, for instance, or Tarpia, if we bribed heavily enough. Then with Roldan once caught and hanged we could deal with them on a new basis.'

Rich was a little surprised at himself for making such proposals. He had never believed he had it in him to contemplate any such vigorous action. He remembered Tarquin in Rome, cutting off the heads of the tallest poppies; he thought of Caesar Borgia in the Romagna, dividing his enemies and striking them down one by one. All that was very well in theory, to a book-learned man; he was genuinely astonished to find himself advocating the actual practice – prepared even, if need be, to put it into execution himself. He hated the thought of fighting just as much as the Admiral did – although he concealed it better – but he was not nearly so averse to this kind of intrigue.

'But how can we bribe them?' asked James Columbus, his foolish jaw gaping.

'The Admiral has more in his gift than Roldan has. Titles. Offices. Estates.'

Rich was searching in his mind for the sort of thing that would appeal to the Garcia he visualized standing before him. 'Some new expedition to seek for the Grand Khan – Garcia would desert anyone in exchange for the command of that.'

He was proposing treachery of the meanest possible sort, he knew. Yet he was only proposing to meet treachery by treachery, and then only when it seemed impossible to employ any other means.

'No one but me sails from Española on any expedition at all,' said the Admiral, instantly. That showed what was necessary to rouse him.

'It need only be promised him,' said Rich, wearily. 'Your Excellency can reconsider it when Roldan is once hanged.'

The Admiral peered at him with narrowed eyes. It was only too obvious that he suspected Rich of planning something more than he had actually suggested – that he was subtly endeavouring to filch from him a little of his precious power and possessions.

'Never!' said the Admiral. 'I shall never allow such a subject to be discussed!'

This was the sort of exasperating deadlock to which Rich had grown accustomed in these last few days.

'As Your Excellency wishes, of course,' he said. 'I am merely making what suggestions occur to me.'

That meeting, like the preceding ones, broke up without anything having been decided. The next one seemed to call even more urgently for a decision, because now there was a new and disastrous development. The sentinel on the citadel ramparts announced a ship – she was the caravel *Rosa*, one of the three which had parted from the main expedition to sail direct to Española and which should have arrived three months back. Anxiously they watched her, running gaily down before the eternal east wind, the Admiral and the Adelantado and the rest of the Columbus clan, Rich and Alamo and the Acevedo brothers.

'She's the *Rosa*!' said Perez with satisfaction.

'She carried most of the horses,' said the Admiral.

'Did she, by God!' said Bartholomew. 'Then that will end our friend Roldan's career, if enough have survived this infernal long voyage they have made.'

'A big "if",' whispered Alamo to Rich.

'Why?'

'I know more about those horses than the Admiral does. The horses that came on board are not the same ones as Their Highnesses paid for. The contractors showed the Admiral two hundred horses on land for his approval, and shipped two hundred quite different horses when they had received it. Four months at sea? Half of them would not survive four days!'

They watched the *Rosa* catch the sea breeze and head for the river mouth.

'No sign of the other two,' said Bartholomew, anxiously. He scanned the horizon unavailingly. 'Lost at sea? Parted company? We shall know soon.'

They knew soon enough; there were three captains on board the *Rosa* with reports to make. It was a rambling story, of losing their way, of finding themselves among the unexplored cannibal islands to the south-eastward, and of finally anchoring at Isabella in the north of the island – Roldan's headquarters.

'Holy Mary!' said Bartholomew. 'What next?'

Ballester, the captain of the *Rosa*, spread helpless hands.

'Half our crew's left us,' he said. 'Sixty men – there had been much sickness, as I said. They took the other two caravels. They took the stores out of the *Rosa*. Those of us who would not join them they allowed to sail round to here. That man with no ears – Martinez – would have made us walk across the mountains, sick though we all were. But Roldan let us take the *Rosa*. He said – '

Ballester checked himself.

'What did he say?'

Ballester had no desire to repeat what Roldan had said.

'Really, sir, it was not important. I could not – '

'What did he say?'

'Well, he said we should soon come sailing back to him after a little experience of San Domingo.'

There was an awkward pause, until Bartholomew changed the subject.

'How many men did you leave at Isabella?'

'Sixty-two. Twenty of them were sick.'

'How many horses?'

'Five.'

'Five? Where are the other hundred?'

'Dead, sir. We were short of water for a long time. And on the voyage – '

'That's all right, man. If Roldan has them, I would rather they were all dead. How many men have you brought in the *Rosa*?'

'Forty-seven, sir. That includes five sick who are likely to die, and two friars.'

The council looked at each other.

'The balance is hardly altered, then,' was Bartholomew's comment. 'We can still fight him.'

Despite the heat and the drumming of the rain outside, Rich found his brain working fast. The newly-landed Spaniards at Isabella would be a source of dissension there, very likely. They would not – gaol-birds though they might be – take kindly to fighting Spaniards the moment they had landed.

They might have slipped easily into mutiny after the hardships of the voyage, but they might hesitate at treason. An immediate move on Isabella would cause them to hesitate, and hesitation is infectious. Roldan's men would hesitate as well. The passive rebellion might be borne down by a bold stroke.

'The sooner the better,' he said, without time to wonder at himself for such advocacy of energetic action.

Everyone looked at the Admiral now, and the Admiral shifted in his seat and eyed them uneasily. With the arrival of the squadron there could be no question of further postponement of the decision. And Rich, watching him, noticed how he gazed first at him and then at the Adelantado; he guessed what wild conclusions the Admiral was drawing from the unwonted circumstance of two of them being of one mind. Rich was paralleling the Admiral's thoughts quite closely, yet even he was surprised at what the Admiral decided eventually to do. The decision was not reached easily. There was argument – of course there was argument – and a little spurt of old man's rage, but it was agreed to in the end. The Admiral was to sail round in the *Rosa* to Isabella, and there he was to make one last effort to recall Roldan and his supporters to their allegiance, and, in the event of their refusal, he was to denounce them as traitors.

'One more wasted month,' sneered the Adelantado, reluctantly agreeing.

Rich thought the same, but in the face of the old man's unreasoning obstinacy there was only one alternative to agreement, and that was to raise a fresh mutiny in San Domingo.

CHAPTER EIGHTEEN

THE Admiral had sailed, and Rich had leisure now for his other duties, to make plans for the future government of the colony, to try to estimate its future worth, to put the final touches on the report to Their Highnesses which had already grown to such inordinate length. It called for a good deal of consideration to discover the right wording of the suggestion that in place of shiploads of gold and pearls Their Highnesses would be better advised to expect sugar and hides, and of the advice that negotiations should be opened with the half-hostile Court of Lisbon for the supply of Negroes.

Still deeper consideration was necessary to suggest a working system of government. There was one precedent to follow in this case – the constitution of the late Kingdom of Jerusalem. The Holy Land, like Española, was to all intents a new country conquered from the heathen by the Christians, and its constitution had been drawn up in the Assize of Jerusalem in clear-cut legal Latin which embodied the deepest thought of the Middle Ages on the knotty problem of how to erect a stable government on the shaky foundation of the feudal system. But the Kingdom of Jerusalem had fallen through its own rottenness, after all. And there was, as Rich came wearily to realize, time and again, that thrice-accursed agreement between Their Highnesses and the Admiral which would hinder any attempt on the part of the Court of Spain to make any laws for the Indies, as long as the Admiral clung so frantically to every bit of the power which that fantastic document had granted him.

At every turn Rich was reminded of the difficulties around him. The Admiral had borne off to Isabella with him the last horn of ink which the island possessed – before Rich could even set pen to paper (and paper was scarce) he had to consult Alamo regarding this difficulty and wait until, out of burnt bones, Alamo managed to compound a horrid sludge which would just answer the purpose. There were two hundredweights of gold, there was a gallon of pearls, in San Domingo – enough wealth to build a city in Spain – and yet he had to live in a wretched timber hut in a corner of the citadel ramparts, where the rain leaked in through the gaps, and where bugs were already well established, and which had the sole merit of being private now that Antonio Spallanzani had sailed with his master to Isabella.

Food was scarce. The fifty men who constituted the garrison should have been amply fed from the surrounding country, where thousands of Indians cultivated the soil under the direction of the Spaniards. But naturally these supplies for the government had to be paid for with government funds, with the gold that came from the fifths and tenths and thirds that were levied on the treasures of the island as collected by the Spaniards outside the town. And when the Spaniards paid it in again, being gold it was subject once more to those fifths and tenths and thirds until it was a most unprofitable business even to sell roots to the garrison, certainly not worth the enormous trouble of bringing them in. In San Domingo the healthy sickened and the sick died and discontent seethed, and the Adelantado dared not use strong measures for fear of further defections to Roldan, and Rich scratched his head unavailingly to try and make some sense out of the tangle of laws and privileges which had already grown up in that part of the island which still remained lukewarm in the government's cause.

There were times when Rich wondered whether he were really awake, or whether he were not deep in some prolonged and fantastic nightmare, from which he would presently awake to find himself safe in bed in Barcelona. All this might well be a dream; in clairvoyant moments he realized how quite unlikely it was that it should be reality – that he should have crossed the ocean, and explored new lands, and ridden in a cavalry charge striking down living men with his sword, and should have taken part in high political debate seriously discussing the hanging of hidalgos. It was a marvellous moment to be invited to the Adelantado's table, there to eat gluttonously of turtle when a fortunate catch had provided several of the creatures. Rich remembered his shuddering disgust at turtles in the Cape Verdes, where lepers congregated to seek a cure by daubing themselves with turtles' blood. Now he was hungry enough to eat them with appetite – that was a nightmare in itself.

The parrot that Malalé had given him in Paria had died long since, while under Diego Alamo's care during his absence at Soco. It had been a disappointing piece of news to receive on his return; in the brief time that he had owned the lovely thing of red and blue he had grown fond of it, with its comic habits and its crowbar of a beak which prized open any buckle which bound it. Rich had an uneasy feeling that this island was fated, that everything Spanish that lived in it was doomed to an early end, whether it should be parrots or codes of law. He was aware of a growing disgust for the place.

And then the *Rosa* came sailing back into the harbour, the Admiral's flag flying at the masthead, and Alonso Perez blowing fanfares on his trumpet, startling the sea birds into flight all round the river mouth. The Adelantado put off hastily from the shore to welcome his brother; everyone else congregated on the beach in anxious expectancy, wondering what had been the outcome of the negotiations with Roldan. They watched for some time before they saw the Admiral descend slowly and painfully into the boat – apparently the brothers had plunged immediately into a long discussion without waiting to return to land.

Apparently, too, the discussion had not been very friendly, to judge by the Adelantado's black brow as he splashed through the shallows to the shore; he stood digging his toes irritably into the sand and meeting no one's eyes while the

Admiral was being helped ashore, feeble, almost tottering, by
Alonso Perez and a couple of Indians. But the Admiral was no
sooner within earshot again than Bartholomew turned upon
him to renew the discussion.

'Have you a copy of this precious treaty, brother?' he
asked.

'Yes,' said the Admiral. He halted in his slow course up
the beach and fumbled in his pocket.

'Oh, it can wait until we reach the citadel,' said Bartholomew. 'Gentlemen, come with us and hear what His
Excellency the Admiral has agreed upon.'

The Admiral fluttered a thin hand in protest, only to call
forth another bitter comment from his brother.

'Why should they not know?' demanded Bartholomew.
'You say the news is to be proclaimed publicly. That is one of
the terms.'

It was only the least of the terms. Bartholomew read the
document aloud in the council room, while Rich and the
others looked at each other in unbelieving astonishment. It
seemed quite incredible that such a treaty could have been
made. Item by item Bartholomew read it out, with its unlettered travesty of legal terminology, its 'whereases' and
'aforesaids' which a group of ignorant people had put in
in an attempt to imitate lawyer's expressions. By the first
clause Roldan and all who followed him were given a pardon
for anything they might have done during their stay in the
Indies. By the second clause they were, each and severally,
to receive from the Admiral a certificate of good conduct.
By the third clause a proclamation was to be made throughout
the island, to the effect that everything Roldan and his
followers had done had met with the Admiral's entire approval. By the fourth clause Roldan was to select who should
be allowed to go back to Spain, and those that he should nominate should be allowed to transport whatever property they
might desire, either of valuables or of slaves. By the fifth clause
the Admiral guaranteed that whoever should remain in

Española should receive, free of obligation, as much land as a horse could encircle in a day, with the inhabitants thereof; the recipients to select both the land and the horse. The sixth clause merely confirmed that Roldan was invested with the office and powers of Alcalde Mayor, but added that these powers – as the original document had merely implied without express statement – were of course given in perpetuity to Roldan and his heirs for ever, as long as the Admiral's viceregal authority and that of his heirs should endure.

The Adelantado interrupted his reading and tapped the document with a gnarled forefinger.

'You did not tell me about this last one, brother,' he said, and then, turning to the rest of the meeting: 'That appears to be all of importance, gentlemen. The rest is merely a résumé of the titles of His Excellency the Admiral of the Ocean and of the Right Honourable the Alcalde Mayor of the Indies; I think I can spare myself the trouble of reading them.'

There was only a murmur in reply, and a shuffling of feet. Rich's mind was already deeply engaged upon a legal analysis of the treaty he had just heard read, and the others were too stunned to speak.

'Would any of you gentlemen care to comment?' asked the Adelantado, but the Admiral spoke before anyone else could open his mouth.

'I will not have the matter discussed,' he said. 'This treaty is your Viceroy's decision, and it would be treason to question it.'

The Admiral sat in his chair, with his hands on his thin knees. He had spoken with an old man's querulousness, and yet – and yet – there was a suspicion of triumph in his glance, a self-satisfied gleam in the blue eyes. It was as if he thought he had done something clever, hard though that was to believe. Rich remembered earlier discussions. Perhaps the Admiral had decided that to retain his power he needed to create some new party for himself which he could play off against the Adelantado's brutal bullying, or against Rich's vague powers.

Or possibly he wanted to send a dispatch to Spain saying that he had arrived to find the island in disorder, and had dissipated the disorder immediately by a few judicious concessions. Or perhaps he knew he had been weak and would not admit it. Or – anything was possible – he might by now have deluded himself into thinking that he had brought off a really creditable coup, just as he believed he had discovered the mines of Ophir and the Earthly Paradise. Meanwhile, Rich saw various loopholes of escape from this treaty.

'Your Excellency signed of your own free will?' he asked. 'You were not coerced into it?'

'Of course not,' said the Admiral, indignantly.

'A promise entered into under compulsion is not binding, Your Excellency,' persisted Rich.

'I know that.'

'And these gifts of land, Your Excellency. Land is a tricky thing to deed away. It is Crown property. I doubt – please pardon me, Your Excellency, but of course we are all anxious to have everything as legal as possible – if Your Excellency's viceregal authority entitles you to dispose of the property of the Crown. The recipients would be well advised to have their title confirmed by Their Highnesses, and until Their Highnesses have given that confirmation I myself, for one, would be chary of entering into any dealings regarding those properties.'

'My agreement with Their Highnesses gives me full powers.'

'Powers can only be expressly given, Your Excellency. Any powers not named are by every rule of law retained by Their Highnesses.'

'Oh, why split these hairs?' broke in the Adelantado. 'Their Highnesses are two thousand leagues from here, the treaty is signed, and there's an end of it for a year or so. Roldan and his men will have the land if anything my brother can do can ensure it. There is no profit in continuing this debate, I fancy, gentlemen.'

Rich was of the same opinion. He escaped from the room as soon as he could and went to sit in the tiny apartment which he shared with Antonio Spallanzani. The *Holy Name* and the *Santa Anna* would be sailing soon, and his report must go in one ship while he sailed in the other. He thought longingly of Spain, of his cool stone house and fountain in the courtyard, the while he sat sweating and fighting the flies. It would be a long voyage home reaching far to the northward to avoid the path of the eternal easterly breezes, but in three months at most he would be in Spain. The King would be at Valladolid or Toledo, and he might be kept cooling his heels round the court for weeks. But six months at most, and he would be home again, in his own house, leading a decent and orderly life. He could sit in his big leather chair reading through the pleadings of law-abiding merchants, or, with a hushed band of students behind him, he could issue his judgements, in stately Latin, to the expectant litigants assembled in his hall.

That was the world he knew and loved, not this mad new world of rain and mosquitoes, of slaughter and mutiny, of mad theories and madder politics. And yet mad though it all was, he was conscious of a queer regret that he was leaving it. He would have liked to have stayed a while longer, even though he knew that he would be bitterly disappointed if some unforeseen circumstance compelled him to stay. He told himself that he was as mad as everyone else in Española.

Meanwhile the report had to be written, and he had to make up his mind what to write. As he repointed his pen he began to form phrases in his mind. He did not want to word them too strongly – the contents of the report would need no emphasis of phrasing.

CHAPTER NINETEEN

ROLDAN and his followers had come to San Domingo under the protection of the free pardon which had been solemnly proclaimed at the foot of the flagstaff. They were swaggering about the place, Roldan and Bernardo de Tarpia and Cristobal Garcia and of all them. They had brought a long train of Indian slaves with them, well set-up and handsome young women, each bearing burdens. Slaves and burdens, in accordance with the recent treaty, were to be sent to Spain in the *Holy Name*; the crop-eared Martinez was to sail with them as agent for all the recent mutineers, and he was to be armed with a long list of the luxuries which he was to buy with the proceeds of this plunder.

Rich's report was completed, signed, and sealed. Rich had given it with his own hands to Ballester, who was sailing as captain in the *Santa Anna*. The action had reminded him – if reminding was needed – of the impermanence of life in this world. He was taking the precaution lest the *Holy Name* with him on board should never reach Spain at all. Perhaps the next week would find him with the saints in Paradise, or suffering the pangs of Purgatory, or – he felt a shudder of fear – more likely cast into the eternal flames of Hell as a result of his recent heretical thoughts. He was in a state of profound dejection and agitation of mind which was not relieved in the least by the suspicious glance which Ballester darted at him when he received the letter; Ballester could suspect only too well what the contents were, and Ballester was one of those who loved the Admiral.

Should anyone of the Admiral's party come to know exactly what was written in his report, Rich knew that his life might be in danger. There were subtle poisons in this island – the deadly manchineel was one – even if it would not be a more simple matter of a knife in his back. He had to set himself for these last few days before the ships sailed to play the part of the conscientious supporter, critical but not too much so – certainly not the man who would write to the King that the Admiral was not fit to govern a farmyard, let alone an empire. It was a comfort to him now that Roldan knew of the letter. Certainly neither the Admiral nor Ballester would dare to incur the penalties of high treason by tampering with a sealed document addressed to His Highness himself – at least, not while an enemy knew that such a letter existed. Rich could not trust either the Italians or the Andalusians, and he waited with impatience during the interminable delays in fitting out the *Holy Name*.

He was walking back in the dark after dining with the Adelantado. The *Santa Anna* had actually sailed with his report on board; the *Holy Name* was almost ready; another thirty-six hours and he would have seen the last of this island. Overhead the stars were brilliant; the moon would rise soon in all her splendour. The cicadas were singing wildly all round him, and the lusty croaking of the frogs in the stream supplied a cheerful bass. Fireflies were lighting and relighting their lamps about his path, far more brilliant and mysterious than their duller brothers of Spain. Altogether he was in a cheerful mood – two cups of the Admiral's wine may have had something to do with that.

A denser shadow appeared in the darkness close at his right hand, and then another at his left. There was a man at either elbow walking silently in step with him; Rich felt the skin creep on the back of his neck, while between his shoulder blades he felt the actual spot where the stiletto would enter. Yet even in that moment he found time to wonder why they were troubling to murder him while his report was on its way to the King and beyond recall.

And then the walking shadow on his right spoke to him with the voice of Garcia.

'Don Narciso,' he said, 'I must trouble you to turn back and come with us.'

'And if I do not, Don Cristobal?'

Both men pressed in close upon him, forcing his elbows against his sides.

'I have a dagger here, Don Narciso. I will use it if you cry out.'

'And I have another,' said the voice of Diego Moret on his left. 'And I will use it, too. There will be one in your back and one in your belly.'

'Turn back with us, Don Narciso,' said Garcia, insinuatingly.

Rich turned; he felt there was nothing else he could do.

'Where are you taking me?' he asked; he had to try hard to keep the quaver out of his voice.

'This is not the time for explanations,' said Garcia, grimly. 'I would prefer you to keep quiet.'

They were walking down the slope from the citadel; the little town lay on their right, and there was only one solitary gleam of light from it. Rich decided they were going to lead him into the forest and kill him there. His body might lie for ever in that tangle of vegetation and never be discovered, even within a mile of the place. But he was still puzzled as to the motive, so puzzled that quite involuntarily he broke the silence with another question.

'What do you want to kill me for?' he asked.

'Be quiet. And we are not going to kill you,' said Garcia.

'Probably not going to,' amended Moret in the darkness on his left.

Even with this amendment the statement was reassuring. The wave of relief which surged over Rich astonished him; he realized that he had been far more afraid than he had suspected at the time. He trembled a little with the reaction, and then battled with himself to stop it. He did not want these two men at his elbows to know he was trembling. They were coming nearer to the trees and the forest.

'There are four horses here, Don Narciso,' said Garcia. 'One of them is for you. The others are for Don Diego and myself and Don Ramon who is waiting for us. There will be no reins for you to hold – the reins will be in my charge. But I hope you can stay in the saddle by holding on to the saddle bow.'

'I can try,' said Rich – the whinny of a horse told that they were drawing near to them.

'Did you find him?' asked an unknown voice.

'Yes,' said Garcia, and then to Rich: 'Mount.'

Rich felt in the darkness for the stirrup, and with the effort usual to him he hoisted up his foot and got it in. By the time he had swung himself into the saddle Moret was already mounted; Garcia sprang into the saddle of the third horse. They began to move along a path; the unknown Ramon who had been waiting with the horses in front, followed by Rich and Garcia, while Moret brought up the rear. The horses blundered along in the darkness; Rich felt his face whipped painfully occasionally by branches, and his knees received several excruciating knocks. For a space his mind was too much occupied with these troubles, and with the necessity of keeping his seat in the saddle, to have any thought to spare for the future, but as soon as the forest began to thin, and the rising moon gave them light to an extent quite remarkable compared with the previous blackness, he inevitably began to wonder once more. Suddenly a new aspect of the situation broke upon him, with a shock which made him sweat and set him moving restlessly in the saddle.

'Mother of God!' he said. 'The *Holy Name* sails tomorrow. You will let me get back in time to sail in her?'

The first reply he had was a light-hearted chuckle from Moret behind; the question seemed to amuse him immensely. Garcia allowed a painful second or two to elapse before answering.

'No, my pretty one,' he said. 'You will not be sailing in the *Holy Name*. Rest assured about that.'

Assured was not at all the right adjective to describe Rich's mental condition. There was bitter disappointment at the thought of not returning to Spain, but his other doubts overlaid that at the moment; he was intensely puzzled. It could hardly be ransom that these kidnappers were seeking; they must know that in the island he possessed practically nothing that anyone could desire. Then it occurred to him that perhaps he was being carried off to give legal colour to some plan they had in mind. They might be intending to force him to construct some binding agreement regarding their grants of land.

'I will do nothing', he announced, stoutly, 'to distort the law for you. I have my professional honour to consider.'

Moret seemed to find this announcement extremely funny, too. He broke into high-pitched laughter again; Rich, who could not see him, could imagine him writhing convulsed with merriment in his saddle.

'Be damned to your professional honour,' said Garcia. 'Do you think a man like me needs a lawyer to chop straws for him in this island?'

'Then why, in the name of God – ?'

They wanted neither his wealth nor his legal services, and he could think of nothing else they could want of him. Unless perhaps – it was a most uncomfortable thought – they wanted him as a hostage. If that were the case his doom was certain; nobody of the Admiral's party would lift a finger to save him. The sweat on his face felt suddenly cold, and he shuddered in the warm night.

'We want you – ' began Garcia, slowly.

'It's too good a joke to spoil yet,' interjected Moret, but Garcia ignored him.

'We want you as a navigator,' said Garcia.

'As a navigator?'

'Didn't you hear what I said?' snapped Garcia.

'But I'm no navigator,' protested Rich. 'I know nothing about it.'

'We saw you on the voyage out,' said Garcia. 'The Admiral was giving you lessons. You looked at the sun every day through his astrolabe, and at the stars each night. You were enough of a navigator to lecture us about it. Or have you forgotten?'

Rich certainly had forgotten until he was reminded of it.

'But I could no more take a ship to Spain – ' he began.

'Spain? Who said anything about Spain? It's west we sail, not east. And I'll warrant you could find your way to Spain, too.'

'Holy Mary!' said Rich faintly. 'Sainted Narciso of Gerona!'

He was too stunned for a space to say more, but slowly realization came to him.

'I will not go with you,' he burst out. 'I will not. Let me go back. Please. I beg of you.'

He writhed about in his saddle, entertaining some frantic notion of flinging himself to the ground and taking to his heels. The sound of a sharp whirr of steel behind him made him refrain; Moret had drawn his sword and was ready to cut him down. He forced himself to sit still, and from that he proceeded to force himself to appear calm. He was suddenly ashamed of his exhibition of weakness; it was especially shameful that he should have been guilty of an undignified outburst before men like Garcia and Moret, whom he despised. And – such is human nature – there was the faint hope growing in his breast already that he might yet escape. 'What is the plan?' he asked, steadying his voice.

'A week back', said Garcia, 'we caught an Indian. He is not of this island, although our Indians can understand him. He is taller and stronger, and his lower lip has been cut off in a V, so that we call him el Baboso, the Slobberer.'

'But what has he to say?'

'He has told us of a land to the north and west, a vast country full of gold. Gold vases and gold dishes. There are vast palaces, he says, reaching to the sky, and the chiefs have their clothes sewn all over with precious stones so that in the sunshine the eye cannot bear their brightness. That is where we are going. We shall bury our arms elbow deep in gold dust.'

'But in what ship?'

'The caravel *Santa Engracia* lies less than twenty leagues from here. Her captain is dead of fever, and her crew tried to run off, but we have caught four sailors who can work the sails, and now we have you to navigate her.'

'My God!' said Rich. 'I suppose Roldan is captain?' Moret giggled again behind him.

'Roldan? Good God, no! Who would want to sail under that lout? It is I who am captain, as you will do well to remember in future. We are twenty gentlemen of coat armour, and we shall carve out our own empire in the west.'

The first thought that came up in Rich's mind as he considered all these amazing statements was that the whole expedition was grossly illegal. Only the Admiral or those licensed by him had any right to explore the Indies; anyone else who should do so offended against not merely the Admiral but against the Crown. The gallows and the block awaited such offenders on their return. But a resounding success and a prodigious treasure might avert the penalty.

The immediate reaction to that notion was one of wonder at the incredible hardihood or rashness of those who had conceived the notion. Twenty gentlemen of coat armour, forsooth, with four sailors and a lawyer, were presuming to sail in a ridiculous caravel to 'carve out an empire' in a land wealthy enough to build palaces reaching to the sky. It would be a very different matter from the conquest of the helpless and lovable Indians of Española.

But this story told by the Slobberer with the missing lower lip had a chance of being true. It sounded a more likely tale than any Rich had yet heard; the facts that the Slobberer was of a different breed, and that he was mutilated in a fashion unknown in these islands, constituted valuable evidence that his story was not like the wild tales which the Admiral had first gathered, of Cibao with its golden mountains and of the valley of emeralds. The Slobberer might have some authentic knowledge of a real kingdom which certainly ought to be found in a north-westerly direction; if not the kingdom of the Grand Khan, then at least a dependency of it.

For a moment Rich felt a sensation almost of pleasurable excitement at the thought of such an adventure. He had to catch himself up suddenly and bring down his thoughts to a matter-of-fact level. How could he possibly navigate a ship from Española to China or Cipangu? Perhaps, as Garcia had in mind, the sailors would know how to trim the sails and attend to the other details of the practical handling of the ship. Perhaps he himself was capable of estimating the speed of the ship, and with the needle he would know something of her course. The astrolabe would give him a notion of their position relative to the equinoctial line; he raked back in his memory to see what he knew of the Admiral's table of the sun's height above the horizon – he could at least make a rough allowance for its variation, or perhaps there was a copy of the table on board the *Santa Engracia*. That would be a check on the other calculation, and would help him in the matter of allowing for currents and leeway and the uncertainty of the needle. Vaguely, very vaguely, he would have some sort of notion as to where they were. He could never hope to find his way back to Española if they wanted to return, but he could at least turn the ship's head and sail her eastward – eastward – eastward until he had found Africa or Spain or Portugal or France or even England. The Old World was too big a place even for him to miss.

Then, like a cold douche, common sense returned again. The whole plan was too mad, too insane. How could he be expected to handle a ship, with only his sketchy theoretical knowledge? There would be all kinds of emergencies to deal with – he remembered how the Admiral had brought the *Holy Name* through the Serpent's Mouth and then through the Dragon's Mouths. He could not handle a ship like that. He knew nothing about beating to windward off a lee shore. He did not have the practised seaman's uncanny knack of guessing the trend of a shoal from the successive casts of the lead. These hot-headed Spanish caballeros had no conception at all of the difficulty of the task they proposed to set him – if for no other reason, they were accustomed to the Admiral's phenomenal seamanship.

'I never heard of such a ridiculous plan in all my life,' he burst out.

'So that is what you think?' replied Garcia. There was a polite lack of interest in his manner.

'Yes!' said Rich. 'And what's more – '

Nobody appeared to listen to what more he had to say. The horses broke into a trot, and Rich, joggling about in his saddle, found his flow of eloquence impeded. He knew then that nothing he could say would deter these hotheads from their plan. Nothing would induce them to set him free to return to San Domingo and the *Holy Name*. He relapsed again into miserable silence, while the horses pushed on in the darkness, trotting whenever their fatigue and the conditions would allow, and walking in the intervals. Fatigue soon came to numb his misery. He was sleepy, and an hour or two on horseback was quite sufficient exercise for his soft limbs. The men of iron who rode with him had no idea of fatigue. The loss of a night's rest, the riding of a dozen leagues on horseback, were nothing to them. Rich bumped miserably along with them through the night; before dawn he had actually dozed once or twice in the saddle for a few nightmare seconds, only saving himself from falling headlong by a wild clutch at his horse's invisible mane.

CHAPTER TWENTY

At dawn Garcia broke his long silence.

'There's the *Santa Engracia*,' he said.

The path had brought them down to the sea's edge here, and the horses were trotting over a beach of firm black sand overhung by the luxuriant green cliffs. A mile ahead a torrential stream notched the steep scarp, and in the shelter of the tiny bay there lay a little ship, a two-masted caravel, her curving lateen yards with their furled sails silhouetted in black against the blue and silver sea. There were huts on the beach, and at their approach people came forth to welcome them. There was Bernardo de Tarpia and Mariano Giraldez, Julio Zerain and Mauricio Galindo – all the hot-headed young gentlemen; Rich could have listed their names without seeing them. There were four or five swaggerers whom he did not know; he presumed they were followers of Roldan whom he had never met before, and the notion was confirmed by the raggedness of their clothing. There were a few depressed Indians, and one with a gap where his lower lip should have been, through which his teeth were visible; this must be el Baboso of whom Garcia had spoken. There were a dozen Indian women whose finery proved that they were the mistresses of Spaniards and not the wives of Indians.

'You found him, then?' commented Tarpia. 'Welcome, learned doctor sailing-master.'

'Good morning,' said Rich.

He was sick with fatigue and fright, but he was determined not to allow the young bloods' gibes to hurt him visibly. If the inevitable really were inevitable, he could cultivate a stoical resignation towards it. His mind went off at a tangent, all the same, refusing to face the present. It groped wildly about trying to recall half-forgotten memories of some learned Schoolman's disquisition on the intrinsically inevitable as compared with the inevitable decreed by God. He slid stiffly off his horse and looked round him, dazed.

'Gold and pearls and emeralds!' said young Alfonso de Avila, clapping him on the shoulder. 'And no grubbing in the earth for them, either.'

It was extraordinary how the lure of easily won gold persisted, despite disillusionments. But young Avila was excited like a child about this new move. He was babbling pleasurably about the kingdoms they were going to assail, and the glory they were going to win; for him the treasure would be merely a measure of their success, just as a lawyer's eminence might be roughly estimated by the size of his fees.

Garcia's voice broke through the chatter.

'Everyone on board,' he said, curtly. 'We may have Roldan or the Admiral on our tracks at any minute. Tarpia, take charge of Rich.'

The longboat lay beside the beach; the Indians pulled at the oars – the hidalgos could not sink their dignity sufficiently to do manual work as long as there was someone else who could be made to do it for them – and within five minutes of Garcia's order Rich was hoisting himself wearily up over the side of the caravel. João de Setubal, the eccentric Portuguese, was there, and three or four others; apparently their duty had been to prevent the escape of the remaining four seamen.

'Here's your crew, sailing-master,' said Tarpia.

The four seamen grinned at him half nervously, half sullenly. It was clear that the new venture was not at all to their taste. Rich looked as sullenly back at them. The sun was already hot, and pained his eyes; he felt the *Santa Engracia* heave under his feet as a big roller lifted her.

'Who are you?' he said. 'What service have you seen?'

They answered him in Catalan, like sweet music after the harsh Castilian. They were fishermen from Villanueva, pressed the year before for service on the Ocean. They could reef and steer, and had spent their lives at sea.

'One of you must be boatswain,' said Rich. 'Which is it to be?'

Fortunately there seemed to be no doubt about that. Three thumbs were pointed at once to the fourth man, the blue-eyed and broad-shouldered Tomas – stoop-shouldered, too, for middle age had begun to curve his spine.

'Tomas, you are boatswain,' said Rich. It was a relief to have found someone on whom he could fob off some of his responsibility.

The second boatload from the shore was already alongside; Garcia had come with it.

'Don Narciso,' he said, 'the horses have to be got on board.'

They were swimming the horses out the short distance from the shore behind the longboat; even at her low waist the *Santa Engracia*'s rail was six good feet above the water's edge. Rich looked at Tomas in a panic.

'Shall I get the slings ready, sir?' asked Tomas.

'Yes,' said Rich.

The sailors pelted up the shrouds; there was tackle already rove on the yards – apparently they had been hoisting in stores and water yesterday. The slings were dropped to the boat, and passed under the belly of one of the horses.

'Here,' said Tomas to a bewildered Indian standing by. 'Tail on.'

The ropes were pushed into the hands of the Indians, and, under Tomas's urging, they walked away with them, and the horse, plunging helplessly, rose into the air. Tomas himself swung the brute inboard, the Indians walking cautiously forward again, and the horse was lowered into the waist. It was amazing how easy it was when one knew exactly how to do it. At a word from Garcia half a dozen young hidalgos took charge of the beasts – there was nothing undignified or unknightly about attending to horses when necessary. To learn how to do so had been part of the education of every hidalgo in his boyhood.

'We are ready to sail now, sailing-master,' said Garcia.

This was all mad, unreal. It must be a nightmare – it could not really be happening to him, the learned Narciso Rich. As though battering with a nightmare he strove to postpone the moment of departure; he felt that if only he could postpone it long enough he might wake up and find himself back in San Domingo, about to sail for Spain in the *Holy Name*.

'But what about stores?' he asked. 'Food? Water?'

'We have spent the last week collecting food,' said Garcia. 'The ship has dried meat, cassava, and corn for forty people for two months. There is forage for the horses, and every water-cask is full.'

'And charts? And instruments?'

'Everything the captain had is still in his cabin. He found his way here with them from Spain when he came with Ballester.'

'I had better see them first.'

Garcia's thick brows came together with irritation.

'This is not the moment for wasting time,' he said. 'Hoist sail at once – you can do the rest when we are on our way.'

Garcia's little eyes were like an angry pig's. He glowered at Rich, his hands on his hips and his body inclined forward towards him.

'I know enough about navigation', he said, menacingly, 'to know we must sail westward along this island before we turn north. I might find I could do without a navigator altogether, and in that case – '

He took his right hand from his hip and pointed, significantly, over-side. Rich could not meet his gaze, and was ashamed of himself because of it. He turned away.

'Very well,' he said faintly.

And even then the prayer that he began to breathe was cut short without his realizing it by the way the problem of getting under way captured his interest – if his active mind were employed it was hard for him to remain frightened. He looked up at the mast-head; the pennant there was flapping gently in an easterly wind; the land wind had dropped and the sea breeze had not begun yet to blow. The ship was riding bows on to the wind; he had to turn her about as she got under way. The theory of the manoeuvre was simple, and he had often enough seen it put into practice. It was an interesting experience to have to do it himself.

'Tomas,' he said. 'Set the Indians to up anchor. And I want the foresail ready to set.'

Tomas nodded at him, blinking in the sun.

'Who'll take the tiller, sir? It'll take the four of us to set sail.'

'I will,' said Rich, desperately. He had never held a ship's tiller in his life before, but he knew the theory of it.

He walked aft and set his hand on the big lever, swinging it tentatively. It seemed easy enough. Tomas had collected a band of Indians at the windlass – from the docility with which they obeyed him it was obvious that they were already accustomed to working under him, presumably during the business of provisioning the ship. The windlass began to clack, the Indians straining at the handles as they dragged the ship up to her anchor against the wind. The seamen were ready to set the foresail – two of them had just finished casting off the gaskets.

'Straight up and down, sir!' shouted Tomas, leaning over the bows to look at the cable.

'Hoist away!' shouted Rich; he swallowed hard as soon as the words were out of his mouth.

The anchor came up, and Tomas rushed back to help with the foresail. As the ponderous canvas spread Rich felt the tiller in his hand come to life; the ship was gathering stern-way. He knew what he had to do. He put the tiller hard over, for the ship had only to lie the tiniest fraction across the wind for the big foresail to wing her round like a weathercock. She lurched and hesitated, and Rich in a sudden panic brought the tiller across to the other side. Tomas was watching him, apparently awaiting more orders, but Rich had none to give. Nevertheless, Tomas kept his head – he saw on which side Rich had at last decided to hold the tiller, and ran with his men to brace the yard round. Rich felt the motion of the ship change as she swung across the swell; a glance at the island revealed the shore to be slowly revolving round him. He struggled wildly to keep his head clear; it was the ship that was turning, not the island. The big foresail was doing its work, and he flung his weight against the tiller to catch the ship lest she swing too far. There was some new order he ought to give to Tomas, but he did not know what it was, so he took one hand from the tiller and waved it in the hope that Tomas would understand.

Fortunately Tomas did so; he braced the yard square and the ship steadied on her course before the wind with no more than a lurch or two. Rich looked up at the mast-head pennant – it was streaming ahead. The shore lay on his right hand, and the ship must be pointing west nearly enough. As he centred the tiller he glanced at the compass, but that was still chasing its tail round and round in its basin; it would be several minutes before it settled down. He experimented timidly with the tiller as soon as he saw that the ship was heading a trifle in shore; the ship answered, but with more of a sullen obstinacy than he expected. It was only with a considerable exertion of strength that he was able to hold her on her proper course.

'Set the mainsail, sir?' asked Tomas. He was so obviously expecting an affirmative answer that Rich was constrained to give him one, but it was with an inward qualm – he had as much as he could do to steer as it was, and he doubted his strength to hold her if more canvas were spread. But the mainsail expanded inexorably while the ropes squealed in the blocks; Rich distinctly felt the ship under his feet gather increased speed as the mainsail bellied out in the wind and it seemed to him as if the tiller would soon pull his arms out of their sockets. And then, as Tomas took his men to the braces, Rich suddenly felt the ship become more manageable. The tiller ceased to be a thing to be fought and struggled with. It became a sweet tool of whose every motion – as his tentative experiments soon proved – the ship was immediately conscious.

Of course, he told himself, he should have expected that. Mainsail and foresail were designed to counterpoise each other almost exactly, so that the tiller and rudder held the delicate balance between two nearly equal forces. A touch, now, and she swung to the right. A touch, and she swung to the left – the feeling of mastery was most impressive. Rich came back to his senses with a guilty start; Tomas was looking at him curiously as he swayed the ship about in unseamanlike fashion, and he hurriedly steadied her. The wind blew on the back of his neck, and he was unconscious of the heat of the sun and of his fatigue. In that triumphant moment he felt as if he could steer the ship for ever. He would rather steer a ship than ride a horse any day – never in the saddle had he felt this superb confidence. But he felt he could not indulge himself at present. He had to make up his mind about what course to steer, and as the numerous factors governing that problem came tumbling into his mind he felt the need for giving it his undivided attention.

'Send a hand to the tiller, Tomas,' he called.

One of the seamen came shambling aft, and took over the steering. He looked at Rich inquiringly for the course; Rich took a stride or two up and down the deck as he made his calculations. He remembered the glimpses he had had of the Admiral's chart – somewhere not far ahead the cape of Alta Vela trended far to the south and would have to be circumnavigated, while soon the wind would shift so as to blow direct upon the shore. It would undoubtedly be as well to get as far to the southward now as he could, so as to have a reserve in hand. And the needle in these waters pointed to the east of north – he would have to allow for that, too. On the other hand, if he set too southerly a course it might take him out of sight of land. Rich suddenly realized that he was not nearly as afraid of that as he was of finding himself on a lee shore during the night. He yearned to have plenty of sea all round him, and it was delightful to discover that he was quite confident of finding Española again should he run it out of sight. He bent over the compass and took in his hand the white peg which marked the course to be set, hesitated for a space, and then with decision he put it into the next hole to the east of south.

'So!' he said.

The helmsman brought the tiller over, and the ship began to swing round. Rich knew that the sails must be trimmed to the wind, but he was vague about the exact wording of the orders necessary. He looked over at Tomas, and saw with pleasure that he was making ready to brace the yards round without orders. Rich nodded to him to continue.

The *Santa Engracia* now had the wind almost abeam; she was lying over to it, with plenty of spray coming over the weatherside, making music through the water, and all the rigging harping together, and the green mountains of Española falling fast astern. Rich looked round to find Garcia staring fixedly at him.

'Our course should be west, along the island,' said Garcia, suspiciously. 'Why are we going south?'

'Because it is necessary,' said Rich, crossly, 'because – '

As soon as he had begun upon it he gave up, before the prospect of all the difficulties, the attempt to explain his technique. He had just performed successfully the feat of getting the *Santa Engracia* under way and on her course, and perhaps his feeling of achievement gave him sufficient elation, combined with his annoyance, to answer Garcia with spirit.

'You want me to navigate this ship,' he said. 'Then allow me to navigate her. If you could do it better yourself there was no need to kidnap me to do it for you.'

'Holy Mary!' said Garcia, 'how quick we are to take offence!'

But he himself had taken none, apparently, and Rich actually forgot him, momentarily, as he looked round the ship of which he was in charge. The feeling of elation still persisted, despite his fatigue – or perhaps because of it, for he was a little light-headed through lack of sleep. The beginning of his captaincy had been marked with brilliant success. Perhaps this business was not nearly as difficult as he had thought it to be. Perhaps he would steer the *Santa Engracia* safely to China and home again to Spain. Perhaps –

The cold fit of common sense broke over him again in a wave. He had been thinking nothing but nonsense – he must beware of these fits of misguided enthusiasm. One such, during his conversation with the King, had been responsible for his ever coming to the Indies. He was acting like a hot-headed boy instead of like a man of a mature forty who had already risen to the topmost height of his own profession. He was quite as mad as Garcia, who was setting out with a single caravel with twenty men and four horses, to find and conquer the Grand Khan. And – it was extraordinary how muddled his mind was now – he had been on the point of forgetting again that he himself was just as involved as Garcia in this mad attempt. Sick despair closed in upon him again.

Tomas had come aft; he hesitated for a moment between Garcia and Rich, and then finally addressed himself to Rich.

'Shall I start the Indians bailing, sir?' he asked. 'She hasn't been bailed today, and she makes water fast. And there's the stores we put in the forehold, sir. I don't like – '

Apparently Tomas had a great deal on his mind regarding the condition of the ship. He talked volubly, while Rich only half heard him. Rich remembered how the captain ought to make a tour of inspection round his command every morning and settle the day's work. He allowed Tomas to lead him forward, and below. He agreed about the necessity for bailing. He looked dubiously at a pile of stores in the forehold, packed in queer containers, half sack, half basket, peculiar to Española, and he left it to Tomas to decide how they should be re-stowed. What with weed and worms and wear and tear the *Santa Engracia* was in poor condition, he was told – Tomas went as far as to say, when they were in the solitude of the after-hold, that he would be dubious about sailing her from Palma to Barcelona on a summer's day.

But Rich was growing more and more dizzy with fatigue and lack of sleep. He tried to display an owlish intelligence as Tomas poured out his troubles, answering his remarks with non-committal monosyllables. He escaped from him in the end and found his way to the captain's cabin under the poop. In a drawer of the little table there he came across the late captain's papers and instruments. There was a roll of accounts of one sort and another, all dealing with the outward voyage and apparently of no more importance. There was a paper of sailing instructions in the handwriting of the Admiral himself, dealing with the problem of finding Española from Spain – Rich's swimming eyes could not struggle with that now. There was a rough chart of the Indies, apparently by the same hand; that might be useful. There was an astrolabe and cross staff, and, in a leather pouch, a table of the sun's declination at weekly intervals throughout the year. That was all Rich wanted to know. He pushed the other things aside, and laid his head upon his arms on the table as he sat on the stool screwed to the deck. And in that attitude, despite the rolling of the ship, he slept heavily for a couple of hours.

CHAPTER TWENTY-ONE

THE voyage went on, somehow. On the third day they doubled Cape Alta Vela and were able to set a westerly course along the southern coast of Española, the old *Santa Engracia*, leaking like a sieve and encumbered with weeds a yard long on her bottom, lumbering along before the persistent urging of the wind. Far on the horizon to the north rose the green mountains of the island. Each day brought its scorching sunshine and its torrential rain, its blue skies and its rainbows.

Each day brought afresh to Rich the strange feeling of the unreality of it all, despite the harsh realism of the ship's routine, the bailing and the constant repairs. He practised diligently each day with astrolabe and cross staff – he told himself that his very life might depend on his skilful use of them, while at the same time he found it impossible to believe. He worked out the little calculation necessary to ascertain the speed of the ship by measuring with his pulse, the time taken by an object thrown overboard from the bow to reach the stern. He pored long and diligently over the Admiral's chart of the Indies, at the long sweep of islands at its eastern end where – as the last voyage had ascertained – lay Trinidad and the mysterious country of the Orinoco and the Earthly Paradise. Westmost of the chain lay Española, divided by a narrow strait from the long peninsula of Cuba which jutted out two hundred leagues or so from the unknown mainland of China or India. So the Admiral had drawn it; Rich was aware that there had been whispers that Cuba was merely another island, the vastest of them all. The Admiral had silenced the whispers by decreeing that any such whisperer would lose his tongue.

But whether Cuba were an island or not, the task Garcia

had laid upon him was to steer the *Santa Engracia* up through the strait between Cuba and Española, and then north-westerly, on and on until they reached the country el Baboso knew of, the land where the temples reached the sky and where worked gold was to be seen everywhere. Rich fancied it must be the land of the Great Khan which Marco Polo the Venetian had visited, but he occasionally had doubts. It might be some new unvisited empire, if it existed at all. If it existed at all – Rich could picture the *Santa Engracia* sailing on and on over the blue sea until her motley crew died of hunger and thirst and disease, himself among them. Or perhaps in that direction there really was an edge to the earth, despite the Admiral's denials, and the *Santa Engracia* might find herself hurtling over it to plunge into the depths. He tried to hint at his fears to Garcia, but Garcia only shrugged his shoulders and laughed callously. Despite his comfortable plumpness, Garcia was a man of iron will and quite without fear – without a heart in his body, Rich came to think.

Certainly without a heart in his body. Three of the sailors – not Tomas – and four Indians were caught the second night by Julio Zerain trying to desert in the longboat; Rich heard the judgement which issued from Garcia's lips the next morning and heard the wild screams of the wretched men as their punishment was dealt out to them. He could not bear to listen – more especially as he would certainly have joined in the attempt if the sailors had taken him into their confidence. He might be screaming there on the deck now, in that case. It was something to thank God for that he had not been allowed the captain's cabin, but had had to sleep in the 'tween-decks with a dozen Spaniards. That had kept him from any such perilous endeavour. He would die – he was sure of it – if ever he were punished in that manner. That morning he knew worse misery of soul than ever since he had left Spain; more could not be said than that.

There was other bloodshed on board. Rich did not know how the quarrel started, but he heard shouts and the clash of steel forward; Fernando Berrocal and Pablo Mourentan had their swords out – the blades flashed fiercely in the sunshine – and were fighting out their quarrel in the manner of hot-blooded youth. Garcia came up from below on the run; he roared like a bull and dashed forward drawing his sword. Tarpia appeared from nowhere, sword drawn, too. Berrocal's blade was beaten out of his hand. Mourentan, thrusting wildly at Garcia in his excitement, received a sword cut on his shoulder which sent him staggering and helpless to the rail.

'Fools!' bellowed Garcia. 'I will have no fighting in this ship. That fool there has less than he deserves. The next man to draw steel will hang. I swear it by the Holy Sacrament.'

He glowered round at the silent crowd and pointed to the yardarm, magnificently animal despite his fat and his rags. Perhaps he remembered the rules on board the *Holy Name* of which Acevedo had once reminded him. He needed every fighting man in the campaign he was planning, and he had come to appreciate not only how easily quarrels may arise in the cramped life aboard ship, but also how easily the whole ship's company might become involved. Rich thought bitterly of the time when he had believed himself to be acquiring the art of managing men – including this same Garcia. He knew now that he could never compare himself with him. He was no man of action; in a great shaking-up like this expedition to the Indies every man found his own level in time.

Seventy leagues to the west of Alta Vela lay Cape San Miguel, the westernmost point of Española; it interested Rich to find that they reached it at the very moment which he predicted. His dead reckoning had been correct, and so was the Admiral's chart – or else they both contained the same error. Rich might at one time have speculated deeply on the philosophy of compensating errors, but nowadays he was too engrossed in hourly problems to waste time. He accepted God's mercy with gratitude and left it at that; as soon as he saw the shore of Española trending away back to the eastward from the bluff green eminence of San Miguel, and knew he had made all the westing necessary, he had to lay a fresh course through the straits, for there was no leeway to spare at all on this next leg of the passage.

No leeway to spare; indeed it became apparent that they would never double Cuba in a single tack. For as they bore northward the wind backed northward as well. Rich and Tomas laid the *Santa Engracia* as close to the wind as they could, striving to make northing while they still had sea room, but she drifted away to leeward spiritlessly, encumbered by her weeds. Rich gazed despairingly at the tell-tale angle which his unaided eye could observe between the trace of her wake and the line of her masts. The cliffs of Cuba loomed in sight, a hard line on the horizon ahead, and still the wind blew from the north. They had to wear the ship round, heading back almost in the direction in which they had come.

Garcia watched the manoeuvre curiously and suspiciously. 'Why back to Española, navigator?' he asked. There was a grim jocularity in his tone. 'I ask you to sail north-west and' – he glanced up at the sun – 'even a poor landsman like myself can see you are sailing south-east.'

Rich endeavoured to explain the difficulty he was encountering. Today there was none of the elation which previously had led him to answer with spirit. He was too frightened of Garcia again now.

'I see,' said Garcia, consideringly, but with still a hint of unsatisfied suspicion in his voice. 'But you do not want to go *too* close to Española, do you? We would not like to lose you, learned doctor – not now that you have proved your worth. And I might add that we will see that we do not.'

Hastily Rich disclaimed any thought of attempting to desert from the *Santa Engracia*, but the words died away lamely in face of the cynical smile on Garcia's face.

'I have no need of further assurance of your loyalty, learned Don Narciso,' said Garcia, with a glance forward to where the previous deserters had suffered.

But he grew more human as he stood beside Rich watching the ship's progress on the other tack.

'These zigzag methods call for much explanation to me,' he said. 'I served for a term in His Highness's galleys against the Moors. We never used them there. The slaves took the oars and we went wherever we wished. When the time serves I will have galleys built for use in these waters. There are slaves enough to be found.'

There were two days when the wind failed altogether, and the *Santa Engracia* wallowed helplessly in the calm, with San Miguel still in sight to the eastward, and the porpoises sported round her as if to show their contempt for her sluggishness, and the flying fish furrowed the deep blue of the water. When it blew again, the wind was still hardly east of north, and day by day the *Santa Engracia* beat back and forth across the wide channel, gaining hardly more than a few yards each day, while tempers grew short on board and the murmuring hidalgos, who had actually come to recognize the shores which encompassed them, asked bitterly how long the blundering incompetence of their navigator was going to keep them confined. Rich began to pray for a southerly wind, which would carry them off towards the mad adventure which he so much dreaded.

CHAPTER TWENTY-TWO

LONG afterwards Rich remembered those prayers; he suspected that it was because of his impiety and incipient heresy that his petition was granted in the fashion which God chose. It was two weeks before the feast of San Narciso of Gerona (who had always stood his friend) to which he had been looking forward as perhaps bringing relief from his troubles. The wind had died away again when they had nearly clawed their way northward to the open sea, and the *Santa Engracia* drifted helplessly with Cuba barely in sight from the mast-head and Española invisible over the horizon. It was oppressively hot, although there was a thin veil of cloud over the sky, through which the sun showed only at rare intervals and then a mere ghost of his usual self. The *Santa Engracia* pitched and rolled in a swell which was extraordinarily heavy for the narrow waters in which they lay. Spaniards and Indians sat helpless about the decks, gasping in the heat; Rich felt his clothes wet upon his back.

He prayed for a wind, any wind, and the wind came. Gently it came at first, only a mild puff, steadying the ship in her rolling and making the sails flap loudly. Rich started from the deck in wild excitement. Those puffs of wind were from the south – a few hours of this would see them through the straits, and free. Tomas noticed the puffs of wind, too; he was having the yards braced round in haste. Soon there was quite a breeze blowing from the southward, piping in the rigging, and the *Santa Engracia* was under full sail before it, heading gallantly to the northward over the grey sea.

But the breeze had brought no relief from the heat, curiously enough. It was a hot wind, a fiery wind. Rich felt his skin still drip even while the breeze blew upon him. There was an Indian on the forecastle chattering excitedly to Tomas, and Tomas was trying to puzzle out what he was saying. He led the Indian aft to where Rich stood with Garcia, and the Indian babbled in panic.

'Hurricane,' he was saying, or some word like that. He was frantic with the desire to express his meaning – it was a most vivid example of the curse of Babel with which God had afflicted the world because of its impiety.

'Hurricane,' said the Indian again, wreathing his hands. 'Hurricane – big wind.'

He pointed up to the sky and waved his arms; the clouds to which he was pointing had a baleful yellow gleam now which was echoed in the sea below.

'Big wind,' said the Indian, and now that he had the Spanish words he had sought he amplified them.

'Big – big – big – big wind,' he said, wildly. He was trying to convey to his stolid taskmasters the impression of a wind bigger than their imagination could conceive. Rich and Tomas exchanged glances.

'Wind's freshening,' said Tomas. It was blowing half a gale, certainly, and the *Santa Engracia* was heaving and plunging before it over the topaz sea.

'You had better shorten sail, Tomas,' said Rich, and then, as bigger gusts came, 'No, heave her to.'

Tomas nodded decided approval and rushed forward; the Indians there were all scurrying to and fro, wringing their hands and wailing, 'Hurricane, hurricane' – there was something about the strange Indian word which filled them with terror. Only two or three were in a fit condition to help Tomas and his men as they battled with the foresail. Rich saw Tomas, clearly frightened now, beckon to some of the Spaniards at hand for assistance, and some of them in the urgency of the moment actually ran to help him. Rich went to the tiller to help the man there heave her to – it was a muddled moment, but the ship came round under the pressure of the mainsail while only the top of one wave came in over the waist amid screams from the Indians. The seamen got the mainsail in, leaving only the lower corner spread; with the yard braced right round and the tiller hard over the ship rode nearly bows on to the wind, meeting the sea with her starboard bow. She was as safe as they could make her, now, and already the wind was blowing a full gale. Garcia came, blown by the wind, aft to Rich, with Manuel Abello, the only one of the old colonists who had joined the expedition, behind him.

'Abello here knows what the Indians are saying,' he shouted in Rich's ear. 'He has seen these hurricanes before.'

Abello was hatless, and his long hair and beard were blown into a wild mop in front of his face.

'Nothing can live in a hurricane,' he shouted. 'Make for land.'

Rich had no words for him. It was not the moment to try to explain that the poor old *Santa Engracia*, hove to before a full gale, could do nothing more now except try to live through it – the Admiral himself would attempt no more. Tomas was clawing his way round the deck with his men, driving the Indians below and making all as secure as might be.

'Why don't you do as he says?' shouted Garcia.

'I can't –' said Rich.

The force of the wind suddenly redoubled itself. It shifted a couple of points and flung itself howling upon the *Santa Engracia* – Rich saw the line of the wind hurtling over the surface of the water. The *Santa Engracia* lay over, took a huge wave over her bows, and then wearily came up to the wind again. The wind was nearly taking them off their feet. They felt as if they were being pushed by something solid, and it was still increasing in force; they had all been dashed against the lee rail, and it was with incredible difficulty that they regained their footing. Rich felt himself being swept away again. He seized a rope's end and began to tie himself to the rail, with great clumsy knots – it seemed mad for a grown man to tie himself to his ship for fear of being blown away, but everything in this world was mad. The deck forward was strangely bare – only Tomas and another man were to be seen there, clutching the rail. The sea they had shipped must have swept the others away. Tomas saw Rich looking at him and pointed up to the mainsail. The small rag of canvas which had been left spread there was blowing out, expanding like a bladder as the gaskets gave way. Next moment the whole sail was loose; a moment later it had flogged itself into fragments which cracked like gigantic whips in the gale with a noise which even the gale could not drown.

The ship must be hurtling to leeward at an astonishing pace, thought Rich, with a mad clarity of mind. He wondered how, when he next worked out the ship's position, he could allow for all this leeway whose pace and direction were quite unknown to him. Then he told himself he would most likely never work out the ship's position again. And he was in mortal sin – he had been intending to confess before sailing in the *Holy Name*. He was frightened now, for the first time since the gale began, and he tried to pray into the shrieking wind.

A huge wave suddenly popped up from nowhere and came tumbling over the poop. Rich felt himself dashed against the rail with terrific force; he choked and strangled and struggled in the water until the *Santa Engracia* shook herself free. Garcia and Abello were gone from beside him, and Rich felt nothing more than a neutral callousness for their fate. The masts went directly after – Rich actually was unaware of the loss of the foremast, but he saw the weather shrouds of the mainmast part and the wind whirl the mast away like a chip. Everything else on deck was going, too – tiller and windlass and boat and all. Only Tomas was still there, bound to the forecastle rail. The *Santa Engracia* was rolling like a spiritless log on the surface of the sea.

A little crowd of people, Spaniards and Italians, came suddenly pouring into the waist, as it rolled awash, from out of the forecastle. The sea took them, too; they must have been driven out of their shelter by the rising of the water within. For the *Santa Engracia* was low in the water by now; the numerous seas she had shipped must have practically filled her, and every sea now was sweeping across her decks and burying Rich in its foam. He realized dully that she would not sink now, for she carried insufficient ballast and cargo for that, and tried to think what would happen to her next as she drifted waterlogged and almost below the surface. Presumably her fastenings would give way under the continual drenching, and she would go to pieces in the end, and that would be the time when he would drown. But while this infernal wind blew and while he was so continually submerged he was incapable of sufficient thought to be afraid any more – it was as if he were standing aside and incuriously watching the body of the learned Narciso Rich battered by the waves.

At nightfall he was still alive, drooping half-conscious in his bonds as the seas swept over him, and deaf to the wild roaring of the wind in his ears. He was not aware of the moment when the ship struck land, although he must have come to his senses directly after. Wind and sea were more insensate than ever in the roaring night; there was white foam everywhere, faintly visible in the darkness, and huge waves seemed to be beating upon him with a more direct violence than before. Under his feet and through the mad din of wind and water he was conscious of a thundering noise as the ship pounded and broke. He guessed that the ship had struck land and in panic, like waking from a nightmare, he struggled to free himself from the rope that had bound him fast so far. The deck heaved and canted, smothered under a huge roller. Then the poop broke clear, hurtling over the reef and across the lagoon. Rich felt himself and the deck tossed over and over, and they struck solid land in a welter of crashing fragments. The wind took charge of him as he hit the beach and blew him farther inshore. He clutched feebly and quite ineffectively at the darkness, while the wind flung him through and over, up the slope. He felt vegetation – some kind of cane – under him. Then he fell down another slope; there was water in his face until he struggled clear. A freak of the wind had dropped him into the lee of a nearly vertical bank, so that the giant's fingers of the hurricane could no longer reach under him and hurl him further. He lay there half-conscious; at rare intervals a shattering sob broke from his lips, while overhead the gale howled and yelled in the pitchy black.

CHAPTER TWENTY-THREE

It was down into the depths of a ravine that the wind had dropped Rich, perhaps the safest place in a hurricane that chance could have chosen for him. There was a stream flowing in the depths – Rich lay half in and half out of it for most of one day until he roused himself to crawl clear. The fresh water probably saved his life, for he was much too battered and bruised and ill to be able to move far. Overpowering thirst compelled him to bend his tortured neck and drink, the first time and at intervals after that; he felt no hunger, only the dreadful pain of his bruises, and he moaned like a sick child at every slight movement that he made. He had neither thought nor feeling for anything other than his pain and his thirst; late on the second day he raised himself for an instant on his hands and knees and looked round the ravine, but he collapsed again on his face. It was not until the day after that the feeble urge of life within him caused him to pull himself to his feet and stand swaying, while every tiny part of him protested fiercely against the effort. He was like a man flayed alive. He had hardly an atom of skin left upon him – his only clothes were his shoes and his leather breeches – and in addition to his innumerable deep bruises he had several serious cuts, caked now with black blood. He was weak and dizzy, but he made himself stagger along the ravine; he could not hope to attempt its steep sides, but after the first few steps progress became easier as his aching joints loosened, until fatigue caused him to sit down and rest again.

He emerged in the end upon the beach at the point where the ravine cut through the low cliff, round the corner from where the *Santa Engracia* had been blown ashore. The dazzling sunshine, in contrast with the comparative darkness of the ravine, blinded him completely for a space – the silver sand was as dazzling as the cloudless sky above. He sat on a rock again with his hands to his eyes while he recovered, but as he sat he became conscious of hunger, and it was the prodigious urge of hunger which drove him again to wander along the beach, seeking something to devour.

For several days, even in that smiling island, the problem of food occupied his attention to the exclusion of all else. The first solution was supplied by the discovery of a bag of unground Indian corn, cast up on the beach from the wreck of the *Santa Engracia*, all that he ever found of her except a few timbers. The grain was soggy with seawater, but he pounded it between two rocks and made a sort of raw porridge out of it which at least sufficed to fill his belly and give him strength to continue his search. Then he managed to kill a land crab with a rock, and ate the disgusting creature raw – he became accustomed very quickly to a diet of raw land crab. Most of the trees in the little island had been broken off short by the hurricane, and at his second attempt to push through the wild tangle to the low summit of the island he found a plantain tree-top full of fruit, tasteless and tough and not very digestible, but of considerable use in keeping his soul in his body – although the very violent reaction of his interior to this stimulating diet made him wonder more than once if the frail partnership were going to dissolve.

There were queer shellfish to be discovered in enormous numbers among the rocks; he ate them, too, and survived. But the catch that really turned the scale was that of a turtle on the beach, crawling seaward after laying her eggs. Rich had just enough strength to struggle with her, avoiding the frantic snaps of her bony jaws, and with one wild effort he managed to turn her over by the aid of a bit of driftwood. The rest of the business was horrible, or would have been if he had not been so hungry – he had neither knife nor fire, and he had to make use of rocks and sharp shells. The lepers on the Cape Verdes had baths in turtles' blood in the hopes of a cure; Rich very nearly did. Nevertheless, it was when he had eaten his fill of the rich food – gorging himself in the knowledge that in that hot sun the meat would be uneatable in a few hours – that he was able to come back to intellectual life again, and cease to be a mere food-hunting animal and become again a man able to think and look about him and to make plans for the future.

He was alone in his little island; of that he was sure by now. He was master of a little hummock of land, a mile long and half a mile wide, rising in the centre to a height of four hundred feet or so, surrounded by a white sandy beach and beyond that by almost continuous coral banks, and covered with the usual dense greenery which was already hastily repairing the ravages of the hurricane. He was unarmed – sword and belt and scabbard had vanished in the storm along with his coat and shirt. He had no tools save sticks and two big nails which he found in a fragment of the *Santa Engracia*. He was not at all sure where he was, but when he climbed as high as he could up the island summit he could see other small islands in the distance, while away to the southward there was a kind of different colouring to the sky and a faint mark on the horizon which he was almost sure must be Española.

He was not very conscious of the curse of loneliness. Indeed, rather on the contrary, he caught himself almost on the point of smiling once or twice at the irony of it that, of all the complement of the *Santa Engracia*, he should be the sole survivor. Garcia with his bull's strength, Tarpia with his skill at arms, Moret, young Avila, Tomas the seaman – the storm had killed them all except him, and he felt no particular regret for any of them save perhaps for Tomas. And even for Tomas he was mainly regretful because with his aid it might have been easier to build a boat.

For he was naturally determined to build a boat. Española lay only just over the horizon, and even if he hated Española he wanted to return there if only as the first stage of his road to Spain. His chances of being rescued if he waited were negligible, he knew – it might be ten years before a ship came even into sight, and with those coral banks littering the sea he knew that any ship would give his little island a wide berth, as unlikely to contain any reward for the danger of approaching it. He had not the least intention of ending his days on a diet of raw shellfish and plantains; he wanted to return to Spain, to his comfortable house and his dignified position. His mind was running on food. He had eaten roast sucking-pig for his last meal in Spain, and he wanted most unbearably to eat roast sucking-pig again, with plenty of wholesome bread – not ship's biscuit, nor golden cakes of Indian corn, but good honest wheaten bread, although barley bread would serve at a pinch. He could have none of these until as a first step he had built a boat and traversed the fifty miles of sea that lay between him and Española. He set himself again to serious consideration of this question of a boat; his recent experiences had had this profound effect upon him, that he was prepared now to stake his life on the work of his own hands in a fashion he would have shrunk from doing a year ago.

There was driftwood in plenty, and he could supplement it by tearing branches from trees. With creepers he could bind it into faggots, and he could bind the faggots into some kind of raft. It would be a desperately unhandy craft, though, and it might take him as much as a week to paddle it fifty miles to Española. It would not be easy to contrive containers for a week's food and water – and would a craft tied together with creeper sustain for a week the working and straining of the big rollers which beat so steadily on his beaches? He doubted it. The thing might go to pieces in mid-ocean, even without a storm to help. He needed something much more like a boat; and in a boat he could use his corn sack as a sail, for there was always plenty of north in the wind in these waters – as he had already painfully learned – and he could make the passage to Española in a single day, then.

Rich was altogether of much too intellectual a turn of mind to have any illusions as to the magnitude of the work before him; it is all the more to his credit that he set himself doggedly at his task, exploring the island for timber that might serve his purpose, and perfectly prepared with shells and stones and his two big nails to dig himself a dug-out canoe from a suitable tree-trunk – his mind was already busy with schemes for tying a keel of rock under the bottom to stabilize the thing and make it not merely less likely to roll over but to save the labour of hollowing it out more than a sketchy amount.

It only took him a single day to discover a suitable tree-trunk, but it took him two weeks to discover stones suitable to work with and to chip them to any sort of edge, for he spoiled nine-tenths of them. He was consumed with a furious energy for the work – his busy mind could not tolerate the empty idleness of the island with only the monotonous beating of the surf to windward and the cries of the birds. He chipped away remorselessly, sparing himself only the minimum of time to hunt for food; he grew lean and hard, and the sun burnt him almost to blackness. He reminded himself that when he was home again at last he would have a delightful time building up once more the corpulence essential to the dignity of a successful professional man. His most exciting discovery was of a thin vein of rock in an exposed scar in the very ravine where he had first fallen. It was of a dark green, nearly black, and when he chipped out a lump and smashed it, it broke like glass into a series of points best adapted for spearheads, perhaps, but with a dull cutting edge which made them possible for use as knives. With infinite patience he quarried out one heavy lump with as perfect an edge as he could hope for. Using that as an axe he quite doubled his rate of progress in the weary business of trimming off the boughs of his tree-trunk.

He went through a period of convulsive labour when he began the process of getting his log down to the beach – even when his canoe was fashioned it would still be too heavy to move with any ease, and it was better to move the log itself where the damage done would be immaterial. He learned much about the use of levers and ramps while he was engaged upon this task; the log lay on the side of a slope so that most of the work was straightforward, but twice he encountered cross ridges which had to be painfully surmounted. He slept each night in the open, hardly troubling to shelter himself under overhanging vegetation, for he was so weary each night that the heavy showers did not wake him. Certainly the winking white fire-flies did not, as they danced round him – nor the ceaseless chirpings of the grasshoppers and the bellowing of the frogs.

Rich had made one miscalculation when he was considering his chances of being rescued. He had only had Spanish ships in mind, and he had never given a thought to Indians in canoes, and so it came about that all his labour was quite wasted. It was one noontide that the canoe came, at a moment when his log was poised on the brink of the last slope down to the beach and a few more heaves upon his lever would have sent it careering down to the water's edge. How long the canoe had been in sight he did not know, for he had been engrossed in his work; it was only when he paused that he saw it, with three men at the paddles, threading its way in through the shoals. He threw himself down into hiding the moment he perceived it – instant decision was easy to him now – and waited until it reached the shore and the three Indians had dragged it up the beach, before he seized his heavy lever and rushed down upon them.

They looked up at him in fright as he arrived, and scattered, squeaking with dismay; they may have recognized him as one of the terrible white men of whom they had heard, but just as likely his mere appearance was sufficiently terrifying to strike them with panic. One ran along the beach and the other two dived into the vegetation, and Rich found himself master of a canoe which, crude as it was, was far better than anything he could have hoped to make in three months. But it was a big boat for a single man to handle, and Española was far away. He would prefer to have a crew for the voyage, and he set himself to wonder how he could catch the Indians.

The Admiral had always managed to play upon their curiosity, he knew – he had studied his reports closely enough to remember that – and somehow he must manage to coax them within his reach. He looked into the canoe; it contained only a crude creeper fishing net and gourds of water and a few cakes of cassava bread – the sight even of cassava bread made his mouth water after his recent diet – nothing by which he could get them into his power. He wanted to eat their bread, but he thought that the sight of a man eating bread would be hardly sufficient to excite their curiosity. He took up his big lever, balanced it upright on his open hand, and walked solemnly down the beach with it. Then he raised it to his chin, and he was able to keep it poised there for a few unstable seconds. He picked up three white lumps of stone and tried to juggle with them – as a boy he had been able to keep three balls in the air at once, and he managed to make a clumsy effort to recapture his old skill. Stealing a glance sideways he saw that the Indian who had run along the beach had halted and was looking back, mystified; he was even retracing a few of his steps, hesitant, just like a child. Rich juggled all the harder, tossing the white stones higher and higher. He took his lever again, and spun it in his fingers, and he sat down on the thick gunwale of the canoe with his back to the land, twisting his lever and working his left elbow as if he was doing something mysterious with his left hand out of the Indians' sight. It was while he was so engaged that he heard soft footfalls on the sand behind him, and whisperings; he was careful to turn round as slowly as possible, lest a sudden movement should scare them away like the wild animals they were.

They were standing in a row, half a dozen yards off, and staring at him big-eyed; they jumped when he turned, and were poised for flight again, but they did not flee. Rich put down his lever and extended his hand in the gesture of peace.

'Good day,' he said soothingly.

They looked at each other, and nudged each other, but they said nothing.

'This is a very charming island,' he said. 'Do you come here for fish or turtles?'

They actually were smiling at the strange noises he made – these children of nature were never far from laughter if the white man had not actually laid his hands on them. He racked his brains in an effort to be more conversational. He pointed south-westwards.

'Cuba?' he asked.

They knew that name, and stirred with recognition.

'Cuba,' said one of them, nodding, and another added something unintelligible.

Rich pointed to the south.

'Española?' he asked, and then, correcting himself, 'Hayti? Hayti?'

They shrank back a little at that – to them clearly the name of Hayti was accursed. But the boldest one managed to nod in reply:

'Hayti,' he said.

The assurance was worth having, even if nothing else came from the interview. One of them stepped forward again, asking a question. He pointed to Rich and then to the south; Rich caught the word 'Hayti' repeated several times – he was being asked if he came from there, and he judged it best to disclaim all acquaintance with the place.

'Oh no, no, no,' he said, shaking his head. 'Me Cuba, Me Cuba. Hurricane.'

They knew that word, too, and there was a faint light of understanding in their faces; they chattered to each other as they debated how a hurricane could possibly have blown this queer bearded stranger all the way from Cuba. One of them

228

sidled past him to the canoe, picked out a cassava cake, and gave it to him. He nodded and smiled his thanks, and ate, the cooked food grateful to his stomach although he did his best not to appear too hungry. The more normal his reactions the easier it would be to win their confidence. He rubbed his stomach and pointed down his throat – a plan was forming in his mind.

He picked up the end of the creeper net and pointed to the sea; they knew something of what he meant. He pointed to the sea again with a sweeping gesture of his arm, and rubbed his stomach again. They grasped what he wanted; this simple stranger needed some fish, and they were perfectly willing to oblige, here on this admirable seining beach. They came fear-lessly forward now; one of them took up the end of the net while the other two, smiling, prepared to push the canoe into the water. Rich smiled, too, and casually picked up his lever and dropped it into the canoe before he bent to help them shove out. The canoe floated, and one of the two Indians prepared to paddle while the other paid out the net; they were only a little surprised when Rich climbed in behind them.

The canoe danced over the small surf as the single paddle drove it slowly forward; the other Indian, standing precari-ously, dropped the net over-side armful by armful. Farther and farther out they went, in a curve, until Rich, watching narrowly, decided that half the net was out and they were about to curve back to the beach. The decisive moment had come. He scrambled forward and seized the whole remainder of the net, and lifted in his arms and dumped it overboard amid the Indians' ejaculations of mild protest. He picked up his lever, poised it menacingly.

'Hayti,' he said, and pointed southward.

They protested much more strenuously at that, piping in their shrill voices and gesticulating despairingly.

'Hayti,' said Rich, inexorably. He swung his club back; he was ready to strike one Indian down if by so doing he could terrorize the other into paddling. The one he menaced screamed and cowered under the impending blow.

'Hayti,' said Rich, again, pointing to the paddles.

They gave way before his snarling ferocity – Rich was desperate now that there was this chance of reaching home. They picked up their paddles and began work; one of them was weeping like a girl. They headed out through the shallows to the open sea, while from the distant beach came the wailing of the third Indian, standing there puzzled and deserted. His voice mingled with the weird cry of the seabirds.

The canoe effected its passage to Española in the course of that night, with Rich steering by the sun while daylight lasted and by the North Star – he had to stand up in the unsteady canoe to discover it low down on the horizon – at night. The steady hours of paddling wore out the frail Indians entirely, even before darkness fell they were sobbing with fatigue and Rich had to goad them to work. Then later he allowed one to rest, sitting hunched up with his forehead on his knees, while the other worked; at first it had been hard to make them understand what he wanted, as they shrank and cowered before him, but they understood at last and paddled alternately while Rich sat in the stern, sleeping in cat-naps of a minute or two each, and waking with a jerk to see that his unwilling crew were still at their tasks and to set the canoe on her course again. The canoe rose and fell with dizzy insecurity over the dark invisible waves in whose depths the stars were reflected and the wind sighed overhead.

Just before dawn there was a sudden squall of wind and rain which blotted the world from sight, and for a few minutes Rich felt for the first time a sense of danger. He turned the canoe bows on into the wind and sea, and had to struggle hard to hold her there, but the odd little canoe, with its thick sides of light wood, rode the waves in a fantastically self-confident manner, threading her way through difficulties as though endowed with an intelligence of her own. Then the squall passed, and with the end of the squall dawn was lighting the eastern horizon, and to the southward there were mountains reaching to the sky, wild and jagged.

'Hayti!' said the Indians.

They turned faces yellow with fatigue towards him, dumbly imploring him not to force them to approach nearer to the accursed land, but Rich hardened his heart. With a stroke or two of his paddle he swung the canoe round towards the island, and then used the paddle to prod them into activity. The canoe danced and lurched over a quartering sea in response to a last effort from their weary arms, and the mountains grew steadily nearer until the white ribbon of surf at the base of the rocks was visible, and then the canoe ran alongside a natural pier of rock and Rich stepped out, so stiff and cramped that he could hardly stand straight.

The Indians still looked up at him apprehensively. They had not the spirit – or else the strength – to try to escape, and they could only sit and wonder what awful fate now awaited them in this land which the white devils had come to plague. Rich returned their gaze, looking thoughtfully down on them. He could still find a good use for the canoe, employing it to take him along the coast until he found a Spanish settlement, but the two Indians were so depressed and apprehensive and pitiful in appearance, that he found it difficult to bring himself to detain them further. He tried to debate the pros and cons of it coldly and practically, but he suddenly thought of what might happen to the poor wretches if his fellow Spaniards laid hands on them.

'Go!' he said, suddenly. 'Go home!'

They looked at him without comprehension, and he swept his hand in a wide gesture towards the horizon and pushed the canoe out a little way from the rock. Still they hardly understood until he turned his back on them and walked a little way inland. When he looked round again they were paddling bravely out to sea again, their fatigue forgotten in their new freedom. Rich found time to hope that they would remember to call at his own island to pick up their marooned companion, and then a great wave of elation caught him up to the exclusion of all other thoughts. He was back again in Española, whence ships sometimes sailed to Spain, and he was the sole survivor of a shipload of men all far tougher and stronger than he. He was all a-bubble with excitement as he breasted the cliff and set out to find his fellow-men.

Rich walked a hundred and fifty miles through the forests before he found what he sought, and he spent sixteen days doing it. There were tracks through the forest, now almost vanished again as the Indians had ceased to use them. Three times they brought him to ruined villages whose decayed huts and deserted gardens had almost become part of primitive nature again, but there he found a few ears of corn and was able to dig up a few roots which kept him alive. The Indian inhabitants, he supposed, had died in battle or of disease, or were toiling away to the south gathering grains of gold in the mountains of Cibao. But the fort of Isabella was somewhere to the eastward, and even though Isabella had been Roldan's late headquarters he would be able to obtain assistance to make his way to San Domingo. So Rich walked through the forest to Isabella.

They gave him help when he reached it; they even were anxious to make him welcome when once he had explained who he was and whence he came. They gave him clothing and food – it was good to set his teeth into meat again – and listened sympathetically while he told them of Garcia's wild scheme to discover a land of gold to the north-westward. They had heard of that land themselves – more than one vague account of it had drifted in to Española. In return they told him their news, of the wild disorders which had spread through the island again; how Anacaona, the mistress of Bartholomew Columbus, had been hanged for treason, and sixteen petty chiefs roasted alive at the same time.

They told him of madness and battle and bloodshed, but what they were most interested in was the fact that a new expedition had just reached San Domingo from Spain. It was under the command of one Francisco de Bobadilla, a High Steward of the Royal household in Spain, and the greatest noble who had as yet set foot in Española. He had some mysterious new powers; he had an army with which to enforce them. At the first news of his coming Roldan himself had made his way to San Domingo. How matters stood between the Admiral and Bobadilla they did not know, but – was Don Narciso acquainted with Don Francisco? That was very interesting. Did Don Narciso wish to repair at once to San Domingo? Of course. They would provide him with a horse and a guide immediately. Was there anything else they could do for him? A sword? Armour? He had only to ask. And if Don Francisco were to consult him on the legality of their recent behaviour, and of their grants of lands and slaves, Don Narciso would go to the trouble of assuring him that at Isabella they were all devoted subjects of the crown, would he not? Rich nodded without committing himself, and took his guide and mounted his horse and rode for San Domingo.

It was five months and a week since Garcia had kidnapped him. The Court of Spain must have acted with unusual promptitude on receipt of his report, and he could guess what sort of orders and what sort of powers had been given to Don Francisco de Bobadilla and at the haste with which he had been sent out. But he hardly cared about that. Soon one at least of the ships which had come out would be sailing back to Spain – perhaps it might already have sailed. That was the rub. Rich urged his horse forward in his panic lest he should arrive too late to be able to sail in her.

CHAPTER TWENTY-FOUR

THERE had been a hazy dream-like quality about many of his adventures when Rich had been experiencing misfortune; there was the same unreality about his good fortune. Rich could hardly believe that this was really he, sitting in the sternsheets of a boat pulling out to the caravel *Vizcaya* on his way to Spain. The boat's side on which his hand rested, the ladder which he climbed, the deck on which he set his feet, all were quite surprising in their solidity, considering how he felt that they might at any moment dissolve like wreaths of cloud. The bustle of the ship making ready for departure, the screaming of the seabirds, were like noises heard in a dream. He was free, and he was returning home; perhaps at that very moment the sucking-pig was being engendered which he would eat as soon as he set foot in his own house again – sucking-pig with onions and a big slice of wheaten bread.

He looked over at the island. For him it was a place of only evil memories, and he never wanted to set eyes on it again; as he decided this he was conscious of the faintest incredible twinge of regret that his adventures were over. It was so incredible that he refused to pay any attention to it, even while he was prepared to admit that if time had been of no value he would have liked on his little island to have completed his own boat himself and sailed her back to Española instead of making use of the Indians and their canoe. But if that had been the case he would not have reached San Domingo for months, and he would not be sailing today in the *Vizcaya,* escaping from these pestilential Indies and on his way to Spain.

The Indies would get on without him – he was of no use

there. Bobadilla had listened with patience to his account of the legal abuses in the island, and to his rough sketch of a system of government, but Bobadilla had his own ideas and would not act on his advice. Perhaps Bobadilla might be able to tame the headstrong mass of his subjects – he had started firmly enough by putting both the Admiral and Roldan under arrest. Certainly no scheme of reform whatever could be put in hand while those two were free. What would happen next, what would be the future of this empire, no one could foretell. He could guess that its boundaries would expand, that island after island would be steadily overrun and conquered, but whether condemned to ruin or prosperity would depend on Bobadilla and his successors. Conquest was certain, as long as Spain could supply restless and daring spirits like Garcia, prepared to attack any kingdom with a handful of men and horses. Someone in the future would take up Garcia's project again, and discover the land of gold to the north-west, and conquer it, even if it should be the kingdom of the Great Khan itself. That would be a notable commerce, the export merely of stout hearts and the import of rich gold; Spain would be wealthy and prosperous then. Rich found himself smiling when he remembered how he had been almost converted by Diego Alamo's prosaic suggestions about establishing a trade in hides and sugar and African Negroes. Now that the island was already receding into his mental perspective he could see things clearer and wonder how he could ever have been carried away by such notions.

A boat was coming out to the *Vizcaya*; presumably it had on board Alonso de Villegio the captain, with Bobadilla's final dispatches for Spain, and they would be under way directly. Villegio was a man of capacity, who had listened, at Bobadilla's side, with much attention to Rich's account of the island. He would be pleasant, sane company for Rich during the long voyage home, and a word in the King's ear (for Rich could be certain of the King's attention for a space on his arrival) could give him much deserved promotion.

But in the stern of the boat, beside Villegio, was a strangely familiar figure. Rich recognized the bent shoulders and the white hair and beard immediately, and only hesitated to be certain because of the unlikeliness of what he saw.

The boat came alongside, and Villegio sprang lightly to the deck, his captain's eye taking in at a flash all the preparations for departure. Then he stood by the rail to help up the man who followed him; another sailor came to help and the head of a third was visible over the side engaged on the same task. And the man who mounted was in need of this help, for he was old and feeble and stiff. Furthermore, as he raised his hands to the rail there was a dull clanking to be heard. The Admiral was coming on board with chains upon his wrists.

Rich was inexpressibly shocked. He had approved of the temporary confinement of the Admiral, on the grounds that it was necessary to keep him harmless until the reforms should be under way. But that the Admiral of the Ocean, the Viceroy of the Indies, the man who had discovered a new world, should be thus publicly put to shame by being packed off home in chains, without either trial or sentence, was a dreadful thing, and the more dreadful because it showed that Bobadilla was a tactless man who would never manage the Indies.

Rich hurried across to where the Admiral still stood by the ship's side, looking about him blindly and unseeing, the chain dangling from his wrists and the land breeze ruffling his white beard.

'Your Excellency,' he said, and bowed low. His heart was wrung with pity as the Admiral peered at him with rheumy eyes.

'Ah, Don Narciso,' said the Admiral, slowly.

All about them was clamour and bustle, as Villegio was giving orders for sail to be set and the anchor to be got in. Farewells were already being shouted from the boat alongside.

'It is dreadful to see Your Excellency treated in this fashion,' said Rich.

'It is not dreadful for me,' said the Admiral. 'This is the sort of gratitude that benefactors can always expect of the world. And Christ had his cross and crown of thorns, while I have only this chain.'

The ship was under way now, with her sails filled with the last of the land breeze, as she plunged southward to make an offing. Villegio returned to them now that the immediate business of departure was completed. He, too, bowed low.

'Your Excellency,' he said. 'I can remove that chain now, thank God.'

'And why?' asked the Admiral. 'What about the orders given by His genuine Excellency, Don Francisco de Bobadilla?'

Villegio snapped his fingers.

'I am at sea now,' he said. 'I am master of my ship, and no orders here have any weight save mine. I shall call the armourer.'

The Admiral restrained him with a gesture, the chain clattering as he put out his hand.

'No!' said the Admiral. 'Never! I wear this chain by order of the King, through his mouthpiece Bobadilla, and I shall continue to wear it until I am freed by the King's own order again. The world will see the sort of treatment the discoverer of the Indies has received.'

Villegio stood hesitant.

'Your Excellency,' interposed Rich. 'Take the chain off now for the sake of your own comfort. You can put it on again when we sight Spain.'

'No, no, no!' said the Admiral. 'I will not!'

Rich and Villegio exchanged glances. They both of them recognized the sort of fanaticism which brooked no argument.

'As Your Excellency pleases,' said Villegio, bowing again. He was already looking round him at his ship; there must have been scores of matters clamouring for his attention.

'I must ask Your Excellency's kindness to spare me for a few minutes again.'

The Admiral motioned him away with superb dignity.

'I understand,' he said. 'I myself was once a captain of a ship.'

As Villegio departed the Admiral rounded upon Rich.

'I had forgotten until now,' he said. 'But I suppose, Don Narciso, that I have you to thank for this treatment. What did you say in that lying report of yours to Their Highnesses?'

'I said nothing but what I saw to be the truth,' said Rich, taken quite aback and only collecting himself slowly; it was the Admiral himself who gained for him the necessary time to take up the defensive.

'Who bribed you?' asked the Admiral. 'What friend at Court have you to put in my place?'

'No one,' said Rich, hotly, stung by the monstrous imputation. 'I have done my duty, that and no more.'

His genuine indignation may perhaps have been remarked by the Admiral.

'No matter,' he said. 'I care not whether you are my friend or my enemy. I am strong enough to stand alone against all the liars and detractors in Spain or in the Indies. Half an hour with Their Highnesses and these chains will be struck off and I shall be Admiral and Viceroy again. I have only to tell them of the discoveries I have made this voyage, of the mines of Ophir, of the Earthly Paradise, of the westerly passage to Arabia. I have only to remind them of the wealth to be won, the new kingdoms to be discovered.'

The dull blue eyes had a light in them now, and the wrinkled face, until now wooden and impassive, was animated and alive. The Admiral had forgotten Rich's presence, and was staring at the horizon and dreaming dreams, just as he had always dreamed them. Rich, gazing at him, realized quite fully that the Admiral was right, that he had only to talk in that fashion, as he undoubtedly would, to Their Highnesses for a few minutes to have all he wanted again. Within a year, perhaps, he would be at sea again in command of a squadron provided by Their Highnesses, and seeking the Fountain of Youth, or the Tree of Knowledge, or the Golden City of Cambaluk. And he would find – God only knew what he would find, but, being the Admiral, he would find something.

Rich glanced astern to where Española's mountains were fast sinking into the sea. There was a magnificent rainbow across them, adding fresh richness to their superb green summits towering above the blue, blue sea. He caught his breath a little at the sight, and felt a fresh twinge of regret at leaving the Indies behind. He had to think very hard about the solid realities of the island to allay that twinge. He shook off his momentary depression. He was on his way home.